HEAD ON

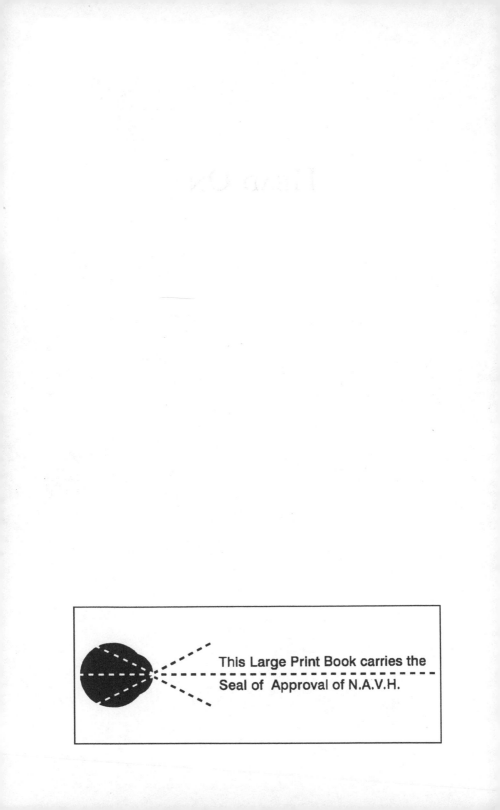

This Large Print Book carries the
Seal of Approval of N.A.V.H.

HEAD ON

JOHN SCALZI

THORNDIKE PRESS
A part of Gale, a Cengage Company

GALE
A Cengage Company

Farmington Hills, Mich • San Francisco • New York • Waterville, Maine
Meriden, Conn • Mason, Ohio • Chicago

Thorndike Press® Large Print Basic.
The text of this Large Print edition is unabridged.
Other aspects of the book may vary from the original edition.
Set in 16 pt. Plantin.

LIBRARY OF CONGRESS CIP DATA ON FILE.
CATALOGUING IN PUBLICATION FOR THIS BOOK
IS AVAILABLE FROM THE LIBRARY OF CONGRESS

ISBN-13: 978-1-4328-5323-5 (hardcover)

Published in 2018 by arrangement with Macmillan Publishing Group, LLC/Tor/Forge

Printed in Mexico
1 2 3 4 5 6 7 22 21 20 19 18

This book is very gratefully dedicated to the editorial and production staffers at Tor Books, who worked on it like rock stars after it was turned in at literally the last possible moment.

Thank you, folks. You are miracle workers and I love you. Please don't strangle me.

And to all the editorial and production staff who work on my books worldwide: You're the reason my books find readers. Thank you for what you do for me.

THE DEATH OF DUANE CHAPMAN

The journeyman Hilketa athlete was looking to make an impression in his final
game. But then he did something unexpected. He died.

By Cary Wise
SPECIAL TO THE *HILKETA NEWS*

By the time Duane Chapman died on the
Hilketa field, his head had already been torn
off twice.

Having it torn off for the third time was
unusual, even for Hilketa, in which the point
of the game is to rip the head off a selected
opponent and then toss or carry it through a
goal at the end of the field. The computer
operated by the officials in the game opera-
tions room — improvised for this exhibition
game between the Boston Bays and the

Toronto Snowbirds in an appropriated stadium luxury skybox — was supposed to select randomly from the defending players on the field who would be the "goat" for the current play: the player whose head the offense would try to remove while the remaining defense players fought them off, with their bodies and with game-approved weapons. With eleven players on each side, it was unusual for any one player to get goat duty more than once or twice a game.

But the operative word here is "random." Sometimes, just by the roll of the electronic dice, a player can be chosen as goat three times in one game. Later examination of the game computer showed it hadn't been tampered with. It selected Chapman, once, twice, three times, entirely randomly.

Nor had it chosen poorly. Chapman was not the franchise player for the Boston Bays — that honor belonged to Kim Silva, who had just signed a five-year, $83-million contract with the Northeast Division leaders — nor was he recognized as a key specialist, like Wesley Griffith, who was known to make the lumbering tank threeps he specialized in look like limber scout models during critical plays.

What Chapman *was,* however, was arguably the Bays' best utility fielder; a jack of all positions and threep body models, even if master of none. "You can put him anywhere and in any body model and he'll get the job done," Bays manager David Pena said, at the evening's postgame press conference. "He's the guy you think of when you think of the phrase 'team player.'"

Chapman had also developed a reputation over his three seasons in the North American Hilketa League of being a wily goat — one who could run down the four-minute clock of the "capo" portion of the play, limiting the number of points opposing teams could get from taking his head. This sort of strategic play-making could be frustrating for fans who had come to see blood — fake blood, but blood nonetheless — but for a canny manager like Pena, this talent played into his ability to stymie opponents, forcing them into errors and bad field strategy.

This much was apparent the first time Chapman was the goat, four plays into the first half. The Bays' Silva started the game with a bang by taking Snowbirds goat Toby Warner's head in the first minute and then spearheading a blitzkrieg into Toronto territory in the "coda" portion of the play, running through the outside goal in only thirty-seven seconds for a ten-point push.

The Snowbirds answered strongly, decapitating the Bays' Gerard Mathis in two minutes, but the three-minute-forty-eight-second scrum in the coda and the resulting inside goal throw-in netted Toronto only six points. Although the Birds smothered the Bays in the next capo, keeping Nat Guzman's head on her shoulders, they still needed five points to take the lead.

When Chapman was chosen as goat the next play, he and Pena didn't let that happen. Instead Chapman, centrally located on the field, faded back toward the Bays' goal and Pena ordered what the history-loving manager likes to call an "Agincourt," funneling the Snowbirds into a gauntlet to get at their quarry.

The Bays' Laurie Hampton and Ouida Kimbrough used the crossbows to snipe out Conception Rayburn and Elroy Gil, two of Toronto's best headtakers, and the rest of the Bays kept the Snowbirds engaged in a melee, leaving Chapman, piloting a general threep, to easily outrun Brendon Soares and September Vigil, piloting tanks. By the time Soares finally pried Chapman's head off, the capo period had ground down to nothing, giving Chapman a small victory.

Chapman wouldn't be so lucky in his second session as goat, in the first play of the second half. This time Rayburn, who later admitted being furious at having been sniped earlier, grabbed a sword rather than his more favored hammer, snuck past Jalisa Acevedo's tank and Donnell Mesa's warrior, and dove straight for Chapman, snapping off his head in a near record twenty seconds from the start of the capo. Forty seconds later Rayburn risked an upper goal; Chapman's head sailed through the hoop and the Snowbirds had scored the maximum possible eighteen points, putting them comfortably into the lead.

In postgame interviews with media, Rayburn said that Chapman had been yelling about the pain of his threep's head being severed. "I didn't pay any mind," he said. "I thought he was trying to distract me, like you do when you're the goat. And anyway, being the goat's supposed to hurt. It's why we leave pain on."

What Rayburn said here is important. North American Hilketa League rules require all players to retain some pain sensitivity in their threeps — rules require at least 5 percent of standard receptivity, and most players tune their game threeps into the 5 to 10 percent range. The argument here is that maintaining some pain receptivity — even at a level below what would register as *truly* painful — keeps the players rooted in reality, and reminds them that their threeps are not invulnerable to physical damage, and are expensive to maintain and repair.

When Chapman's head came back to his

threep after the play, the first thing he did was walk over to Pena and report an anomaly with his body. Pena referred him to Royce Siegel, the Bays' sideline technical support lead.

"He said he was feeling more pain than usual," Siegel told the press in the conference after the game. "I did a diagnostic on the threep and there was nothing that showed up as a problem." Siegel then pinged Alton Ortiz, Chapman's care provider, who was watching over his body in Philadelphia. (Chapman, unlike most of his teammates, did not have his body travel to events, due to autoimmune issues. He piloted his threep remotely using dedicated connections to minimize lag.) Ortiz reported nothing unusual on his end. Chapman returned to the field for the next play, on offense.

When asked why he didn't sub out Chapman after he reported playing in increasing pain, Pena said, simply, "He didn't ask."

Why didn't he ask? There are several possible reasons. The first is that Chapman, like many journeyman athletes, had performance bonuses he was aiming for to pad out his standard contractual rate. Although this was an exhibition game, and its stats wouldn't go to the season records, they would go to Chapman's contractual quotas. He was getting an early start at a salary increase, in other words.

The second reason was why the Bays and the Snowbirds were playing in the capital in the first place: The NAHL was expanding into Washington, D.C., as well as Philadelphia, Austin, and Kansas City, and would have an expansion draft at the end of the season. For a player like Chapman, an expansion draft could be a chance to move up into a key role at one of the new teams. The Washington game had the entire NAHL brass at it, along with several potential new franchise owners and investors, including Washington, D.C., favorite son Marcus Shane, as well as their prospective management and coaching teams. Chapman might have thought that staying in the game was the best way to come to their attention and make an argument for being in their expansion draft selections.

And then there's the third reason, as Kim Silva said, after the game: "You play through the pain. Always."

This is a mantra for every athlete in every sport, of course. But it's even more so for the athletes of Hilketa. They know they are both more and less than your average athlete — they are also Hadens, that small percentage of citizens whose bodies are inactive while their minds move freely through the world, both in the online venue of the Agora and in the offline world, through which they navigate in their threeps.

It's these threeps — machines designed arguably better and more efficiently than human bodies — that have led many, including non-Haden professional athletes, to state that Hilketa athletes aren't athletes at all, but something along the lines of glorified video game players.

This naturally rankles Hilketa players, the game's fans, and many Hadens. At the minimum, if NASCAR drivers can be considered athletes, so too can Hilketa players. But ask any Hilketa athlete and they will tell you that there's physicality to the sport. Even if their bodies are immobile, the effort required to pilot their threeps for the ninety minutes of each game (not to mention practices and other related work) takes a physical and mental toll. They work hard. They feel aches and fatigue. And when the hits come hard and fast, they feel the pain. Real pain, for real athletes.

But they know how many people would deny that pain *is* real. So they play through, more than they might otherwise, more than non-Haden athletes might, to make the point.

For some or all of these reasons, Chapman went back onto the field.

Seasoned observers of the game could see

right away that there was something going on with Chapman. ESPN commentator Rochelle Webb pointed out how he started to hang back on the Bays' next offensive drive. "Chapman's keeping to the backfield, which isn't where you usually see him," she commented. *Washington Post*'s Hilketa reporter Dave Miller noted on the site's live simulcast that Chapman picked up the crossbow as his weapon for the play. "He's done that maybe three or four other times in his career," Miller noted, "probably because he can't hit the broadside of a barn." Miller was right; Chapman shot his bolt at the Birds' Sonia Sparks and missed her by a country mile.

On a normal night, Chapman's lack of engagement might be the top story of the game — or at least enough of a reason for Pena to finally bite the bullet and take him off the field — but right around the time Chapman decided to loiter in the background, Silva made it clear why the Bays were paying a premium price for her, racking up twenty points in the next two offensive plays and single-handedly thwarting Elroy Gil's upper-goal attempt.

Almost no one was looking at Chapman during this remarkable run, and those who were confined their comments to asides, minor color commentary filling out the edges of a star turn.

And then Chapman became the goat for the third time.

At first it looked as if Chapman was doing what he always did when he was goat: ducking, weaving, evading, running the field to run down the clock.

Then the *Post*'s Dave Miller saw it. "Chapman is calling a time-out? There are no time-outs in Hilketa."

"Chapman's putting his hands out at Rayburn," Webb said on ESPN, as the Toronto star bore down on him. "He looks like he's trying to say 'Don't hit me.' "

Rayburn didn't hit him. As Chapman scrambled backward from his grasp, he collided with September Vigil, one of Toronto's tanks.

With one massive tank arm, Vigil hugged Chapman's threep to her.

With the other, she reached down and tore off his head.

"I didn't know," Vigil said afterward, and anyone who doesn't believe threeps can convey emotion simply did not see Vigil in her personal rig, sitting there in obvious shock. "Duane screamed when I took his head, but we all scream when that happens. We're *supposed* to scream. You want to distract and confuse the other player. I thought he was trying to make me lose focus."

Vigil didn't lose focus. She tossed the head to Rayburn, who ran it in for eight points.

By this time Siegel knew something was wrong with Chapman. "I got a call from Alton, Duane's caregiver, telling me his heart rate and brain activity were all over the place," Siegel said. "I pulled up his physical stats on my glasses and confirmed it. Alton was yelling at me to disconnect him from the threep. He was convinced something was going haywire with it. But it wasn't the threep. Or if it was, I couldn't tell." Siegel pulled the plug on the threep anyway.

From the point of view of the spectators and other players, nothing special had happened. Players had been unplugged from their threeps before, when there were connection issues or major damage. A cart came onto the field during the reset and took the headless threep away to scattered applause. Pena called in Warren Meyer as a substitute for the remaining minutes of the game. There was nothing to suggest that 140 miles away Duane Chapman was suddenly fighting for his life.

It was a fight he would lose minutes before the end of the game, which the Bays would win, 58 to 41. Pena was informed by Alton Ortiz as the final seconds counted down.

After a game players normally head to the press zone for interviews almost immediately, pausing only to switch to their personal threeps. That didn't happen this time. Both the Bays and the Snowbirds were sent, still in their game threeps, to the home and visiting locker rooms, where Pena and Snowbirds manager Linda Patrick quietly informed their players of Chapman's death.

Nearly every Bays and Snowbirds player withdrew from the postgame press scrum, heading home stunned. Only Pena, Siegel, Silva, Rayburn, and Vigil remained to meet with reporters, who were now independently receiving reports about Chapman.

"We don't know what happened yet," Pena said, at the press conference, when asked how it was that Chapman died. He said it would take days or possibly weeks to figure out what caused an otherwise healthy Haden athlete to suddenly die. Washington police and medical examiners would look into it, as well as the FBI's desk for Haden affairs, and the league itself.

When Pena was asked how Chapman's death would affect the league, the manager looked at the reporter who asked the question like he was a bug. "At the moment, I couldn't give a damn about that," he said.

The right answer, but the question wasn't out of line. The Bays-Snowbirds exhibition game was meant to be a showcase for what has been the quickest-growing major sport in North America, with four new franchises up for grabs in the next year; representatives from China, Russia, and Germany attended with an eye toward creating one or more international leagues in Europe and Asia. What should have been a triumph for the league, including a star turn by Silva, the league's biggest draw, had now been overshadowed by the league's first athlete death.

As for Chapman, the journeyman player who had hoped for his star to rise, he has found his way into Hilketa's record books in another, more tragic, fashion.

"It's unbelievable," the visibly emotional Pena said, near the end of the press conference. "But it's also just like Duane. He gave everything to the game. Everything to the league. He never wanted to leave the field."

He never did. Until he left it forever.

CHAPTER ONE

I almost missed seeing Duane Chapman die. I didn't know it at the time. All I knew was that I was running late for the "special exhibition game experience" that I was supposed to be having along with my mother and father. The North American Hilketa League really really really wanted my dad to be a minority investor in the league's upcoming Washington, D.C., franchise, and thought wooing him in a luxury skybox would do the trick.

I was doubtful about this — Dad knew his way around skyboxes, as both a former NBA player and current real estate billionaire, and didn't see them as anything particularly special — but I did know that my flatmates, Hilketa fans all, were glowing green with envy that I was attending the game. This had been literally the case with the twins, Justin and Justine, who for the last three days had set the LED piping of their threep to pulse green at me anytime I walked past them. I thought that was overdoing it, personally.

I had left the house in time to make it to the start of the game, but public transportation had other plans for me. I spent the first half of the game in a tube, surrounded by increasingly agitated passengers.

Where are you, my mother had texted me, once the game had started.

Stuck on the Metro, I sent back. *The train stopped fifteen minutes ago. We're all looking at each other deciding who to eat first.*

I think you're safe, she replied.

Don't be too sure, I sent. *I can see some of them sizing up my threep to part it out for battery power.*

Well, if you survive, try to hurry up, Mom texted. *Your father is being swarmed by German businessmen and I'm being condescended to by PR flacks. I know you won't want to miss any of that.*

I hear there's a game going on too, I sent back.

A what now? she replied.

Eventually the train decided to move again, and ten minutes after that I was heading into the stadium, threading my way through other Metro stoppage victims, rushing to see the second half of the game. Some of them were in Boston Bays white and blue, others were wearing the Toronto Snowbirds purple and gray. The rest were wearing Washington Redhawks burgundy and gold, because this is Washington, D.C., and why wouldn't they.

"I can help you," a gate attendant said to me, waving me over. She had very little traffic because most of the attendees were already in the stadium. I flashed my ticket code onto my chest monitor and she scanned it.

"Skybox, very nice," she said. "You know where you're going?"

I nodded. "I've been here before."

The attendant was about to respond when there was a commotion behind us. I looked over and saw a small clot of protesters chanting and waving signs. HILKETA DISCRIMINATES, read one of the signs. LET US PLAY TOO, read another one. EVEN THE BASQUE DON'T LIKE HILKETA, read a third. The protesters were being shuffled off by stadium security, and they weren't happy about it.

"I don't even get that sign," she said to me, as they were being hustled away.

"Which one?"

"The Basque one." She pronounced the word "baskee." "The other ones I get. All

23

the Hilketa players are Hadens and these guys" — she waved at the protesters, none of whom were Hadens — "don't like that. But what does that other sign even mean?"

"The word 'Hilketa' comes from the Basque language," I said. "It means 'murder.' Some Basque people don't like that it's used. They think it makes them look bad."

"Why?"

"I don't know. I'm not Basque."

"Everyone's got a word for murder," the attendant said.

I nodded at that and looked back at the retreating protesters. Some of them saw me and started chanting more forcefully. Apparently they were under the impression that because I was a Haden, their grievances were my fault. A couple of them had glasses on and were looking at me in the fixed sort of way that indicated they were either storing an image of me or trying to call up my public information.

Well, this was a new threep and I didn't keep my information public when I wasn't working, so good luck, there, guys. I thanked the gate attendant and headed in.

The particular skybox I was going to was a large one, designed to fit a few dozen people, a buffet, and a full-service bar. It was basically a hotel conference room with a view of a sporting field.

I glanced around, looking for my parents. I found Dad first, and this was not entirely surprising. As a former NBA player, he towered above most other people in most rooms. And as Marcus Shane, one of the most famous humans in the world, he was generally thronged.

As he was here — two concentric rings of admirers arrayed themselves around him, holding drinks and looking up at him raptly as he related some story or another. Dad's natural habitat, in other words.

He waved when he saw me but didn't wave for me to come over. I knew what that meant. He was working. A few of the people who were thronging him glanced over to see who he had waved at, but seeing only an anonymous threep, they turned their attention back to Dad. That was fine by me.

"Oh, good. Here, take this," someone said, and shoved a glass at me.

I looked up and saw a middle-aged suit. "Pardon me?" I said.

"I'm done with this," he said, waggling the glass.

"Okay. Congratulations."

The man peered at my threep. "You're catering, yes?"

"Not really." I considered flashing my FBI identity information at the suit and then enjoying the fumbling that would follow. Before I could, someone in a white blouse and an apron appeared. "Let me take that," he said, taking the suit's glass.

The suit grunted. "And bring me another. Jack and Coke." He walked off in the direction of Dad.

"Sorry about that," the catering staffer said.

"Not your fault." I looked around the room. "Interesting, though."

"What is?"

"A skybox full of non-Hadens, here for a game played by Hadens, and the first thing that dude does when he sees a threep is hand over his drink glass." I nodded to the glass the caterer had in his hand.

"I better go get him another one," the caterer said.

"Do. Try not to spit in it." The caterer grinned and walked off.

I walked over to the glass wall partitioning the inside of the skybox from its balcony and went through the door there, going to the balcony railing and taking in the roar of the spectators. If the size of the crowd was any indication, the league wasn't wrong to want to expand into Washington. The stadium was jammed to the upper decks.

"I still don't know what's going on," a man said, next to me, to another man standing next to him.

"It's not complicated," the second man said, and pointed at the field, to a threep whose head was ringed with flashing, blinking red lights. "That threep's the goat. That's the player the other team wants to rip the head off of. They try to take his head, while his team tries to keep him from having his head ripped off."

"And when the head is taken, they try to punt it through the goalposts."

"Punt it, toss it, or carry it through, yes."

"And everyone has swords and hammers and bats —"

"They have those because that shit's just fun."

The first man stopped to consider this. "Why 'goat'?"

The second man began to expound on this, but I went back inside to find Mom.

Who I found in the seats facing toward the field, drink in hand, smiling tightly while some young and overenthusiastic dude chatted her up. I recognized the smile as the one Mom used as an alternative to murdering someone. I went over to her, to save her from the overenthusiastic dude, and to save the overenthusiastic dude from her.

"Chris, finally," Mom said as I came up. I bent over to receive a peck on the cheek. She turned, acknowledging her seatmate. "This is Marvin Stephens. He's with the league's PR department."

Stephens stood and held out a hand for me. I shook it. "A thrill to meet you, Chris," he said. "I'm a big fan."

"I didn't know FBI agents had fans," I said.

"Oh, well, not of your FBI work," Stephens said, and then produced a slightly startled look. He was worried he'd made a faux pas. "I mean, I'm sure your FBI work is good."

"Thank you," I said, dryly.

"I meant when you were younger."

"Ah, you meant when I was famous for being famous."

"I wouldn't put it *that* way." Stephens's startled look was back. "I mean, you were a symbol for Hadens everywhere."

I thought about poking at Stephens a little bit more, and finding out just how many permutations of his startled look I could get out of him. But it wouldn't have been nice.

And anyway, he wasn't wrong. When I was young, I *was* a symbol for Hadens everywhere, the poster child for an entire group

28

of humans, all locked into their bodies by a disease and using machines and neural networks to get through the world, just like I did, and do. Being a poster child was a nice gig, until it wasn't. Which is why I stopped doing it and went to work for the FBI instead.

I could have explained this all to Stephens, who was still standing there, looking increasingly worried that he'd just stepped in it. Stephens was just trying to be complimentary, just like lots of other people who unintentionally blurted out a reminder I currently resided in the "where are they now" category of fame and then thought it was a bad thing, instead of something I hoped for and planned to happen.

But that would have taken time and it would have meant having a long conversation of the sort that didn't mix well with a sporting event.

"I was," I said. "Thank you for noticing."

Stephens relaxed and sat back down.

"Marvin was explaining the game of Hilketa to me," Mom said, waving toward the field, on which the Bays and the Snowbirds were currently going after each other with melee weapons. "In *detail*."

"It's an amazing game," Stephens said to me. "Are you a fan?"

I shrugged.

"Chris was more into video games growing up," Mom said.

"Hilketa is a video game too," Stephens said. "In fact, the NAHL sponsors several virtual leagues to help train our athletes and to find new talent. Hadens and non-Hadens both."

"I ran into some non-Hadens protesting outside," I noted. "They didn't seem to feel they were well represented in the league."

"Well, there's a skill gap," Stephens said. "Non-Hadens still lag behind in piloting threeps. It's a reaction-time thing."

"Is it."

"That's the official response, anyway." Stephens got that startled look again. He realized what he'd said and how he'd said it. I wondered how long he'd been in his job. "I mean, it *is* the reason. It's not just an excuse. The NAHL is open to qualified athletes regardless of Haden status."

"Good to know."

"It's just that piloting threeps is tricky. You know . . ." He motioned to me, or more accurately, my threep. "Without a neural network, getting around in a Personal Transport requires a lot of skill and attention." Stephens pointed out toward the field, to a Toronto tank threep that was pounding the hell out of a Bays player with its fists, to cheers. "When I started this job, they put me in a VR getup and had me try to pilot a tank threep around an open field, so I could get a feel for how the players did their job."

"How did you do?" I asked.

"I walked it into a wall," Stephens admitted. "Several times. I just couldn't get the hang of it. So it doesn't surprise me that we don't have non-Hadens playing the game at a professional level yet. It's the one place Hadens have the advantage over the rest of us." The startled look returned. "Well, I mean, not the *only* place. . . ."

Mom glanced over at me on that one and then tinkled the ice in her glass at Stephens. "Would you be a dear and top off my drink for me," she said, and Stephens practically fell over himself to grab the glass and extricate himself from the situation.

"He seems nice," I said, watching as he sprinted toward the bartender.

"He's clueless," Mom said. "I'm sure he was assigned to me because he was the only apparatchik the league could spare to babysit the spouse of the man they wanted to extract money from." She motioned with her head to Dad, who'd grown another ring of admirers. "I'm sure they thought he'd be relatively harmless."

"Do they not know who you are?" I asked.

"They know I'm Marcus' wife." Mom did a hand movement that was her rather more elegant version of a shrug. "If they missed out on what else I am, that's their problem."

Mom, that is, Jacqueline Oxford Shane, on the board of Shane Enterprises, executive vice president of the National Haden Family Association, ferocious fund-raiser, and scion of one of Virginia's oldest and most politically connected families, who dated the current vice president before she met and married Dad. Rumor was the VP still regretted ever letting her go. I didn't regret it. I wouldn't be here if she'd stayed with him.

I tilted my head at Dad. "So how's he holding up, anyway?"

"He's fine," Mom said. "He's doing his thing."

"His 'special exhibition game experience' is apparently being mobbed by international businesspeople."

"You didn't think we were invited to this because the league was trying to impress your dad, did you?" Mom said. She waved at the businesspeople. "We were invited so he could impress *them.*"

"Does that mean Dad is going to invest in

the new franchise?" I asked.

Mom did her shrug wave again. "We're looking at the numbers."

"How are they?"

Before Mom could respond, two gentlemen appeared, gave slight bows, and then one spoke in Japanese.

"Mr. Fukuyama apologizes for the intrusion, and wishes to know if you are a player in the Hilketa game," the second man said, clearly the translator.

I had known what Mr. Fukuyama said because my onboard translator had given me a translation as soon as it recognized Fukuyama was not speaking English at me.

I stood and gave a small bow. "Please tell Mr. Fukuyama that I regret that I am not."

"This robot is not a player," the translator told Fukuyama, in Japanese.

"Damn it," Fukuyama said. "I was promised that I would get to meet players on this trip. Why they think I will invest in an Asian Hilketa league when they can't even show me the goods is beyond me."

"Perhaps you will meet a player after the game, sir," the translator said.

"I better." Fukuyama nodded his head at me. "Get this robot's autograph anyway. I promised my grandson I would get one from a player."

33

"But this is not a player," the translator said.

"My grandson won't know the difference."

The translator reached into a suit pocket and produced a small notebook and a pen. "Please, an autograph?" he asked, in English.

"Of course," I said, taking the pen and signing the notebook with it, adding "I am not a Hilketa player" in English below the signature. I closed the notebook and handed it and the pen back to the translator. He and Fukuyama bowed and departed.

"You're famous," Mom joked to me.

"It's a step up from when I came into the skybox and someone shoved a drink glass in my hand."

"Who did that?"

"That one —" I pointed to the suit, now in the outer ring of my father's admirers.

"Oh, *him*," Mom said. "I've met him. Smarmy little jerk."

"You were talking about the league numbers before we got interrupted," I reminded her, to get her off the topic of the smarmy suit. "You were about to tell me how they were."

"They're marginal."

"Ah, that good," I said.

"The NAHL likes to call itself the fastest-growing major sport in North America, but all the other major sports are decades old, so that's just marketing," Mom said. "Hilketa's attendance and merchandising are growing but the league spends a lot. Your father has questions about the value proposition of investing in a franchise."

"You mean, *you* have questions about it."

"We *both* have questions about it," Mom said. "The league just doesn't appear to realize your father and I talk to each other."

"That's going to end well."

"We'll see." Mom looked up at me as if she suddenly remembered something. "Where's Leslie?" she asked. "I thought she was thinking of coming with you."

"She's busy," I said. "Leslie" in this case was Leslie Vann, my partner at the FBI, where we were part of the Haden affairs division.

"She's busy? Doing what?"

"Avoiding sunlight. It's a Sunday, Mom."

Mom snorted, delicately, at this. "Leslie needs fewer late nights, Chris."

"I'll let her know you've volunteered to be her life coach."

"I just might take the job. Leslie is lovely" — and here I did an internal smirk, because in the year I'd been partnered with Vann, "lovely" was an adjective used about her exactly once, right now — "but she's aimless."

"She likes aimless."

"Yes, well. If it makes her happy, I suppose. Look, here comes the problem child again." She pointed to Stephens, who returned with Mom's glass.

A roar went up from the stands. Not because Mom got her drink, but because on the field, Duane Chapman's head was ripped clean off.

Mom grimaced. "I hate when that happens."

"The player is fine," Stephens assured her. "It looks violent, but that's a threep body. The player and his *actual* head are as safe as can be. He's a Haden, after all."

My mother looked at Stephens, blankly and silently.

"Which, uh, you *knew,*" Stephens said, awkwardly.

Mom continued to stare blankly at Stephens.

"You know, I'm going to check in with my boss to see if she needs me for anything," he said, and sprinted off again.

Mom watched him go, and then returned her attention to the game, where Duane Chapman's headless threep sprawled on the

Hilketa playing field. Meanwhile his head, carried off by the opposing team, was making its way down the pitch, one threep-crushing meter at a time.

"It disturbs me to see a headless threep body on the field," she said. "It makes me think about you."

"None of my threeps ever lost its head," I said.

"There was that time you rode your bike out in front of that truck," Mom pointed out. "When you were eight."

"In that case it was less my threep losing its head than it was it hitting a truck and disintegrating and losing *everything*."

"That's my *point*," Mom said. "Threep bodies aren't designed to have body parts removed."

I pointed to the field, where the Snowbirds and the Bays were literally going after each other with swords and war hammers. "*Those* threep bodies are," I said. "Decapitations and severed limbs add to the drama of the game."

As if to accentuate the point, one of the Snowbirds slashed viciously at a Bay, whose arm lopped right off. The Bay responded by bringing a mallet down on the Snowbird's threep skull. Then both of the players ran off in the direction of Duane Chapman's head. The entire exchange brought more cheers from the crowd.

Mom grimaced again. "I'm not sure I like this game very much."

"All my flatmates do," I said. "When they found out I was coming to the game they plotted about how to kill me and take my ticket. They're fans."

"But *you* don't like it very much, do you?" Mom asked. "You shrugged when Stephens asked you if you were a fan. And I don't remember you being much for it growing up."

"I liked basketball better."

"As you should," Mom said. "Basketball's done very well for our family. But that's not the question."

I paused and tried to frame an answer.

The long version of which would be:

I have Haden's syndrome. I contracted it when I was so young that I have no memory of not ever having it. Having Haden's syndrome means you are locked into your body — your brain works fine but your body doesn't. Haden's affects about 1 percent of the global population and about four and a half million people in the United States: roughly the population of Kentucky, in other words.

You can't keep the population of Kentucky

38

trapped in their own heads — especially when one of the victims of the syndrome was Margaret Haden, the then first lady, for whom the disease is named. So the United States and other countries funded a "moon shot" program of technologies, including implantable neural networks to let Hadens communicate, an online universe called "the Agora" to give us a place to exist as a community, and android-like "Personal Transports," better known as "threeps," that let us walk around and interact with non-Hadens on a near equal basis.

I say "near equal basis" because, you know. People are people. Regrettably, many of them aren't going to treat someone who looks like a robot exactly the way they'd treat a person who looks like a standard-issue human. See Mr. Smarmy Suit handing me a glass the second I walked through the door as an example of that.

Not only that, but threep bodies are literally machines. Despite the fact they're generally rated to operate within the usual human range of strength and agility, threeps in sports are generally a no-go. Have a coworker in a threep for your office softball team? Fine. Playing shortstop for the Nationals? Not going to work. Yes, there were lawsuits. Turns out, in the eyes of the law, threeps are not the same as human bodies. They're cars, basically.

So here's Hilketa. It's an actual sport, designed to be played by people operating threeps — which meant Haden athletes. And it's a popular sport, even (and, actually, *especially*) with non-Hadens, which means the Hadens who play the sport have become bona fide celebrities outside of Haden circles. In just a decade since its inception, the NAHL fields twenty-eight teams in four divisions across the United States and Canada, averages 15,000 spectators a game in the regular season, 95 percent of whom are non-Hadens, and has athletes earning millions and becoming posters on kids' walls. That matters, for Hadens and for everyone who cares about them.

Of course, I thought as I watched Duane Chapman's head sail through the goalposts, giving the Snowbirds eight points, the reason Hilketa is so popular is that the players score points through simulated decapitation, and go after each other with melee weapons. It's team gladiatorial combat, on a football field, with a nerdy scoring system. It's all the violence every other team sport wishes it could have, but can't, because people would actually die.

In doing so, it makes the players something other than fully human. And *that* matters too, for Hadens and everyone who cares about them.

Basically, Hilketa is both representation and alienation for Hadens.

So: It's complicated.

Well, for a Haden. For non-Hadens, it's just cool to see threeps pull off each other's heads.

"It's *okay,*" is what I finally told my mom.

She nodded, took a sip of her drink, and then motioned toward the field. "What's going on down there?" she asked. Now that the play was done, Duane Chapman's headless threep was being loaded onto a cart and sent off the field. From the Bays sideline, another threep came in for the next play.

Before I could answer, I got an internal ping from Tony Wilton, one of my roommates. "Are you at the stadium?" Tony asked me.

"Yes. In a VIP suite."

"I hate you."

"You should pity me. It's mostly filled with corporate suits."

"Your life fascinates me. Be that as it may, you should access the stadium Haden feed if you can."

"Why?"

"Because there's something really weird

41

happening with Duane Chapman. We're watching the pay-per-view Haden feed. One minute he's there and the next he's not."

"He was taken off the field. His threep was, anyway."

"Right. But player stats and vitals are supposed to be live for the whole game whether they're on the field or not. All the other player S&Vs are live but his. People are talking about it. I want to know if it's just a glitch in the feed we're getting."

"I'll check," I said. "Let me get back to you." I disconnected and turned back to Mom, who had noticed the pause.

"Everything all right?" she asked.

"I have to check something," I said. "Give me a second." She nodded.

I opened up the Haden view of the game.

The game field, previously green and blank, exploded with data.

Data on the players, on the field, and on the sidelines. Data about the play currently being executed. Data about the field itself. Data about the stadium and attendance. Current data, historical data, projections based on data coming in real time, processed with AI and by viewer sentiment.

This view of the data, and the game itself, could be displayed from any angle, up to and including the first-person view from the players themselves. Thanks to the over-whelming number of cameras framing the game and the amount of data otherwise fill-ing in and modeling any gaps the cameras missed, one could virtually walk the field while the game was afoot and plant one's ass down in the very center of the action.

That's the Haden view of the game.

To be clear, the Haden view was not ac-cessible only to Hadens. Aside from being discriminatory, it would also be bad busi-ness for a sport whose fan base was mas-sively skewed toward non-Hadens. People pay extra for the Haden view, and it would be stupid to limit access to 1 percent of the possible fan base. Even in the stands at the live event, the faces of non-Haden specta-tors glinted with the glasses streaming Ha-den view information into their eyeballs.

The reason it was called "Haden view" was that the user interface was designed with Hadens in mind — people so used to living in an alternate electronic reality that what seemed like mad chaotic data overload to non-Hadens was the Haden equivalent of a standard spreadsheet. Non-Hadens could use it and view it, but it wasn't *for* them. They simply had to manage it as best they could.

Ironically this became a selling point for

the Haden view. It seemed "exotic" to non-Hadens and made them feel like they were getting a glimpse into what it was like to be one of us, and to get access into the deeper areas of our life and experience.

And, well, sure. It was like that, exactly in the way going to Taco Bell is like living in a small village deep in Quintana Roo. But then, Taco Bell has thousands of locations, so you tell me.

In the Haden view, I pulled up the player stats and vitals for the Boston Bays.

Tony was right: All the data for every Bays player was there, in exhausting detail — every single possible in-game statistic, from meters run in the game to the amount of damage their threep had taken, and where, and how close they were to losing a limb or having their threep shut down entirely — to every conceivable bit of career or historical data, relevant or otherwise. Not to mention health data, including heartbeat and some limited neural activity.

Which might seem strange at first glance. Haden athletes play Hilketa in threeps, not with their physical bodies. But threeps have full sensory input and output. A Haden feels what their threep feels, and that's going to have an effect on their brains. And like anyone else, Hadens are affected physically

44

by their emotional states. Our hearts race when we're in the middle of the action. Our brain activity spikes when we feel danger or anger. It's all there for us.

And it was all there for every single player on the Boston Bays.

Except for Duane Chapman. His stats and vitals were nowhere to be found.

I scrubbed back several minutes to when I knew Chapman had been on the field. His player box was there but the data from it was gone. Someone had retroactively gone back and pulled all the data for Chapman out of the feed.

Which was stupid. Thousands of people would have been recording the game's Haden view data for their personal use. They weren't supposed to — "Data feeds provided by the North American Hilketa League are the exclusive property of the NAHL and may not be recorded or stored in any form or fashion without the express written consent of the NAHL and its governing bodies," as the boilerplate read — but they did. Whatever the NAHL was trying to erase was almost certainly already being shared, in the Agora and other places online.

But they did it anyway. They had to be doing it for a reason.

I glanced over to where Dad was, surrounded by his throng, and saw a couple of the people there being grabbed by apparatchiks and pulled out of Dad's adoring circles. I did a face recognition on a few. They were NAHL bigwigs.

One of them, leaning in to hear the apparatchik whispering in his ear, noticed me looking at him. He turned his back to me. A minute later he walked out the door, followed by several others.

"Uh-oh," I said, out loud.

"What is it?" Mom asked, looking up at me.

"I think something really bad just happened on the field."

"With the player who had his head torn off?"

"Yes," I said. "His information was wiped off the Haden view feed and a bunch of NAHL executives just left the skybox."

"That's not good," Mom said.

"I don't know if it's entirely legal," I said.

"Leaving the skybox?"

"No." I glanced at Mom to see if she was making a joke. She wasn't, she was just trying to process what I was saying to her. "Removing data from the feed. If it was an official data stream for the league, they could be tampering with information they're

46

legally obliged to keep."

"What does that mean?"

"It means I might have to go to work," I said, and then opened a line to my partner.

She took her time to answer. "It's *Sunday,* you asshole," Leslie Vann said to me, when she finally picked up.

"Sorry," I said. "I think we're about to get some overtime."

"What happened?"

"I think something bad just happened to a player at the Hilketa match," I said.

"Jesus, Chris," Vann mumbled. "That's the whole point of the frigging *game.*"

"Not this time," I said. "I think this one may be a special case."

Vann grunted and hung up. She was on her way. I went back into the skybox to see the PR people begin to deploy on the would-be investors.

CHAPTER TWO

"Well, this is fun," Vann said, as she walked up to me. Around us, the corridors of the stadium were in chaos as league apparatchiks hustled would-be investors into private areas for discussion, Metro cops and stadium security managed crowds shocked to learn about the death of Duane Chapman, and press members flitted everywhere, looking for stories to file.

"Are you caught up on the news?" I asked.

"I heard about the player death on the way here. They did a live broadcast of the press conference. Did you listen?"

I nodded. "Well, I did that between trying to get someone to talk to me."

"They shutting you out?"

"Not exactly shutting me out. Just not paying attention to me as they run by."

"You need to be more forceful."

"I think I need to not be in an android body."

"There's an irony for you, considering where we are."

"The whole day has been like this so far, to be honest."

"I bet." Vann stepped back to avoid being collided into by a hurtling apparatchik. "Why didn't you stick with your parents? I'm sure they're somewhere in this maze being fluffed by a Hilketa league executive. You could have listened in."

"One, that's an image I never needed in my brain and I will make you pay for it," I said. Vann did not seem impressed by the threat. "Two, I foolishly thought that someone might actually be willing to help out an FBI agent."

"Yeah," Vann said. "So, why don't you try to locate your parents and find out what the league has been saying to them about this little event, and meanwhile I'll grab one of these flunkies passing by and make them give me someone to talk to."

"I don't think I'll be able to find them in this place."

Vann stared for a minute. "It's called a *phone,* Chris." She strode off in search of someone to threaten.

I have no idea where we are, my mother texted back when I sent to her. I felt a moment of real, if futile, vindication at this. *But*

49

not too far from the skybox, I think.

I'll come find you, I sent, and then looked down the endless corridors. I remembered I was a trusted contact for my mother and pulled up her location on an internal screen.

It told me she was at the stadium. Thanks, that was helpful.

"Hey."

I looked up to see a young woman in a suit jacket staring at me. "Yes?"

"You were in the skybox earlier, right?"

"I was."

The young woman sighed in relief. "I was told to gather everyone. Come with me, please." She beckoned me with a wave. I was curious enough to follow.

She led me to a small conference room that was jammed with the German, Japanese, and other potential investors, none of whom looked particularly pleased to be there at the moment. "We're going to begin the investor conference in just a moment," the young woman said, and then slipped out.

I looked around at the crowd. Middle-level rich people looked the same wherever in the world they were from. These ones were mostly male, mostly middle-aged, and mostly looking like they shouldn't have to be here wasting their *time.*

The door to the room burst open and a man walked in. He was the suit who had tried to give me his empty glass back in the skybox.

"I've met most of you before but for those I've not, I'm MacKenzie Stodden, head of NAHL franchisee relations," he said, once he'd gotten to the lectern set up near the far wall of the room. "And to begin I want to thank you for being with us here today at what is now one of most successful pre-season games ever."

"What the fuck are you talking about?" one of the would-be investors asked. He was not Japanese or, I suspected, German. He sounded like he was from Jersey. "You just had a player die on the goddamned field."

"In the final moments of the game," Stodden said. "Prior to that moment, the game had the highest real-time and streaming numbers we've seen for a pre-season game, and the highest number of Haden view purchases by a significant percentage."

"And then your player fucking died," Jersey said.

"Yes," Stodden said. "A tragic accident which everyone in the league feels shocked and deeply saddened about." He said this in a tone of voice that registered neither shock nor sadness. I recognized the tone as one you would get out of a salesman of some really high-end product, trying to close a deal. Which I suppose was exactly what he was. "Duane Chapman was admired and respected across the league, and in the league's season opener this Friday night in Boston, we'll be doing a special pregame segment to honor him and his career. But neither I nor the league want this accident to overshadow the investment proposition Hilketa offers to you as potential franchisees, both here and in the international leagues we plan to create."

"How did the player die?" someone asked, in what sounded to me like a Russian accent.

"The medical examiner in Philadelphia will be examining Chapman tonight," Stodden said.

"That's not an answer. You must already know."

"It would be irresponsible for me to speculate."

"And it would be irresponsible for me, or anyone else here, to invest in a league that will not share information."

Stodden sighed. "Look," he said. "This is not something we want to see in the press, but Duane and his wife were having trouble and he had taken to . . . well, I guess 'self-

52

medicating' is the euphemism that we would want to use, here. It had begun to affect his performance in pre-season practices. He was given a warning, and we thought it was working. We may have been wrong."

"There's a difference between being high, and dying during a game," Jersey said.

"I'm saying it's possible that his usage affected his physical well-being long-term, and we saw the results of that today."

"So the problem is him, not the league," someone else said, and it was impossible to tell whether the statement was meant to be sincere or sarcastic.

"The league has been in business for over a decade," Stodden said. "In all that time, with all the equipment and training that we use, and with all the product partnerships that we have, we've never had a player die. We're confident that, as tragic as Duane's death is, this is literally a glitch. An anomaly. And something you, as franchisees, will not need to concern yourself with as we move forward with expansion plans."

"You want us just to forget it ever happened," the Russian said.

"Of course not," Stodden said. "We want you to have confidence that the league will investigate this tragedy and take steps to ensure it can't happen again. We'll come out of it quickly, both stronger and better."

"What happened to Duane Chapman's feed?" I asked.

"Pardon me?" Stodden peered over to me and seemed momentarily confused at the appearance of a threep in the midst of his investors.

"The players have a data feed with their physical stats that streams through the entire course of the game, including heart rate and brain activity," I said. "When Chapman's threep was carried off the field, his data feed disappeared. Just his, no one else's."

"You're . . . you're from *catering*," Stodden said, recognizing me, sort of.

"Actually, I'm from the FBI," I said, and suddenly every head in the room locked on to me. "And I'd really like to know what happened to that data feed."

"That was one way to get their attention," Vann said to me. The two of us were standing around in a now-deserted private skybox, waiting for a league representative to come talk to us. I had caught her up on recent events. "I was just threatening peons to get higher up the chain of command here, but what you did works too."

"I think it's interesting that this Stodden

54

character could simultaneously say they didn't know why Chapman died and also blame him for his own death," I said.

"You said his job was franchisee relations, right?" Vann asked. I nodded. "Then it's not his job to tell the truth. It's his job to keep the money from bolting."

"I think I ruined that plan," I said.

"Yes, well," Vann said. "Now you know why we finally have someone important coming to talk to us."

The door to the skybox opened and a man and a woman walked into the room. The woman came up to Vann, smiling, hand extended. "Agent Vann. I'm Coretta Barber, NAHL associate vice president for publicity." Vann shook her hand, and Barber came over to me to shake hands as well. "Agent Shane. And this is Oliver Medina, general counsel for the league. Shall we sit?" She motioned to a small, round bar table. We sat.

Barber turned to me. "I understand you caused a bit of a commotion at an investor meeting, Agent Shane."

"I didn't intend to," I said. "I was just curious what happened to that data feed."

"You're aware that meeting was meant to be private and confidential," Medina said.

Vann jumped in. "One of your own people

led Shane into the meeting."

"I wasn't asked if I was an investor," I said. "I was asked if I was in the skybox earlier. Which I was."

"You know who Shane's parents are," Vann said. "You can't imagine they wouldn't *talk* to their own kid."

"Nevertheless, I expect you to treat the information you learned as privileged," Medina said.

"You can expect anything you want," Vann said. She turned to Barber. "But this is now an FBI investigation. Speaking of which, maybe you can explain why you were trying to cover up the details of Duane Chapman's death by pulling his data feed."

"Of *course* we weren't trying to cover up what happened to Duane Chapman," Barber said. "We couldn't have covered it up. We were simply protecting his privacy, and the privacy of his family."

"His *privacy,*" Vann said.

"That's right." Barber nodded.

"Forty thousand people in the stands watched Chapman die, Ms. Barber."

"Forty thousand people watched a threep being taken off the field," Barber said. "It's not the same thing."

"You broadcast your players' heart rate and brain activity to eighty thousand people a game for $29.95 a pop," Vann replied, "or $39.95 for three games in a single day. If you could sell the data on when your players peed, you'd do it."

Barber frowned. "I think you're making light of a serious and tragic situation."

I jumped in. "What Agent Vann is trying to say is that data privacy isn't something the NAHL has been very concerned about before."

"I don't think that's accurate."

I shook my head at this. "I checked to see whether the NAHL had ever redacted a data feed of a player before. You've got eight years of Haden view data available and in all that time you've never pulled a data feed."

"We've never had a player die on the field before this."

"Is that the protocol?" Vann asked. "Someone *dies,* you pull the feed? Is that in the NAHL bylaws somewhere?"

"I would have to check," Barber replied, flustered. "But my point is once it became clear that Duane was in trouble, it made sense to pull the feed."

Vann squinted at Barber. "Why?"

Medina spoke up. "So his family wouldn't have to learn he died from a goddamned data feed, Agent Vann. So that one of us could break the news to them, not a sports-caster or some random troll from the Ag-ora."

Vann looked over to Medina. "Uh-huh."

"You don't seem particularly sympa-thetic," Medina said, to Vann. "Perhaps you would have preferred some troll tell his mother, or his sister."

"If you were trying to avoid that, you could have just cut the feed from that point," I said. "But you took down the whole feed. Everything from the moment the game started."

"And?" Medina asked.

"You had a player die. You have a live feed of data relating to his physical status. Then you took it down. Who knows what you've been doing to it since."

Medina smirked. "Because we would tamper with data that people already have."

"No one's data feed but yours is official," I pointed out. "Not even your broadcast partners' feeds."

"And no one has any data from after the moment you pulled it," Vann said.

"Duane's death was an *accident*," Barber said.

"Yes," Vann said. "If only we had a verifi-able data feed to help confirm that. But we don't, so we can't. Which is why *we're* here,

Ms. Barber. The minute the league pulled that feed, we had to assume something *other* than an accident."

"If you're suggesting that the league is in any way implicated in a wrongful death, we'll be stopping this conversation now," Medina said.

Vann turned to me. "Look, it's a lawyer."

"I actually knew that," I said.

"Mr. Medina," Vann said, turning back to the lawyer, "by all means, stop this conversation now. And when you do, I'll do what *I* do, which is to get warrants for every single bit of data relating to Duane Chapman's death, and also everything else I think is even vaguely related to his death, which will be many things. I will also tell the Washington, D.C., and Philadelphia Police Departments to warrant up as well, and between the three of us we'll be very noisy about it. Which I'm sure is a thing that your league would love to have happen right now, while you're trying to keep potential investors, who are already nervous about a dead player, from bailing and taking their money with them."

Barber looked appalled. Medina, on the other hand, just looked annoyed. He got it.

"Or?" Medina asked, finally.

"Or, for starters, you can tell us why you

59

actually pulled that data."

Medina looked at Barber and nodded. She sighed. "Deputy Commissioner Kaufmann ordered it pulled," she said. I looked up the name. Alex Kaufmann appeared in my vision, youngish.

"Why?" Vann asked.

"Because he's stupid," Medina said, and then held up a hand to preempt Vann's objection. "I know. But it's actually the truth. He saw the feed, realized Chapman was dying, and panicked. He ordered the technical director to pull the feed. She wasn't happy about it but she didn't have any choice."

"Who is the technical director?" I asked.

"Giselle Hurwitz," Barber said.

"Is she here?"

"I think so. She may be back at the hotel by now."

Vann turned to Medina. "And she'll talk to us."

"I'll let her talk to you, yes."

"And Chapman's data?"

"What about it?"

"We'll need it."

"Why?"

"Did you *miss* the entire conversation we just had about the potential for the data to have been compromised?" Vann said.

"We need our own people to look at it now," I said. "We have to be sure. And we need to see what happened after the feed was down."

"I'm worried about it getting out," Barber said.

Vann smiled. "This is your privacy gambit again."

Barber flared at this. "Look, it's not just a bullshit line. The last thing we want is Duane's family to find this data feed floating around with people speculating about it."

"So you're not going to put it back up?" I asked.

Barber opened her mouth but Medina quickly put his hand on her shoulder to silence her. "We'll be returning the game portion of Duane's feed to the overall data set very soon. We can't certify the game stats until they are in there. The rest of it I feel comfortable keeping out of the public eye for now."

"We need all the data," Vann repeated.

"Giselle will have it," Medina said. "She'll give it to you. You can verify it if you want. And, Agent Vann."

"Yes?"

"Later, if I see it out there in the world, I'll come find you."

CHAPTER THREE

The lobby of the Hilton looked like a press conference had exploded inside of it. The lobby itself was filled with reporters and other various grades of journalists looking for someone, anyone, to get a quote from, while outside the lobby, television and streaming journalists and their crews jostled each other for space to do their one-shots.

"This seems excessive," Vann said to me as we got out of the taxi we took to the hotel.

"It's the league's first player death, at the last pre-season game," I said. "And the league was actively courting new money. It's national news."

Vann grunted at this and we went into the lobby through the revolving door. As we came out of the door, a couple dozen sets of eyes looked at us and a secon later, through their glasses, identified both Vann and myself as FBI agents, and me as, well, me.

"Oh, *here* we go," Vann said, and then we were surrounded by press yelling questions at us.

"Why is the FBI investigating the death of Duane Chapman?" shouted one journalist, as we trudged toward the elevator bank.

"No comment," Vann said.

"Is there reason to believe there was foul play in Chapman's death?" shouted another.

"No comment." Vann jabbed the elevator call button.

"Agent Shane, your father may be investing in the league, is it appropriate for you to be part of the FBI investigation?"

"No comment," I said.

"Chris, are you dating anyone?"

"What?" I said. "Really?"

"You're still famous!"

"Jesus. No comment," I said. Vann grabbed me into the elevator and glared at the reporters to keep them from blocking the doors.

"You're still *famous*," Vann said to me, mockingly, after the doors closed.

"I'm really *not*," I protested.

"I don't think it's something you get to vote on."

"I'll pass anyway."

"You used to do that every day?"

"I had my share of press gaggles when I

was growing up," I said. "But not for something like this."

Vann nodded. "A firehose would solve the problem."

"In the short run," I agreed. "In the long run it would just make more trouble. Reporters don't forgive being firehosed." We exited the elevator.

Giselle Hurwitz was a Haden and her "room" at the Hilton was a charging closet with an inductive floor mat. We met in a conference room the league had reserved for meetings.

"Thank you for meeting me here," she said, after we had made our introductions and sat. "I didn't want to bother with the lobby."

"Completely understandable," I said.

"Did Medina explain why we're here?" Vann asked Hurwitz.

She nodded. "You want Duane's data feed."

"We also want to ask you about why it was pulled."

"Oh, *that,*" Hurwitz said. Her threep was one that had facial movement in it. She pulled a frown. "That was all Commissioner Kaufmann. I warned him against it."

"What did he do?"

"He freaked out. Me and Taylor, my assistant director, were monitoring the player feeds in the broadcast booth when he came in and told me to pull Chapman's feed out of the data stream. He slammed open the door and the first words out of his mouth were 'Pull Chapman's feed. Pull the whole thing.' "

"You saw that Chapman's vitals were all over the place by then?" I asked.

"Sure, but we've had that happen before," Hurwitz said. "I mean, we haven't had anyone *die* before. But we've had players affected during games. Last season we had Clemente Salcido have a seizure during a game. He was with Mexico City. His threep just dropped and shook, and his brain activity was spiking all over the place."

"And no one told you to cut the feed then."

"We were told to *highlight* it," Hurwitz said. "We can take any individual player data and pin it so everyone who has Haden view sees it. The broadcast director had us pin it and then feed it to our broadcast affiliates. He said it was great drama. He was kind of an asshole."

"What happened to the player?" Vann asked.

"Salcido was benched for the rest of the season and then dropped. The league's insurance carrier didn't want to cover him for play. They were worried his next seizure would kill him."

"Did what was happening to Chapman look like what happened to Salcido?" I asked.

"I don't remember," Hurwitz said, and spread her hands. "Sorry. It was a while ago. And I'm a tech person anyway, not a doctor."

"Can you get us the feed for Salcido's event?"

"Sure, but that's my point. I don't *have* to get you the feed for that. You can get it yourself. It's in the league's public data archive. We don't pull feeds. Not before tonight."

"So why now?" Vann asked.

"You'd have to ask Commissioner Kaufmann."

"You didn't ask why?"

"Of course I asked why. And he said, 'Pull the fucking feed or you're fired.' He's the boss. Or one of them, anyway. I wasn't going to lose my job over it." Hurwitz nodded to me. "*You* know why."

I nodded back. A year ago Congress passed the Abrams-Kettering Bill, drastically cutting back government assistance and coverage for people with Haden's. It's

66

not a cheap syndrome to have, even with government assistance.

A year isn't a lot of time, but it's enough time for a lot of Hadens to notice the economic floor was suddenly tilting out from under them. Hurwitz's gig as a technical director for the NAHL probably paid well, and it wouldn't do for a league that relies on Haden athletes to give its Haden employees a rough ride on benefits.

But these days she and most other Hadens were working without a net. The rationale behind the Abrams-Kettering Bill was that advances in technology and medicine meant Hadens were now playing on a more even field along with everyone else, and that the government could scale back the services it had provided them over the last couple of decades.

It was a nice theory. Hurwitz's comment suggested in practice there were some issues.

But what did I know. I was a government employee with excellent benefits. And a ridiculous trust fund.

"You didn't worry that you'd get in trouble for pulling the feed?" Vann asked.

"No," Hurwitz said, then amended, "Well, a little. But there were six other people in the broadcast booth. They all heard Commissioner Kaufmann order me to pull Chapman's feed. I figured it would be hard for him to pin it entirely on me if it became a problem." She paused. "*Is* it a problem? I mean, I *know* it's a problem, or you wouldn't be here. But I want to know if it's a *problem* problem. I don't want to lose my job."

"There's a problem," Vann said. "I don't think it's your problem. It might be Alex Kaufmann's problem, though."

Hurwitz seemed to relax at that. "Well, he's staying here at the hotel. In case you wanted to ask him."

Vann smiled at Hurwitz. "Did you just throw your boss under the bus, Ms. Hurwitz?"

There was the smallest of mechanical noises as Hurwitz's threep made a smile. "He threatened to fire me today, Agent Vann. I think it's okay to make him sweat a bit."

Kaufmann didn't answer his phone but texted back to me a minute later. Apparently he was screening his calls. *I've been expecting you,* he texted. *I'm literally just about to hop into the shower. Can you come up in fifteen minutes? Room 2423.*

"He'll meet us in fifteen minutes," I said,

to Vann. We were returning to the lobby.

"Good, I need a smoke."

"Have you thought about quitting?"

Vann gave me a look.

"You should quit, you know," I said.

"I'm going to keep giving you this look."

"Yeah, I know." The elevator opened up and we exited the lobby so Vann could have her cigarette. The journalists who accosted us earlier were occupied with a league executive. We escaped the lobby unscathed.

"Have you looked at the data yet?" Vann asked me as she puffed.

"No," I said. Hurwitz sent it to me directly, threep to threep. She pulled it straight out of the NAHL's data cloud and I downloaded it directly into my threep's local memory. "I was going to contract Tony to look at it. He'd know whether it's been tampered with."

Vann nodded. In addition to being my flatmate, Tony Wilton was a high-end computer nerd who regularly contracted with the federal government. He was smart, easy to work with, and already in the vendor system, and when he got paid, some of the payment went toward the communal rent. So in a way it was like getting cash back.

"But it's all there," Vann said.

"It's all here as far as I can tell," I agreed.

69

"And soon enough we'll see what it has to say about Chapman dying."

"It's going to show that Chapman had some sort of seizure, like that other guy."

"Salcido," I prompted.

"Right." Vann puffed again. "Hadens have a higher incidence of seizures because of what the syndrome does to the brain and because of the neural nets we stick in there." She looked at me. "Have you ever had one?"

"A seizure?"

"Yeah."

"No. How about you?" When Vann was a teenager she had contracted Haden's and suffered through both the early flu-like stage, and then the much more painful second phase, which resembled meningitis. Unlike many whose progression went that far, she was not locked in, nor did she suffer significant mental damage or cognitive impairment. To all outward appearances, she came out of it just fine.

Nevertheless her brain was rearranged by the disease. And she had a neural net in her head, a souvenir from her days as an Integrator, one of the fully ambulatory humans who could let a Haden borrow their bodies to do things for which human bodies were desirable, or required.

"No," she said, and then held up her

70

cigarette. "But then again I self-medicate."

"So if the data shows he had a seizure, what then?" I asked.

"Then it's just bad luck for Duane Chapman."

"There'll be an autopsy too. That was covered in the press conference."

"Right. Which will likely confirm that it was a random seizure."

"That doesn't explain why Kaufmann freaked out like he did."

"He's probably an idiot, like the lawyer said. Saw one of his players dying on the field, remembered the league was wining and dining potential investors, including your dad — how did that go, incidentally?"

"Mom said that she and Dad went home. A league flunky was begging him not to leave yet. I think after this they need his credibility more than they did before."

"After this, your dad could probably ask to be made commissioner and they'd give him the job and a parade."

"I don't think he'd want the job."

"That's because your dad is smart. So, we go visit Kaufmann, he admits he over-reacted and is an idiot, which is sad for him but not actually a crime. And then we'll be done with our end of things."

"Okay," I said.

"Which means you will have dragged me out here, on a Sunday, for nothing."

"Sorry."

"I was sleeping."

"It was four thirty in the afternoon when I called. I'm not going to feel too bad about that."

"I had a late night."

"Mom says you might be having too many of those."

Vann smiled. "She's not *my* mom." She dropped her cigarette and crushed it out. "Come on. Let's go talk to Kaufmann."

"We'll be early."

"I want to get back to sleeping. If Kaufmann's not fully dressed he doesn't have anything I haven't already seen elsewhere."

The door to room 2423 was unlocked. The bolt, which normally would have secured the door, stuck out, keeping the door from closing entirely. Behind the door was the sound of the shower, still running. "I told you we were early," I said.

Vann ignored me and knocked on the door, calling Kaufmann's name, and did both a second time when he didn't answer. He didn't answer the second time, either. Vann unholstered her sidearm and prepared to enter the room, then looked at me. "Where's your weapon?"

72

"It's at home," I said.

"You're working."

"I wasn't," I reminded her. "Then I was. It wasn't convenient to go home."

She reached down to her ankle and produced a small pistol. She handed it to me.

"You actually have an ankle holster," I said to her, after a moment of staring.

"Yes. Come on." We entered the room, cautiously.

There was no one in the main hotel room, which didn't entirely surprise me, as the shower was running. The bed was rumpled and slept in. On the floor by the bed were various articles of clothing: a shirt, suit jacket, slacks, tie. A wallet and a pair of glasses were on the dresser, by the TV.

Something was missing from that collection.

"Chris," Vann said. I looked up and she pointed into the bathroom.

What had been missing was a belt. One end of which was knotted around the showerhead, still running, the pipe of which had been pulled out of the wall.

Just not enough to keep Alex Kaufmann from being strangled on the other end of belt. He was very clearly dead. Vann went in and checked, to be sure.

"Well, shit," Vann said, coming back out

of the bathroom. She holstered her weapon.

I looked at her. "We're not still going with the 'it's just bad luck' theory anymore, are we?"

Vann looked my threep up and down. "New threep."

"Yes."

"How is it for recording and mapping?"

"It's got all the bells and whistles. I've been recording since we entered the room."

Vann nodded. "Map it. Map the entire room, including in there." She pointed into the bathroom. "I want to get as much information as possible before Metro police gets in here and starts fucking up the scene. And then I'm going to need you to do something else."

"What's that?"

"Go to Philadelphia."

"Tonight?"

"Yes," Vann said. "We need to talk to Duane Chapman's wife. Before someone from the league convinces her not to talk to us." She motioned to Kaufmann's body. "After this, the league's urge to shut everyone up is going to be very strong."

CHAPTER FOUR

I got back home an hour later for my trip to Philly. A welcoming party was waiting for me in the foyer.

"Tell *everything*," the twins said. Or one of them, anyway — Justin and Justine shared a threep and you never quite knew which of them was operating their threep at the time, and after a while you stopped wondering and just thought of their threep as "the twins." I was told there was a reason the twins shared their threep, and I had been promised early on it would be explained to me, but a year after moving into the house I shared with them and three other Hadens the reason had yet to be revealed. Honestly at this point I sort of enjoyed speculating more than knowing the actual answer.

"Chris can't tell everything," Tony yelled from the front room. "It's classified."

"It's not classified," I yelled back. I returned my attention to the twins. "But I probably don't know anything more than you do about Duane Chapman right now."

"There are *rumors,*" the twins said, backing up to let me into the house.

"That I don't doubt." I walked into the front room, where the threeps of Tony and Tayla Givens, two of my other flatmates, were shooting pool. Elsie Curtis, the final roommate and our most recent addition to the house, was on a work gig in Singapore and kept different hours from the rest of us. We rarely saw her around these days.

Well, that's not true. We saw her every single day. Her body was in her room, along with her local threep. We checked in on her a few times a day, changed her various bags, and the one of us who was an actual doctor — that would be Tayla — would make sure there were no outstanding biological issues that needed to be addressed. Elise checked on all of us, too, usually while the rest of us were asleep.

That was the whole point of the house: six Hadens, living together and looking after each other's bodies. It was cheaper and friendlier than hiring in-home staff, especially now that Abrams-Kettering had cut off medical subsidies to Hadens. These days every bit helped.

For the rest of my housemates, that is. My physical body still resided in my parents' house in Northern Virginia, along with two full-time caretakers. I had been planning to move my body to the communal house at some point, but I was confronted with the optics problem of having two personal caretakers while the rest of my flatmates had none, or dismissing my caretakers and then being responsible for two people I'd known and cared about for years losing their jobs. Jobs they wouldn't be able to easily replace, because the Abrams-Kettering Bill meant there was less money for Hadens for home care.

It was easier to maintain the status quo. Cowardly, perhaps. But easier.

Not that my flatmates minded all that much. One extra pair of eyes and hands paying attention to their bodies, one fewer body for them to take care of on a day-to-day basis. Plus I paid for the biggest room in the house. Really, I was a model house-mate.

"We saw you on the news," Tayla said. She was lining up a shot on the pool table. "You and your partner being mobbed while you were waiting for an elevator."

"And then the two of you finding that NAHL executive dead in his hotel room,"

77

Tony said.

"There are *rumors,*" the twins repeated.

"I'd rather not add to any of those," I said.

"People are saying you wouldn't be involved if there wasn't a murder."

"That's not true," I told the twins. "We're involved because Duane Chapman died under unusual circumstances."

"So did the executive," Tony pointed out.

"Murder is an unusual circumstance," the twins noted.

"Not *that* unusual," Tayla said. She worked at a D.C. emergency room, so she had standing to opine.

"There's nothing to say it's murder," I said. "In either case. It's unusual, that's all. And Chapman's threep was in D.C. while his body was in Philadelphia. That's an interstate issue. When it's an interstate issue, we get called in."

"And they didn't even have to call you in," Tony said. "You were already *there.*"

"Damn it." Tayla had flubbed her shot. Tony was now lining up his. "At the very least, you've had a busy day today," she said.

"It's going to get busier," I said. "I have to go to Philly. I need to interview Duane Chapman's wife."

"Jesus," Tayla said. "That's no fun."

"The rumors say they were estranged,"

the twins said.

"Do the rumors say why?" I asked.

"The usual. Infidelity. Stupidity. Group-ies. Stress because he's Haden and she's not."

"How are you getting to Philly?" Tony asked. He sank his shot.

"The FBI office there has a visitor's threep. I'll use that. Also, Tony, I need to talk to you privately before I go."

"I'm busy humiliating Tayla at the mo-ment," Tony said, and then shanked his shot. His ball clicked against the eight ball, which had been in front of the left side pocket. The eight ball sank into the pocket. "Shit."

"You were saying?" Tayla said, to Tony.

"Chris cursed me," Tony said, and then looked over to me. "You totally cursed me."

"Sorry."

"I demand compensation."

"Well, as it happens, the thing I wanted to talk to you about can probably take care of that."

The Philadelphia FBI's guest threep was a late-model Sebring-Warner Galavant, which was mildly surprising to me. The Galavant was a midprice, midspecced model, and since the FBI's loaner threeps tended to be gotten through civil forfeiture, they were usually either barely functional basic models, gotten from street-level miscreants, or high-end luxury gigs, gotten from miscreants higher up. With the Galavant, either some suburban Haden had gotten tangled up in a questionable enterprise, or the Philly FBI office actually bought a guest threep, and this was what they could get past the bursar.

The loaner threep was stored in a storage closet. When I accessed it, the first thing I noticed was that it was at 13 percent power. I looked down and saw that the threep had been displaced off its induction plate, shoved over by a pile of boxes.

"Well, crap," I said out loud. I shoved the boxes back, and stood full on the plate to see if it was a high-speed charger, and got nothing. I followed the power cord. It was unplugged. I cursed and plugged it in and got back on the plate. It informed me that a full charge would take eight hours.

The door to the equipment opened and an older gentleman peered in. "Hello?"

"Do you know if there's a high-speed induction plate somewhere in this office?" I asked.

"A what now?" the man asked.

I suppressed an urge to groan. "Are you

an agent here?"

"No, uh —"

"Agent Shane."

"No, Agent Shane. I'm custodial staff. Nearly everyone else is at home. It's Sunday evening. I didn't even know you were here. I just heard noises."

"Sorry."

"It's fine. I just thought the rats might have come back." He held open the door to let me out.

I exited the storage room into a hallway and called up a map of nearby fast-charge induction plates open to the public. There weren't any. The FBI office was in a part of Philadelphia's downtown. The area had lots of federal buildings and museums, but not a lot of places open on a Sunday evening. Looked like I would be trying to coax a charge out of the Bureau car that I'd reserved.

"I don't have any notice of a reserved car for you, Agent Shane," the lobby security officer said to me, when I went down to find out where the cars were.

"I sent in the request at the same time I requested the threep," I said.

"I'm sure you did," the security officer said. "But unfortunately that request never got to me, so I can't unlock one of the vehicles for you to use."

I posted up my FBI ID on the Galavant's small chest monitor. "You can check to see I am who I say I am. I mean, beyond the fact that the only way I can access this threep is to use the FBI's encrypted network."

"I believe you," the security officer said. "But I literally cannot unlock a car for you without an authorization code."

"I sort of need a car," I said. "Not only to get where I'm supposed to go but to charge this threep."

"I can call you a cab. Maybe you can charge in there."

I resisted the urge to throw a fit, because the lobby security agent wasn't doing anything wrong. "Please," I said.

Five minutes later the cab appeared at the front of the FBI's building. I went out of the lobby and tapped the passenger-side window. "The cab wouldn't happen to have an induction plate in it, would it?"

"A what?" The cabdriver appeared confused.

"Never mind." I gave him the address of Duane Chapman's town house. As we drove along, I shut down every possible threep system I could to conserve energy. This was going to be a long night, but if I didn't watch my power usage, it would also be a paradoxically short one.

The Chapman town house was thronged by reporters and journalists and also by Hilketa fans, wearing Boston Bays colors. Philadelphia itself didn't have a Hilketa team yet, although it, like Washington, D.C., was slated for an expansion team. Pittsburgh had the Pitbulls. The fact that Pittsburgh had a Hilketa team before Philly was a source of irritation to many Philadelphians.

I put my FBI ID on my threep's chest screen and pushed my way through the mass, making my way up the steps. The door opened before I could knock and a man in nursing scrubs peered out. "Agent Shane?"

"That's me."

The man nodded. "Come inside, please."

"I'm Alton Ortiz," the man said, once we were inside. He'd held out his hand for me to shake, and I did. "I was one of Duane's caretakers."

"I know," I said. "I'm very sorry for your loss."

"Thank you. It's been a rough day."

"I'm sure it has."

"I know you're here to see Marla, but she's busy at the moment."

"Is she talking to the Philadelphia police?"

"No, she did that earlier. This is a league representative."

"Hmmm," I said. The whole point of talking to her now was to do so before the league tried to hush her up. I made a mental note to contact the Philly police and see who was working the death on their end, to see if our stories matched up. "Is it a lawyer?" I asked Ortiz.

"I think so? I know he's here to talk about her survivor benefits." Ortiz motioned to a front sitting room. "If you like you can sit here and I'll let her know you're waiting."

"Actually, I'd like to see Mr. Chapman's room, if that's all right."

Oritz seemed to think about this for a moment, then nodded again. "All right," he said. "The police have already been through it, though."

"I'm sure they have. Don't worry, I'll be unobtrusive."

Duane Chapman's room was on the first floor of the town house, where a traditional dining room might be. This made a bit of sense, as the kitchen area could be used as both a storage and sitting area for caretakers. Along the wall were three threeps, one a standard luxury threep, one designed for heavy-duty recreational use, and a gaudy, vaguely ridiculous-looking thing that I recognized as a "formal" threep, something to wear to galas and events. Near the back of the room sat a now empty creche, a model I didn't recognize.

"It's Labram," Ortiz said when I asked him about it. "The company makes them specifically for the league. All the players have one."

"That's a very specific endorsement deal," I said.

Ortiz shook his head. "It's not that. Labram creches have special systems and monitors to transmit information and to make sure there's no cheating going on."

"Is there a lot of that in Hilketa?"

"It's a professional sport, Agent Shane. Lots of players would give it a shot."

I nodded to the empty creche. "What about Chapman?"

Ortiz smiled and shook his head. "Naw, man. Not Duane. Duane was straight-edge as they come." He motioned to an IV bag, unhooked now and dangling by the creche. "He only used league-approved supplements and IVs."

I walked over and looked at the IV solution bag. Labram was also the brand name on it. "Was Chapman straightedge outside of his career?" I asked.

"What do you mean?"

"There are rumors that he was struggling with sobriety." I motioned my head to a picture on the wall, a portrait of Marla Chapman. "Because of troubles at home."

Ortiz's face darkened a bit at this. "I don't think I need to be talking about that," he said.

I held up a hand. "I'm not asking because I want to hear the latest gossip. I'm asking because I want to know why your friend died playing a game that shouldn't have killed him."

"I'll let you talk to Marla about that," Ortiz said, after a minute. "But I'll tell you this, Agent Shane. I was with Duane most of the time he was awake and all the time he was on the field, practicing or playing. No one would know better than me if he was doping, professionally or recreationally. I saw nothing like that. That wasn't his thing."

"So what *was* his thing?"

"Like I said, I'll let Marla talk to you about that. Speaking of which, let me see if she's ready for you."

I nodded and Ortiz exited, toward the kitchen, where Marla Chapman was talking to the league rep. I took the opportunity to quietly map the room for future examination.

When I was done I drew my attention to Marla Chapman's photo on the wall. She was young and attractive in a mostly standard American cheerleader way. She was non-Haden, which made it unusual for her to have married someone who was. Most of the time when there was a mixed marriage of this sort, it was because one partner had contracted the disease at some point after the wedding. There was no bar to Hadens and non-Hadens hooking up, dating, or getting married — you're consenting adults, do what you want and be happy about it — but as with any time partners come from wildly different backgrounds, there are challenges.

And if the rumors were true in this case, the challenges might have been too much for this particular marriage.

Ortiz came back into the room. "Marla will see you now," he said. I followed him into the kitchen, bumping into the league rep as I entered, and whom Ortiz escorted out of the house. He didn't seem entirely happy as he exited. But then, seated at the kitchen table, Marla Chapman didn't seem entirely happy with him. She looked over to me, and the "not entirely happy" theme

87

continued.

"Mrs. Chapman, I'm Agent Chris Shane of the FBI's Haden affairs division," I said.

"I know who you are," Chapman said, and looked away. She held a small glass in her hand and fiddled with it, running a distracted finger around the rim. "Duane used to be a *fan* of yours." She motioned to an unoccupied chair at the table for me to sit in.

I sat. "I'm very sorry about your husband's death."

"Thank you." Chapman's voice was distant and guarded.

I motioned back to where the league representative had gone. "I hope everything is okay with you and the league."

Chapman glanced over to the door and smirked. "Oh, that prick," she said. "It was fine. He was just trying to bribe me."

"How so?"

"With my survivor benefits."

"Was he threatening to withhold them?"

"He can't. That much I know. But he's offering me extra to stay quiet. A settlement."

"The league can't keep you from talking to us," I said.

"Not you." Chapman pointed in the direction of the front door. "*Them.* The press camped out on my stoop."

"Why would he do that?"

"Because in public the league would rather have Duane be a tragic figure than the cheating son of a bitch he was." Chapman looked at me and, while obviously attractive, was haggard and drawn. "Agent Shane, may I ask you a question?"

"Yes."

"A personal question."

"All right. I'll answer it if I can."

"When is it you can say a Haden is a cheating son of a bitch?"

"I'm afraid I'm not following the question," I said.

Chapman motioned to my threep. "Well, look at you," she said. "You're walking around in a machine. If you're in a machine, and you're fooling around with someone else, are you *really* fooling around? Is it sex? *Actual* sex?"

She took a hand and gestured toward the room where her husband's creche resided. "What I want to know is whether you think I should be allowed to be angry with my dead husband for screwing around on me, or if I should just be a grieving widow because sex doesn't count if you're in a machine for it."

I stared for a minute. "Mrs. Chapman —"

"Marla."

"— I don't think I'm qualified to judge your relationship with your husband."

"Sure you are. You're a *Haden.* So was my husband. He was one since he was three years old. We met in college. I dated a guy in a threep. You wouldn't believe the crap I got for that, by the way. At Thanksgiving the first year I dated Duane, I had a cousin ask me what it was like to date a walking vibrator."

"What did you say?" I asked.

"I didn't *say* anything. I punched the crap out of him, though."

I smiled inwardly at this. "That seems fair," I said.

"I always said I was in love with Duane for who he was, and the fact he was in a threep didn't matter." Chapman fiddled with her glass some more. "And then he joined the league and the *others* started happening. He would deny it, and there was no way to prove it, was there?" She motioned to me. "You go off into the Agora or can port yourself into a different threep if you want. You could say you were sleeping or playing a game or whatever and none of us would ever know. At least not until you fuck up and the landlord of the apartment you're renting for your *adventures* calls your business line to tell you that the neighbors are complaining about the noise, and your wife takes the call instead of you."

"I'm sorry," I said.

"So am I. But I'd still like you to answer the question."

I thought about it for a minute. Then I said, "You had certain expectations and understandings with your husband, Mrs. Chapman. About intimacy. About who you both spent your time with and how that time was spent. If your husband went against that, then he was unfaithful to you. Whether it counts as 'sex' is immaterial to that."

"So you *would* say he was a cheating son of a bitch."

"Yes," I said. "If he was doing that, he was a cheating son of a bitch."

"Thank you," Chapman said, and drained her glass. "Now. What are your questions for me?"

"Were you here today when your husband had his attack?"

"No. On game days we have too many people in the house. Alton, his caregiver. You met him." I nodded. "Whoever the league sends over to monitor Duane and Alton so they don't try to cheat, or whatever. Duane's pals from the neighborhood, who watch the game in the living room on our one-hundred-inch screen. They get a kick out of being able to yell at Duane whenever he screws up a play. There are usually five or six of them. So, no. I go out to shop or have lunch or see a movie with friends and come back when the game is done and everyone's cleared out."

"So today —"

"So today I went to see a movie with my friend Karen and I turned off my phone." A pause here while Chapman fiddled with her empty glass and her eyes welled with tears that almost but did not spill over. She looked away, blinked, and then looked at me again. "And then when I turned my phone back on I learned that Duane was dead."

"Before you left the house, did you say anything to your husband?"

"Just that I was going to see a movie."

"So no arguments."

"No. Well," Chapman amended, "not *today*. We've argued before. A lot, recently."

"About that apartment."

"No, not that. I'm sorry, I should have been more clear. Duane didn't know I knew about his extracurricular activities there. I just found out about it this last week. I didn't want him to know I knew. I was going to make it a surprise element of the divorce proceedings."

"Mrs. Chapman," I said, "maybe you should have a lawyer present right now."

"Why?" Chapman said. "I didn't *kill* him, Agent Shane. I wasn't even here when he died. And you can *believe* me when I say that I wanted him alive. I wanted to drag him through divorce hell. I don't need a lawyer."

I changed the subject. "Did Duane have any addictions?"

"Aside from sex? No. He never drank or did any drugs, even in college. He was aiming for the league even then. He said he didn't want to blunt his edge."

"What about sharpening his edge, then?"

"You mean performance-enhancing drugs?" Chapman shook her head. "He never did any of that either. The league checked out everything Duane put into his body through a feeding tube or IV. They checked what came out, too. That creche of his monitored everything. Alton had to ship the first bags of urine and feces after a game to the league for testing. And not just Duane had to do this. It's every one of their players. Duane wouldn't risk it. He knew he wasn't a star."

"It's the players who aren't the stars who might take the risk," I said. "They know how quickly they can be out of the league."

Chapman shook her head again. "You don't know Duane. He wouldn't. The league has a special nutritional supplement that they used — every player got it, except for the stars who had their own supplement deals. But even *they* had to get their supplement formula approved. It's the only extra thing Duane ever put into his body."

"What's in the supplement?" I asked.

"I don't know. Vitamins, electrolytes. Duane always said it was basically Haden Gatorade. Why are you asking?"

"You husband died in a very public fashion. I'm sorry to put it this way, but we need to make absolutely sure it was accidental, not something else."

Chapman nodded and motioned toward the room her husband's body had been in. "Everything Duane put into his body is in there," she said. "And if you talk to Alton again, he'll be able to give you a schedule of what got put in when."

"Thank you, I will," I said. "I'm also interested in that apartment you spoke of."

"What about it?"

"If it's something he kept from you, there might be things in there he didn't want you to see."

"You mean, aside from the people he was

94

screwing?" Chapman asked.

"Yes, aside from them," I said.

Chapman shrugged. "So go look."

"We'd need to get a warrant," I said. "From a judge here in town."

"You don't need a warrant," Chapman said. "I can give you permission to go inside."

"If he kept its existence from you, it might be leased through a third party."

Chapman laughed at this. "You would think that, wouldn't you? But I told you, when I got the call from the landlord, it came on the business line. We have a pass-through corporation for endorsements and investments. Duane and I co-owned it. He rented that apartment through the corporation. I'm on the goddamned lease."

CHAPTER FIVE

"I thought you said your cab had a charge plate," I said to the new driver, as I got into the cab.

"I have a charger back here," he said.

"It's a charge port for a phone," I said.

"Right, a charger," he agreed.

I sighed and gave him an address, on Natrona Street in the Strawberry Mansion neighborhood. He punched it in and let the autodrive take over, and then stared into his phone. I glanced into my power level at the moment. I was down into single digits now. Great. I put up a map to see if there were any public charging stations between me and Duane Chapman's secret apartment and found two, both in closed shops. Philadelphia was not impressing me.

An interior window popped up with a New York number I didn't immediately recognize. I debated about answering it but curiosity got the better of me.

"I'm Laurie Wilkerson from *The New York Times*," the person on the other end of the line said. "I was hoping I could talk to you about the investigation of the deaths of Duane Chapman and Alex Kaufmann."

"How did you get this phone number?" I asked.

"Are the two deaths linked somehow?" Wilkerson asked.

"No comment," I said, and hung up and immediately switched my phone settings to "passive," which would log calls and texts rather than take them except from a specific list of contacts. I looked at the call log, which was suddenly filling up with texts and call requests, then closed it and pinged Vann. "My number has apparently just been leaked to the press," I said to her.

"No fucking kidding," she said. "My phone has been a mess for the last ten minutes. You were lucky you called when you did. I was about to turn my phone off."

"What happened?"

"Things are nuts over here," she said to me. "This has blown up into a national scandal. Apparently our dear director has had to jump in with a quote." Vann was not fond of Gibbs Ablemare, the current director of the FBI. "It was no less stupid than anything else he's said in the last year and a half. He said he's giving the Chapman investigation the highest priority."

"Does that mean we're off the case?" I asked.

Vann snorted. "It means we better not screw it up, or we'll be looking for new jobs. For one of us, that will be a problem. How are things on your end?"

I caught Vann up on my end. "Plus I'm almost out of power on this threep and there's nowhere to charge."

"Charge in your cab."

"The cabs of Philadelphia are strangely Haden-unfriendly. Not to mention the rest of the town."

"Well, you're going to the secret love nest of a Haden. I'm guessing there will be charging opportunities there."

"I think that might be inappropriate," I said.

"More inappropriate than powering down in the middle of an investigation?"

"You have a point."

"It's wireless induction. You can just say you didn't know you were standing on a plate."

I ignored this. "Do we have anything new on the investigations?"

"Kaufmann's been cut down and is at the medical examiner's here. They're going to get to him sometime tomorrow. I didn't get much of a sense of urgency from them about it. They think it's a straightforward suicide."

"I mean, so do we?"

"Right, but they don't have the director of the FBI breathing down their necks because he just said on national TV he's making it a priority."

"Fair point."

"Damn right it is. At least the Philly ME is more on the ball. They already have someone examining Chapman's body and will have a preliminary report for us tomorrow."

"So I'll need to come back."

"I'll be there too. I'll want to take this report in person."

"Why?"

"Because we have the FBI director breathing down our necks now."

"I'm sensing a theme in your conversation."

"I don't know why." Vann's sarcasm was unmistakable. "Also, I've had Chapman's game threep impounded. The Bays' tech director said there was nothing wrong with it but I want to be sure. Does your flatmate know anything about threeps?"

"Tony?" I said. "Sure. He's done contract

coding for at least a few of the big Personal Transport companies."

"Add an examination of the threep to his to-do list."

"What is he looking for?"

"For starters, anything that would amp up Chapman's pain sensitivity."

"That's going to take a while. Threeps are complicated and both their hardware and software are usually proprietary."

"Are you saying we'll need a warrant to look at it?" Vann asked.

"No, just that there's going to be a lot of backward engineering involved."

"We'll get in touch with the manufacturer and see if they want to play nice."

"They're going to be worried about liability," I said.

"Then we'll make them worry about impeding a federal investigation."

"That's friendly," I joked.

"FBI director," Vann began.

"Breathing down our necks," I finished. "Yeah, no. I get it."

"I figured you would. Wrap up what you're doing and get back soon. I've got us scheduled bright and early in the imaging room. You, me, your flatmate Tony."

I checked my internal map. "We're almost there. I have to get the landlord to let me in. I'll look around and map it out, and note anything useful or notable for collection tomorrow, when we come back to town."

"Seems simple enough," Vann said.

"Don't jinx it," I said.

We turned onto Diamond, which connected to Natrona, and saw a building on fire.

"Hey," my driver said. He pointed out the windshield to the burning town house. "Isn't that your destination?"

The building was definitely my destination, definitely on fire, and the crowd that had gathered was yelling at someone.

"I am not fucking going back into that thing," a man, short and lumpy, was saying. "I barely got out myself."

"It's your building," one of the crowd said. "You're the landlord."

"I'm not the landlord, I'm the manager."

"So you're going to let her die?!?"

"The fire department is coming!"

"They're not going to get here on time!" someone else yelled.

"They're on York Avenue, for chrissakes," the manager said.

"They closed that station down two years ago, you asshole!"

"I'm not going in!"

"I'll go in," I said, loudly.

Everyone turned to look at me. "I'm an FBI agent," I said.

The manager pointed at me. "Let the Fed go in!"

"Who's still in there?" I asked

"The old lady on the third floor," a kid said to me.

I turned to the manager, who nodded. "Shaniqa Miller," he said. "Everybody else is out but her."

"Everyone?"

"Yeah," the manager said. "I'm ground floor, the Waverlys are on first" — he pointed to a couple sobbing at the curb, a small curly dog licking one of their faces in an attempt to comfort its owner — "and Shaniqa's on third."

"What about the second floor?"

"That guy's dead," someone in the crowd said.

"Not from the fire!" the manager yelled back.

I held out my hand. "Keys."

The manager handed over a key ring with several keys on it, color-coded. "Third floor is the red keys."

"How long has the fire been going?"

"Like five minutes," the manager said. "Out of fucking nowhere."

102

I looked at the building. The entryway doors were blown out with glass everywhere. Smoke poured out the door and out of the windows.

"This is a bad idea," I said to myself, and jumped through the shattered doors.

I turned off my senses of smell and pain but could still feel the heat as I climbed the stairs. The first-floor apartment was wide open and in flames. The second-floor apartment — Chapman's — had its door closed. If Shaniqa Miller's apartment had its door closed, I had a decision to make — opening it could create a column of oxygen rushing through the stairwell, feeding the fire. In a rush to save Miller, I might end up killing her instead.

The problem was moot when I reached the third floor. Miller was on the landing, unconscious, her door ajar behind her. I'd guessed she had tried to make it down the stairs and was overcome by smoke before she'd even gotten to the first stair. Either that or had a heart attack or something else equally grim.

Well, now was not the time to speculate. The fire was still gathering strength. I bent down, picked Miller up in a fireman's carry, and headed down the stairs as quickly as possible, individual steps groaning under the weight. I had to open the ground-floor doors this time to get through with her on my back.

Crowd members rushed up and relieved me of Miller, carrying her away to a safe distance from the burning building. I turned my sense of smell back on and was hit by a wave of scorched plastic and hot metal scent. I figured the Philly FBI branch was not going to be happy with what I did to their threep.

Someone touched me on the arm. It was a kid, who solemnly pointed to the windows of the second floor of the building. There was something moving there. I looked closer.

"Chapman had a goddamn *cat*?" I said, out loud, to no one in particular.

"Are you gonna go get it?" the kid asked.

Oh, come on, I thought, but did not say out loud, and turned to the nearest adult. "How long until the fire department gets here?" I asked.

"This is Strawberry Mansion," she said to me. "By the time they get here, this building's gonna be gone."

Well, I needed to get in there anyway, I thought, and then found the manager in the crowd. "What color key for the second floor?" I asked.

"Green," he said. "You're going back in there?"

"There's a cat," I said.

"I wouldn't," he warned.

"Yeah, but you're an asshole," someone said from the crowd. The manager scowled and shut up.

The second trip up the stairs was hotter and more precarious and smoke-filled than the first. I fished the green keys into the door lock, unlatched the door, and prepped myself to open and close it as quickly as possible to keep the burst of oxygen from adding another layer of ignition to the flames, cracked the door —

— and then saw a flash at my feet as the cat shot out of the apartment and zoomed down the stairs. I slammed the door shut and raced back to the stairwell in time to see the cat rocketing out of the shattered front doors of the building. I looked dumbly to where the cat had exited and then re-membered where I was. I went back to the apartment door and quickly let myself in.

The apartment was filled with smoke and threeps, and the threeps on display in the front room made it clear what they were meant for. One of them was anatomically male, a second anatomically female, and then there were two threeps that were

105

neither but had an area on their lower abdomen that featured ridges and grooves — three grooves separated by two arcing ridges. That was new to me.

I photographed them as I mapped through the apartment as quickly as I could, seeing that it was, after all, on fire. The plan was to map now, examine closely later. Which was a good thing when I got to the bedroom, which was filled with toys, and the spare room, which was a dungeon, and the kitchen, which was less of a kitchen and more of an erotic art gallery.

I wasn't judging. It's just that there was a lot to take in.

But I was also aware that on the surface, and through the smoke, there wasn't much here that was going to be useful. Chapman clearly had his kinks, but kinks were probably unrelated to his death. This visit had been dramatic but only really that.

But you don't really believe that, some part of my brain said.

And I didn't. Coincidence does happen, but Chapman dying and a Hilketa league executive killing himself and Chapman's secret love nest burning down all within a span of eight hours was a little much to take.

"I'm missing something," I said, out loud, and decided to take another swing mapping through the apartment on the way out. I looked up to start mapping.

One of the threeps from the front room was standing in the hall, looking at me through the smoke.

What the hell, I thought, stepped forward, and then was deeply confused as the floor gave way from underneath me. Gravity dropped me into the first-floor apartment of the Waverlys, which was substantially more on fire than Chapman's had been. I rolled over and looked up through what remained of the Waverlys' ceiling, and Chapman's floor, to see the threep looking down at me. Then it disappeared.

My threep informed me I was on fire.

Well, there's a sign, I thought. I picked myself up to get out just in time for my threep's internal systems to warn me I had another thirty seconds of power available to me.

"Fuck," I said, and sprinted toward the front windows. The plan was to jump through them and get the threep clear of the fire and collapsing building.

It was an excellent plan, marred somewhat by the fact that the threep's power management system had egregiously overestimated the power left in the threep. I made it as far as the Waverlys' front room, tastefully appointed in modern-era furniture, and fire, before the threep collapsed. The last thing I saw through the threep was the Eames lounge chair the threep had collided with, which was on fire, and which was now spreading the fire to the threep. Then I was kicked out of the threep entirely, left to float in my liminal space, the private area all Hadens had in the Agora, our online network.

I hovered in my liminal space for a couple of minutes. Then I sighed inwardly and pulled up a window to Avis, the rental service I had an account with.

"Welcome to Avis," the rental bot in the window said. I wouldn't get a human until and unless my request got complicated. "How may I help you?"

"I need to rent a threep," I said. "And a car. Both in Philadelphia, and as close to the Strawberry Mansion neighborhood as you can get."

CHAPTER SIX

"You look tired," Vann said to me the next morning, as I wandered into the FBI's basement imaging room. She, along with Tony Wilton and Ramon Diaz, the imaging lab technician, were waiting for me.

"I'm in a friggin' robot body," I said. "How do I look tired?"

"You're slumping."

"I'm not slumping." I straightened up.

"Uh-huh." Vann went back to her coffee.

"Chris didn't come back to the house until two A.M.," Tony said.

"You're telling on me?" I said to Tony, incredulously.

"I'm giving context."

"You were up then too," I protested.

"*He's* not slumping." Vann pointed at Tony's threep.

"In Chris's defense, I was not the one leaping into burning buildings, rescuing

109

little old ladies and cats from flames," Tony said.

"And then having to file police and fire reports because your borrowed threep burned up in the fire," I said.

"Which reminds me that when we go to Philadelphia later, we have an invitation from the director there to pop into her office and explain why you let a fifty-thousand-dollar threep burn down to the metal," Vann said to me.

"You can tell her that if they had the fucking induction plate plugged in, this wouldn't be a problem."

"No, *you* get to tell her. This should be fun."

"Guys, we should get started," Diaz said. "The room's booked in an hour and you have lots you want to get through."

Vann nodded and turned to Diaz. "Bring up the hotel room."

Diaz fired up the imaging equipment, and out of the projectors came what I had mapped the day before: Alex Kaufmann's hotel room, translucent and half-sized, including the bathroom, which featured Kaufmann's body hanging from the showerhead.

"Whoa, Jesus," Tony said. His hand went up in front of his face.

110

"Sorry," I said.

"I think I should get extra for having to see that."

"Quiet," Vann said.

"You were there after our people and Metro police arrived," I said to Vann. "How did it go?"

"Well, Metro police didn't fuck it up, which was a miracle." Vann pointed to Kaufmann's virtual corpse. "Our people, Metro police, and the ME's people all agree it looked like a suicide. No obvious marks on his body that suggest a struggle or fight with a third party, no indication in the room of anything like that either. We have to wait for an official ruling, obviously. We got into the room a little more than ten minutes after we had texted, and he was dead when we got to him."

"So basically he would have sent me a text and in the next minute or so taken his belt and strung himself up," I said.

"You think we pushed him over the edge?"

"Maybe?" I pointed to Kaufmann's phone, on the toilet lid. "But I think he might have already been in process, and picked up the phone when I texted."

"He interrupted killing himself to answer a text," Vann said, skeptically. "Not to mention bringing his phone with him into the

111

bathroom when he killed himself."

I pointed to the pocket I knew Vann kept her phone in. "You take your phone with you everywhere." I looked at Ramon. "I bet you do, too." I didn't bring Tony in on this one because he had a threep. Our phones were built in.

"I definitely take my phone with me when I'm in the bathroom," Ramon confirmed.

"Yeah, but you're going to the bathroom to take a crap, not kill yourself," Vann said, to Ramon. He shrugged.

"My point is that it's an automatic behavior," I said. "He probably didn't even think about it."

"So Kaufmann freaks out about the feed, has it pulled, goes back to the hotel, undresses, takes his belt and his phone into the bathroom, wraps the belt around the showerhead pipe and his own neck, responds to a text, tells us to come up in fifteen minutes, then kills himself."

"Right."

"Sounds complicated," Vann said.

"Does it matter?" I asked. "Whether he was planning to kill himself before we called, or after?"

"We're trying to figure out why he might have killed himself, so yes. Also, there's this —" Vann pointed to the door, with its

112

extended bolt. "He wanted to make it easy for someone to get into his room. Was that meant for us? Or for someone else? And if someone else, who? And why?"

"You interviewed the NAHL people," I said. "What did they have to say about it?"

"They were all shocked," Vann said. "As in actually shocked, not just saying they were shocked. Apparently Kaufmann was on the bottom of anyone's list of people to hang themselves in a hotel bathroom." She pointed to Kaufmann's image. "No history of depression, generally enthusiastic about life, all that. Apparently a 'go-getter.' "

"What does that mean?"

"I think it means he was an asshole, just an enthusiastic one who did his job and got things done."

"We he married or in a relationship?" I asked. "If something was going wrong there it might have contributed to his hanging himself."

Vann shook her head. "No. Has parents and a sister. The league notified them. I'll touch base with them today or tomorrow."

"Did anyone check his phone?" Tony asked. "If he was wanting to be in touch with his family or someone else, he might have called or texted before . . ." Tony waved his hand in the direction of the apparent

113

suicide scene.

"The phone was locked," Vann said.

Tony glanced over at the phone. "I can think of several ways to get into that sort of phone."

"I think with two different law enforcement agencies on the scene, no one wanted to be the one to attempt an unconstitutional search."

"Point," Tony said.

"I put in a warrant request before I got here," Vann said. "When it clears we'll take it to his service provider."

"If the phone was given to him by the league, you might not need the warrant," Diaz said.

Vann looked toward me at this and raised her eyebrow. "I'm on it," I said. I gestured to the room again. "Was there any chance anyone came into the room before us?"

Vann nodded to Diaz, and a virtual screen popped up that showed the hallway outside of Kaufmann's room, running on fast forward. "This is the security feed from the floor for the hour ahead of our arrival. This is Kaufmann —" She pointed to a sped-up version of him popping into his room. "No one else in or out of his door until we show up. Other people going in and out of rooms, but it's just him and us here."

114

"Did the forensics people have anything to add?" I asked.

"They said that it's a hotel room, so it's going to take them a while to process fingerprints and other data. The hotel chain has the service staff fingerprints on file so that at least will help us trim down the number of people who we'll know were in the room. But at least for now there's no reason to think this is anything other than what it looks like."

"Where is Kaufmann's body now?" I asked.

"With the D.C. medical examiner's office. They're processing him today. They'll send along a preliminary report including initial toxicology scans. So we're waiting on warrants, forensics, and the medical examiner."

"Yes," I said. "To be fair it's nine thirteen on a Monday morning. We'll probably get the warrants first. And I'll check with the league as soon as we're done here."

Vann nodded and looked over to Tony. "You're up."

Tony looked over to Diaz, who wiped the hotel room from the viewing area. In its place a long teal-and-orange ribbon popped up, with two columns, one for heart rate and the other for brain activity, one on top of the other. Vann looked over at Tony,

115

questioningly.

"It's the visual design the league does for the stats," he said. "It was easier to use it than extract out the raw data to present it visually."

"It's ugly," Vann said.

"It's meant to pop."

"Ugly does pop," Vann agreed.

"Okay, so, there's three places I want to show you on this data." The visual data scrolled forward quickly and then slowed. "Duane Chapman was goat three times in the game. That means he was the defensive player whose head was selected as the ball."

"You're mansplaining Hilketa to me now," Vann said.

Tony held up a hand, imploringly. "Look, not everyone follows the game."

"I don't," Diaz volunteered. Tony motioned at Diaz, as if to say, *See.*

"Go on," Vann said.

"So, here's the first time." Tony pointed. "You see the heart rate go up and the brain activity jiggle around a bit. That's because it hurts a little when the head gets pulled off. Not a lot, they dial it down, but enough that it motivates the player to avoid it. So right around the level of an open face slap, pain-wise. It's reflected in the vital signs — a sharp spike, which comes back down because once the head's off the threep, the threep's sensory system is shut down."

"Why?" Diaz asked.

"Because in the early days of the game they found out if they didn't do that, some opposing team players would stomp on the downed threep just for the hell of it. Because some people are real dickheads."

"So the heart and brain activity go up, and then they come back down," Vann said, getting Tony on track.

"Right, but now look at the second time Chapman's the goat." The data flashed by and then stopped. "This time the heart and brain activity spikes are substantially higher, and they don't come down as far as they did the first time, once the head is off the threep. To the extent this data correlates with pain, he's in a whole lot more of it, and it's not entirely going away."

"Someone dialed up the pain receptivity in his threep," I said. Hadens with threeps can increase or decrease the threep's pain receptivity. It's stupid to dial it down to zero — as with a human body, you can damage yourself really badly that way, and repairs are expensive — but reducing that receptivity can come in handy at times. You can also go in the other direction, but, really. Few do.

"You would think so, but the Bays' sideline tech director says the threep checked out. At least that's what he says in a story I read this morning. And that's data the league *would* have. They're always auditing threep adjustments and data feeds because the temptation to tweak the threeps out of standard setup is huge."

"So it's like car racing," Diaz said. "Everyone has to race basically the same-model car."

"Right," Tony said. "In this case it's one of four models and there are some other modifications that are allowed, but everything has to be within a certain range. Step out of the range, and everyone gets penalized. And in this case the tech guy would probably get fired. He's not going to lie about it in a press conference."

"If it's not the threep then what is it?" Vann asked.

"I'm not sure, but whatever it is, it's significant." Tony started the feed scrolling again, but more slowly. "Chapman's stats never really settle down after the second time he's the goat. In fact, they start being more erratic and on an upward stress path. So when he's goat for a third time, right *here*" — Tony pointed to a third, substantial spike in the data — "his vitals were already close to what they were in the second spike. And after this third spike, things get really messy."

Tony was right. After the third spike, Chapman's vitals kept spiking, wildly and chaotically. "Here's where the feed was shut off," Tony said, pointing to a marker in the data stream. He pointed to another marker past the first. "Here's where he went into cardiac arrest. And here" — another marker — "is where his brain activity shut down entirely."

"When he died," Vann said.

"When death was likely inevitable, yes."

"So you're saying Chapman died from too much pain," I said.

"Well, no," Tony said. "We know he was in pain because at the press conference last night we were told that." He waved at the ribbon, now still. "These data don't explicitly show any sort of pain, but strongly imply it. But these data are incomplete. Especially the 'brain activity' data, which measure a sort of generalized brain state, not any system or section of the brain in particular."

"It's for show," Vann said.

"Basically," Tony agreed. "It gives the league something to sell. It lets you see something was going on with Chapman's brain. But nothing specific enough to say anything with accuracy."

"Except to say he was in pain."

"Except to say that this data supports everyone's assertion that he was in pain," Tony amended. "And anyway, pain is a symptom. Technically, I'd say Chapman died of the cardiac arrest. A heart attack. You'd have to check with the Philadelphia medical examiner for confirmation of that."

"In your opinion, has this data feed been tampered with?" Vann asked.

"No, or if it has the person who tampered with it is really good at what they do," Tony said. "That's a preliminary assessment, based on a couple hours' examination. I'll run more detailed tests on it later. But even if it was tampered with, it's been tampered with to show pretty much what we already knew: Chapman died not long after his threep was taken off the field. So if it *was* tampered with, the question is, why?"

"This brings us back to our original theory that Kaufmann pulled the feed just out of sheer panic," I said.

Vann shook her head. "We never stopped thinking it was panic. The question we don't know is, *why* he panicked about it. And why he killed himself over it."

"If he did."

"He did," Vann said, and tilted her head

up at the ribbon of data. "If in every other moment of his life he was a smug, cocksure bastard, and everyone I talked to last night said he was, then it's something *here* that made him do a hard turn."

"So what do we do now?" I asked.

"We hold that thought and you show us what you got in Philly."

I nodded and ported my information over to Diaz, who wiped Tony's data and brought up Chapman's burning apartment. Smoke, fire, and particulate matter was frozen in the air.

"Whoa," Tony said.

"I know," I said. "I was there."

"What did you find?" Vann asked.

"Nothing, I thought. It just looked like a basic groupie den."

"And you know what a groupie den looks like, how?"

"You recall I was famous for a while, yes? This isn't entirely new to me."

Vann cocked her head at me. "Did . . . *you* have a groupie den, Chris?"

"You're joking."

"I am, but I'm maybe five percent actually curious."

"I'd go as high as ten percent," Tony said. Diaz looked quietly uncomfortable.

"You are both terrible people, and also,

no," I said. "And anyway, that's what I thought it was, until someone else showed up and activated one of the threeps."

"Which one?" Vann asked. I pointed to one of the ones with the grooves in it. She peered at it. "I don't recognize that model."

"I don't recognize any of the models," I said.

"That looks like a Van Diemen," Tony said, pointing to the threep with a penis.

Vann blinked. "And you know this how?"

"Obviously because I've been in close proximity to one."

"Go on," Vann said.

"You want to know my sexual history?"

"No." Vann made a swatting motion. "I mean, tell us more about this company."

"Not much to it," Tony said. "There's a market for these, the big guys don't want to officially touch them, so Van Diemen licenses their tech and makes modifications. Makes models with both sexes."

"And that?" Vann pointed to the one with ridges.

Tony shrugged. "I've never seen one of those. But it looks like it's basically for the same purpose."

Vann looked over to me. "Chris," she said.

"Already on it," I replied. I had pulled up a screen on the company. "They're based out of Baltimore."

"What happened to those threeps in Chapman's apartment?" Vann asked.

"They got burned up. I had the Philly police impound the remains."

"We'll bring the one that moved with us tomorrow and hit Van Diemen on the way back from Philly," Vann said. "Do you have anything else?"

"I have Chapman's town house footage, with his room."

"Let's see it."

I sent it over to Diaz, who popped it up. We all looked at the room.

"Yes, that's a room," Vann said, finally.

"That was kind of my thought as well," I said.

"Anyone else?" Vann asked Tony and Diaz.

"Actually," Tony said.

"Yes?"

"Can you zoom in on the IV bag?"

Vann nodded to Diaz, who zoomed in on the bag. She glanced over to me. I shrugged.

Tony pointed at the bag. "That's not right."

"What's not right about it?" Vann asked.

"It's the wrong brand," Tony said.

Vann frowned. "I don't know what that means."

"The IV is full of supplements that the

123

league allows the players to have during the game, to keep them alert and whatnot. Right? Well, the top Hilketa players have endorsement deals for their IV supplements. The ones that don't use the league-endorsed supplements. That's Tigertone. But the bag says Labram on it. Chapman didn't have an endorsement deal with Labram."

"Okay, and, so?" Vann said. "Maybe Chapman just wanted a change."

Tony shook his head. "That's not how endorsements work. The NAHL could get sued for Chapman not using Tigertone during a game. And Chapman could be fined by the Bays for it, unless he had his own endorsement deal. He didn't."

Vann nodded. "So you're wondering why the switch."

"And what's in the bag," I added. Then I paused and turned to Diaz. "Bring up Chapman's secret apartment again, please."

Diaz did. "Bring up the front room full size," I asked. He did.

"What are you looking for?" Vann asked.

"That," I said, and pointed to a box in the corner of the room, near one of the threeps, partially obscured by static smoke. "It says 'Labram' on it."

"That could be anything."

I nodded. "It could be anything, but it's

124

specifically *something*." I pointed to a shipping code on the top of the box. "We can follow up on that. And while we're at it —" I asked for Diaz to go back to Chapman's town house, and zoomed in again on the IV bag. "Each bag has its own serial number. It will tell us when it was produced and what batch it was part of. If we know that much, we might know whether it was shipped to Chapman directly or if he got it from someone else."

Vann frowned. "You think it might have something to do with his death."

"I don't know," I said. "But if Tony's right and it's not supposed to be there, then we should probably try to figure out why it is. We don't know why Chapman's body freaked out during the game, and we can't take any explanation for granted. We have to find out about what was going on with his body, and what was going on with his threep. So we get that bag and test it. Then we need to get a medical report from the Philadelphia medical examiner. Then we need to talk to the people in charge of the threeps at the Boston Bays."

"You talked to Chapman's caregiver?"

"Alton Ortiz. Yes."

"And he didn't say anything about the IV being different."

"No."

"Maybe we should ask him again."

"We can do that, along with checking with the Philly ME. In the meantime we should get someone from our Philly branch over to Chapman's town house to collect that bag as evidence."

Vann smiled slightly at this. "Let me do that. I don't think they want to do anything nice for you yet."

"Fair point."

"We also need to go back to Strawberry Mansion and talk to some of the people in the building. Find out what was going on in that love nest of Chapman's, and why the building burned up."

"Yes," I agreed. "Now, what do we do about Kaufmann?"

"Oh, him," Vann said, and then looked at me. "I don't know, Chris. What do we do?"

This was not Vann actually being confused about what to do next. This was Vann the senior partner, quizzing her junior partner, me, about the job. This was how our working relationship had started, a year earlier, and how it had continued. I suspected that we could be working together for a decade and I would still get the quiz.

"Get the warrants or clearance from the league, and get the medical examiner here

126

in D.C. and the forensics teams to expedite their examinations."

"And what about what connects Kaufmann with Chapman?"

"You got me," I said. "And anyway my day's already scheduled out."

Vann smirked. Then she turned to Diaz. "Bring up the hotel room again." Kaufmann's hotel room zoomed into view. "I think we missed something," she said, to me.

I looked at the room again, studying it. "I got nothing," I said, after a couple of minutes.

"This is where your being a Haden is giving you a blind spot." Vann pointed to the bed. "The bed's a mess."

"Okay, so?"

"Pull up your security feed," Vann said, to Diaz. He pulled it up and put it into its own virtual screen again, and once more put it on fast-forward. "Here's Kaufmann coming into the room. It's about forty-five minutes before we arrive."

"So he took a nap," I said.

"Not a lot of time. And he'd had a stressful day."

"All the more reason for a nap."

"From how everyone described him, he doesn't strike me as the napping type."

"His room might not have been made up from the morning," Tony said.

"Does that hotel security feed of yours go back further?" Vann asked Diaz.

"I've got about six hours of it," he said.

"Run it back and see if the room got serviced."

Diaz zoomed the feed back until the service cart appeared and the staff, in reverse, went into the rooms and back out of them again. In short order the cart was in front of Kaufmann's door and the staff member inside. "That answers that," Vann said.

"It's not exactly conclusive," I suggested. "Your hunch about his personality type notwithstanding, maybe Kaufmann really liked his catnaps."

Vann ignored this. "Has the room been released yet?"

"To the hotel? I don't know."

"Find out. If it's not, get a forensics team back over there. If it has been, get a forensics team back over there anyway. And get the hotel to keep their staff out of the room next to Kaufmann's, too, until we our people can look at it."

"Why?"

Vann pointed to the visual of the room. "Look again," she said.

I suppressed the urge to gripe and looked again. This time, after a minute, I saw it.

"The interior door," I said.

"The interior door," Vann agreed. "Which opens up into the next room, if someone wants to rent both and make a suite out of them. Or, maybe, if someone wants to take an adjoining room to be able to get from one room to the other without making a public scene about it."

"Still thin," I said.

"Probably." Vann smiled, without much joy. She looked like she was up against her time limit for needing some nicotine. "But let's be sure. And let's get a name on that room. If we're lucky, maybe they won't have checked out yet. Let's get that done before we head to Philly."

"And by 'let's get that done' you mean 'you do it,' don't you."

"Yes," Vann said. "Yes I do."

"Then you drive to Philly. And back."

"I was going to do that anyway. Because while we're driving, I have something else I want you to do."

"What's that?"

"Talk to your parents."

CHAPTER SEVEN

The agency vehicle we usually drove around in was in the shop. Vann went to get another out of the motor pool. I didn't want to wait with her while she argued with the staff there over which car she got. She would get cranky and the motor pool would get cranky back and I would end up like the kid who felt sad that Mommy and Daddy were fighting. I told her to pick me up in front of the main entrance, and headed out of doors to enjoy a typically muggy Washington day. Around me people were already visibly sweating. I turned down my heat sensitivity and felt mildly smug about being a Haden.

And then stopped feeling smug when a small pack of reporters fell on me, shouting questions about the case. My threep had been recognized.

"I don't have any comments," I said, holding up my hands.

"Come on, Chris," one of the reporters

said. I scanned his face and the database came up with Dave Miller, who wrote about Hilketa for the *Post.* "Your press people aren't being very helpful."

"Maybe that's because it's an ongoing case and we don't like talking about those," I suggested.

"If it's an ongoing case then it suggests that there's something going on besides a natural death, right?"

I cocked my head at Miller. "That's a nice leading question," I said. "Are you going to ask me when I stopped beating my partner next?"

"You're confirming you have a partner?" Miller asked, cracking a smile as he got the allusion.

"What about Commissioner Kaufmann?" asked another reporter, this one popping up as Cary Wise, from the *Hilketa News.*

"Well, see, that would *also* be an ongoing investigation, wouldn't it?" I said. "And what do we know about ongoing investigations?"

"You could tell us off the record," Wise said.

Everyone in the small press scrum groaned and looked at Wise. "What?" Wise said, looking around.

"You're new at this, aren't you?" I asked.

"No," Wise said, defensively.

"Now you've just guaranteed Chris will never say anything to anyone on *or* off the record, moron," said another journalist.

"Ding," I said, and then pointed to the various security cameras around us. "Here's a pro tip: Don't ask an FBI agent to go off the record, in public, in front of microphones and video cameras, in front of the *actual FBI building*."

"When will the FBI have a statement?" This question from Leona Garza, from WTTG.

"Ask our press folks."

"We did. They didn't say anything."

"Maybe ask them to speak off the record," I said.

"What about the protesters yesterday?" Wise asked.

"What protesters?"

"The ones protesting the Hilketa game yesterday," Wise said. "Are they being investigated in conjunction with yesterday's events?"

I paused for a second. "That's a fairly random question," I finally said.

"They're not just random protesters," Wise said. "They've got some serious funding."

"Uh-huh, *okay,*" Miller interjected, and

then positioned himself in front of me and Wise. "If you can't tell us about the investigation, Chris, can you at least tell us about saving that woman from a fire last night in Philly?"

There was a honk. Vann had pulled up in our car.

"My ride's here," I said, and walked through the mini-scrum, waving. Miller protested not getting an answer. I kept waving until I got into the car.

"You're popular," Vann said, as I got in.

"It's not me, it's our case." I buckled up and then looked at the car. "This is nice. Nicer than our usual car."

"Yeah, well," Vann said. She pulled away from the curb. "They tried to give me that goddamned Fiesta. I was going to shoot somebody."

"It's just a car," I said.

"Spoken like someone who doesn't have to worry about their spine being compressed for three hours on the way to Philly. And three hours back."

"We can get someone from the Philly Bureau to cover for us," I said. "Handle the little chat with the director there by video."

"Nice try getting out of that," Vann said, smirking. "And anyway, I know the person covering Haden affairs there. Rachel Ramsey."

"And?"

"We're going to Philly."

"I've been your partner for a year and in all that time I'm not entirely sure I've ever heard you say anything nice about anyone else in law enforcement," I said.

Vann fished a cigarette pack out of her suit jacket pocket. "I don't hate you."

"That's reassuring."

"I'm going to smoke on the way."

"You know they hate it when you do that. I get yelled at by the motor-pool people because they think yelling at me will change your mind about doing it. I tell them it won't. They yell at me anyway."

"Sorry."

"It's why they tried to give you the Fiesta. What happened to your electronic cigarette?"

"It broke."

"Get a new one."

"They're expensive."

"And cigarettes are cheap at twelve bucks a pack? I question your budgeting skills."

"Did the press get anything from you?" Vann asked, changing the subject.

"No," I said. "I can handle a scrum, and this was a small one. Although one of them asked a weird question. It was a reporter from some outlet called the *Hilketa News.* You heard of it?"

"Not really."

"There were protesters at the game saying that Hilketa is discriminatory. Wise — the *Hilketa News* reporter — implied they weren't just cranky dudes. That they're organized and funded by someone."

"Well, fuck," Vann said.

"The protesters being funded?"

"No. I can't find my lighter."

"The motor pool staff will be happy to hear that."

"We're stopping at a convenience store."

"You're driving," I said. "Stop wherever you want."

"So these protesters are being funded," Vann said. "So what?"

"I think Wise's implication is that there's something sinister about it."

"And?"

"No other 'and,' just wondering if we're investigating them as well."

"I think we're going to be busy enough. And anyway, the protesters aren't wrong, paid or not. Hilketa *is* discriminatory."

"Ah, that's crap," I said. "It's the least discriminatory major sport in the country. There's no gender or racial or sexual barrier to play."

"It helps a lot to be a Haden."

"That's like saying that there's discrimination in basketball because there's no one on the Washington Wizards roster shorter than six feet tall."

"An artificial neural network in your head isn't a de facto requirement in order to play in the NBA."

"No, you just need generations of genetic selection to make you two meters tall," I countered. "In both cases something entirely not up to you has to come into play. Genetics or a virulent disease requiring you to get a dangerous implant in your brain to get along in the world. One of these is worse than the other."

"None of which doesn't mean Hilketa isn't discriminatory," Vann said.

"Jesus, Vann," I said. "I'm getting the feeling you were one of those 'I'm just playing devil's advocate' assholes in college."

"I wasn't, but I punched a few of them." Vann carefully placed her cigarette back into her pack. "You interrupted me to be outraged before I finished my actual thought. Which was, the protesters weren't wrong, it is discriminatory, and also, who gives a shit, because it's not *legally* discriminatory, and it's mostly discriminatory on the basis of

136

skill, just like every other major sport. It helps to be more than six feet tall in pro basketball, but there have been enough players who haven't been, to say skill can compensate. I'm pretty sure it's the same for Hilketa."

I was quiet for a moment. "So what you're saying is that I yelled at you for nothing."

"Pretty much."

"But you argued *back*."

"Yes, well . . ." Vann stuffed her cigarette pack back in her jacket pocket. "I'm a little edgy at the moment."

"We need to find you that convenience store."

"We really do." Vann took back control of the car. "I know where one is near here. While I'm doing that, go visit your parents and have a talk with them. By the time you get back, I'll be less jittery."

So I went to visit my parents.

Which was easy to do because unlike most Hadens, I had more than one threep.

My "main" one, a Sebring-Warner 680XS, was the one in the passenger seat of the FBI car on the way to Philly. I'd gotten it when I traded in my 660XS, which had been relatively new, but which, thanks to my gig, I put a lot of wear and tear into. The 680XS had, as I noted to Vann earlier, all the bells and whistles.

My second threep was a Kamen Zephyr, a nice model although this particular threep was extensively refurbished. This one stayed at my parents' house, because I liked visiting my parents and sometimes I didn't feel like dealing with traffic in my 680XS. Also, my biological body was still at my parents' place, even though I rented my room in D.C. and my main threep stayed there. If I needed to quickly engage with my biological body in some way, I'd pop into the Zephyr.

(I had a third threep, too: a Brummel Maier-Vonn III, which was kept in the family vacation home in the Jackson Hole valley. It was specifically designed for skiing and winter sports. The MVIII is essentially a snowmobile for Hadens. I've mentioned the family was wealthy. We do obnoxious wealthy things from time to time, like have vacation homes in Jackson Hole and own ridiculously specialized equipment. I don't even like skiing all that much.)

The ability to switch from one threep to another almost instantly could be disconcerting for non-Hadens. It felt a little like teleportation to them. I explained it now and again by saying it's not really any different from switching between a phone and a tablet, but admittedly there's a scaling issue between looking at one screen and then at a different one, and seemingly moving one's consciousness from one machine body to another. Which could be half a planet away. Which really *was* kind of like teleportation, come to think of it.

The secret is that neither I nor any Haden ever really goes anywhere. We're always in the same place: in our bodies. Mine was in suburban Northern Virginia, in a sunny room at my parents' house, in a top-of-the-line creche, with a full-time caregiver watching over it at all times, and a spare threep sitting in an induction chair, in case I want to use it. Which I did, now, to visit with my mother and father.

I didn't just drop in. Despite the fact that my biological body was in the house, I now spent most of my conscious time at the home I shared with Tony and my other flatmates. Other than actual physical emergencies involving my body, I tried to give my parents a heads-up when I was coming over. There was always a risk of dropping in at an inappropriate time. This is a phrase that works on many different levels, but in this particular case it would mean popping in on Dad when he was trying to do business.

But when I pinged Mom about coming over, she simply said, "Do. I think your father could use your perspective with one of his visitors."

I found out what that meant when I caught up with Dad and his visitors in the trophy room. It was the room in which Dad kept the memorabilia from his NBA career and his business life. The point of it was to humble the millionaires and billionaires he met with. It usually worked. Sure, you might be a billionaire. But were you a billionaire with four NBA championship rings, like Dad? Probably not. Sit down.

"Chris!" Dad smiled widely at me when I came in, and got up from the couch where he was sitting with his two visitors, an older man and a younger woman. Both looked somewhat familiar. He crossed the room and gave me a hug. "Good to see you, kid."

"I know, it's been so long," I joked.

"You're kidding with me, I get that, but I didn't really get to see you yesterday, now did I?" Dad said.

"No, I guess not," I admitted.

Dad nodded and motioned toward his guests. "You'll recognize Wendell Gordon, the North American Hilketa League commissioner, and this is Amelie Parker, who is the CEO of a start-up named MobilOn."

Now I recognized where I knew both of them. Gordon I'd seen yesterday, at the game. He'd been the NAHL executive who looked directly at me when his apparatchik was talking in his ear, telling him about Duane Chapman. It's possible that he might not have known that threep was me at the time.

Parker I recognized not because of Parker, whom I had never met before, but because the woman in front of me was an Integrator, a person Hadens hired to borrow their bodies. Integrators had a neural net in their brains as well, which allowed Hadens to connect with their bodies and then control them, with some small assistance from the Integrators themselves. Integrators are fairly rare — there's only about 10,000 of them in the United States — so they tend to have multiple clients who use their services at different times.

This particular Integrator was Lena Fowler, who was relatively new to the D.C. area. I recognized her because one of her clients was someone Vann and I investigated for wire fraud a few months earlier. That client pleaded guilty and was now serving three years in a Haden-specific federal penitentiary. She would not be using Fowler's services again for a while, at least.

"Mr. Gordon, Ms. Parker," I said, nodding to both. As was customary, I did not acknowledge Fowler, because she was working for a client, and the client was presenting. I looked over at Gordon. "My condolences on Duane Chapman and Alex Kaufmann, sir."

"Thank you."

"And thank you for the league's cooperation with the Bureau's investigation of their deaths."

Gordon was momentarily surprised and then made the connection of what it was that I did, and the fact that I was in the luxury suite the day before. "Yes, yes. We're happy to assist."

"As a matter of disclosure, you understand I cannot give you any information about the current state of either investigation, nor am I able to share such information with either of my parents."

"Yes, of course," Gordon said. I nodded again at that.

"Both Wendell and Amelie are here to try to make a hard press for me to join the Washington Hilketa franchise as a minority owner," Dad said. "And that's 'minority owner' in more than one way. Isn't that right, Wendell?"

Gordon looked nonplussed at what Dad

said, but then recovered. "Yes, I suppose that's correct." He turned to me. "Hilketa is one of the nation's fastest-growing sports, and we're proud of the diversity of our players and fans. But one area we could do better in is ownership."

"He means that nearly all the NAHL franchise owners are white and male, and almost none of them have any personal connection with Hadens in their own family," Dad said, smiling.

"That's an artifact of the early rounds of funding and ownership," Gordon said, hastily. "We were ambitious but perhaps not entirely wise in those early days. We're looking to this expansion round of franchise ownership to do a bit of course correction."

"So you're interested in my dad being a part owner of the D.C. team because he's black and because I'm his kid," I said.

"Yes," Parker said, interjecting before Gordon had a chance to attempt to fumble through an answer to that question. "And if those were the *only* reasons we were interested in your father — in both of your parents, really — then you would be absolutely right to call the league out on its tokenism. Just like you could call them out on tokenism for me because I'm a Haden. But in both our cases, it's not just that. I mean, come on, Chris." Parker motioned toward Dad. "This is *Marcus Shane*. Four-time champion with the Wizards. If anyone's an actual living icon of Washington, D.C., it's your dad. He knows more about the city, and the *business* of the city, and the sports life of this town, than anyone else."

"Now that's what's called a quality buttering up," Dad said.

Parker smiled and laughed. "Thank you. I try."

"Amelie, maybe you can tell Chris about MobilOn." Dad turned to me. "Amelie's about to do a second round of funding for her company, and independent of whatever happens with the league, I'm considering making an investment. I'd be curious as to what you think of her business model."

I leaned in to Dad and got close to his ear. "I'm actually here to speak to you, you know," I said in a low voice.

"I know. This is almost over." We moved our heads away and then Dad motioned to Parker. "Do the elevator pitch, Amelie."

"Two words," Parker said. "Time-share threeps."

"Come again?" I said.

"It's simple," Parker continued. "With the passing of Abrams-Kettering, we're in a unique moment in the history of Personal

144

Transports. Before AK" — I found myself slightly unsettled by the Abrams-Kettering Bill being referred to in a jargon-y acronym — "ownership of threeps was limited to Haden families, for the use of Hadens, and the purchase price largely subsidized through tax credits and low-interest loans. Now those subsidies are gone, which means the real-world price has gone up. That's bad for a lot of Hadens, who now can't afford a threep, and for the makers of threeps, who are seeing their sales fall through the floor. MobilOn helps solve both those problems."

"By renting threeps to Hadens?"

"By offering a subscription that allows access to threeps."

" 'Renting' is shorter," I said. "And there are already places to rent threeps."

"That's where the difference is." Parker smiled. She was well into the meat of her presentation. "You rent a threep if you're traveling to another city and you don't want the expense of transporting your own threep, or if your primary threep is getting maintenance. With MobilOn, you get rid of the personal threep entirely."

I had an internal shudder at that. "Why?"

"Because thanks to Abrams-Kettering, personal threeps are too expensive for a lot of Hadens," Dad said.

"Right," Parker acknowledged Dad's point. "We could discuss the philosophical aspects of that and be here all day, but at the end of it, it wouldn't change the fact that a lot of Hadens — a lot of *us,* Chris — can't afford to buy and maintain their own threeps. Nor should they! How much time do Hadens actually spend in their threeps on a daily basis?"

"I'm in mine constantly. I'm an FBI agent."

Parker made a motion with her hands, acknowledging the point. "You may not be our core user demographic," she allowed. "But our studies show that more Hadens are spending less time in threeps. They're spending more time in the Agora" — and here she acknowledged Dad, who a year ago made a major financial investment in the Haden community's primary online space — "and otherwise doing their business through the virtual world. I know *I* do. I hardly ever use my threep anymore."

I was tempted to point out that Parker was saying this while using an Integrator, the cost of which was exponentially higher, on a per capita basis, than using a threep with any regularity. I decided not to. "And you think this will be popular with people who have owned their own threeps all this time," was what I said instead.

"We know that Hadens, like everyone, appreciate value. And we also know that the makers of Personal Transports would be delighted to have a mass buyer of threeps until the next market comes."

"She means non-Haden users of threeps here," Dad pointed out.

"Yes," Parker said. "Now that AK has opened up the market to non-Hadens, it's just a matter of time before they start using them. Older people. Those with non-Haden mobility issues. Able-bodied people who want to travel to faraway destinations but can't take the time or make the financial investment for a full vacation. There's an explosion of threep use less than a decade out. Some of these new users will want to own their own threeps. But others will just want access."

"So your business model is to use Hadens' reduced circumstances to reconfigure the threep manufacturing industry to your specifications, just long enough for the Hadens to become an afterthought to the threep manufacturing business entirely," I said.

"I'm not the one who passed AK, Chris." Parker was using a tone of voice that suggested she was often in a position of having to sound like she was very sorry that circumstances had come to this pass. "We work in the world that exists. In the world that exists, this isn't just the reality, it's an opportunity."

"What do you think, Chris?" Dad asked.

I nodded to Parker. "I think you have your finger on the financial pulse of our times, Ms. Parker."

Parker smiled at this.

"Now, what do you *really* think?" Dad asked, after he had said his goodbyes to Gordon and Parker and promised them they would hear from him soon about the franchise.

"I hate every single possible thing about it," I said.

Dad nodded. "I thought you might." He motioned with his head in the direction Parker and Gordon had exited. "But she's not wrong, you know. Demand for threeps has cratered. Hadens are spending less time out in the physical world."

"That's because they can't afford their threeps anymore," I pointed out.

"Amelie does tend to gloss over the arrow of causation there," Dad allowed. "But either way you point that arrow, it makes an argument for a service like MobilOn."

"It feels like bloodsucking," I said. "She's

not doing this to help Hadens. She's doing it to be first in line when everyone *else* wants to rent a threep."

"You think Hadens will get pushed to the side with her business model, then."

"We're already being pushed to the side. And threeps are more important to Hadens than she's saying. They're not just a service."

Dad nodded again, then looked over at me. "I knew you wouldn't like it," he said. "I told Amelie I thought you wouldn't. She told me she was curious what you might think, which is why I made her tell you about it when you showed up today. But you seem to like it even less than I thought you would."

"I'm in a bad mood," I admitted. "Vann and I were talking about the people protesting Hilketa because there are no non-Haden players and I hear about this start-up, basically about making Hadens rent their meat world identity until the non-Hadens come around to marginalize them entirely. I feel like we're slowly getting nudged out of our own space."

"Join the club," Dad said. "Well, sort of. You and I, we have some breathing room."

"I've been thinking about *that* part of it, too," I said. "So, you going to invest in the company?"

"I'm going to think about it some more," Dad said. "Now, let's you and I and your mother talk. What are you looking for?"

"The same thing you just wanted out of me, Dad. I want some perspective."

CHAPTER EIGHT

Vann jumped A little when I popped back into my threep, causing the car to swerve until the lane assist kicked in. "Jesus," she said.

"You knew I was coming back," I told her.

"Right, but you've just been sitting there motionless for ninety minutes, and then suddenly you *twitch.*"

"Sorry."

"It's fine. What did you get out of your parents?"

"The NAHL is definitely still pushing the 'difficulty at home' and 'self-medicating' angles."

"Did you let your parents know otherwise?"

"No," I said. "It's an ongoing investigation."

"Check out the ethics on you," Vann murmured.

"You're not surprised, I hope."

"No, just reminded you and I are very different people. But also, the NAHL might still not be wrong, at least in terms of forbidden substances."

"You mean because of that switched IV bag of supplements."

" 'Supplements,' " Vann said, and I could hear the quotation marks around the word. "That's what I mean, yes. It's entirely possible there's something in there that wasn't approved by the league."

"Something that would increase his pain sensitivity and give him a heart attack."

"I'm sure that wasn't the intended effect," Vann said.

"I can't think of anything that would do that."

"Well, neither can I, Chris, but that's not really our area of expertise, is it?"

I thought about that for a second. "Hold on," I said to Vann, and made a phone call.

"I was sleeping," Tayla Givens, my flatmate, said to me as she answered.

"It's noon," I said.

"I'm a doctor at a hospital," she said. "I have long shifts. I'm going to have another long shift real soon. You're lucky you don't keep your body at the house or I'd walk my threep over to your room and punch you."

"Sorry. I have a quick question. Medical

related."

"Medical related for you, or for your job?"

"For the job."

"Does this mean I get a consulting fee, like Tony?"

"Sure, if you want to fill in all the federal government contracting forms and submit to the required background check. I can send you all that paperwork today."

Tayla groaned. "What's your stupid question?" she asked.

"You know about Haden-specific pharmaceuticals, right?"

"Yes, because I'm a doctor and a Haden."

"Can you think of any that we know increase a Haden's susceptibility to pain?"

"You mean, aside from the ones that would do the same to anyone, not just Hadens?"

"Right."

"As an intended result, no. That's not something we generally aim for, medically speaking. As a side effect, I can think of a couple. Not their specific names, because you woke me up and my brain is fuzzy."

"Would any of those also be used as a performance enhancer?"

"Like, say, on a Hilketa field?" Tayla asked.

"It doesn't have to be a Hilketa field."

"Right."

"This is entirely a hypothetical question."

"Of course it is," Tayla said, and the sarcasm in her voice was notable. "The short answer is no. The longer answer is more complicated and for a question you didn't actually ask."

"What question is that?"

"Whether any drug can increase a Haden's susceptibility to pain."

"I did ask that!" I protested.

"No, you asked if we *knew* of any drug that did that. The question is whether any known drug *could* do that, or whether increasing pain sensitivity is the drug's intended function or a known side effect."

"What's the difference?"

"The difference is that every Haden brain is significantly different," Tayla said. "The disease rearranges our gray matter differently in each case, and each brain recovers differently from the attack. As a result every Haden brain is idiosyncratic. It's one of the difficulties of Haden-specific medicine. We can't just assume that any one Haden isn't going to have that same reaction to a drug as another Haden, or as a non-Haden patient."

"So you're saying that *aspirin* could make a Haden more pain-sensitive."

"Probably not aspirin or a drug designed

to lessen pain. But any other drug idiosyncratically decreasing pain tolerance? It's possible, sure. Likely? No. But possible. That's why we call it 'idiosyncratic.' "

"So theoretically a Haden could take a performance enhancer that has no known side effects to anyone else, and have a reaction to it no one else ever has."

"Yes," Tayla said. "Performance enhancer or any other drug. And now you know why your doctors have always been very, very careful with your medicines, Chris."

"Can you get me the names of the drugs we know have pain-enhancing qualities for Hadens?"

"That's actual *work,* Chris."

"You'd be my favorite flatmate."

Tayla groaned again. "Whatever. I'll see what I can come up with. Not now, though. I'm going back to sleep. And I'm blocking your call signal."

"Fair enough. Sweet dreams."

Tayla grunted and disconnected.

"So basically anything could have made this happen," Vann said, after I caught her up on the conversation.

"Basically," I agreed. "And, if there was something different in the supplement bag, something knowingly put in there, Marla Chapman and Alton Ortiz lied to me."

155

"Or they didn't know."

"Marla Chapman, maybe," I said. "Duane was keeping secrets from her. But how could Ortiz not know? That's part of his job."

Vann shrugged. "Ortiz is on our schedule today, so we ask him again. Much less nicely this time. But first we go to Philadelphia's medical examiner. No point going 'good cop, bad cop' on Ortiz if there's nothing there."

"Having nothing hasn't stopped you from doing that before," I noted.

"Yeah, but we have a busy schedule today," Vann said. "And I don't want to be in Philadelphia any longer than I have to."

"Drugs? What kind of drugs?" asked Sara Powell, the medical examiner assigned to Duane Chapman. We met her in her office, which was all right by me. I didn't actually like visiting the morgue.

"You tell us," Vann said.

"Well, if you're talking recreational, our initial toxicology work-up didn't catch anything like that in Mr. Chapman's system," Powell said. "And nothing in my initial examination suggests any long-term abuse of drugs or alcohol."

"No cirrhosis of the liver or anything like that."

"Definitely no cirrhosis. Mr. Chapman's liver looked pristine. This isn't unusual for Hadens. Statistically fewer of them drink than the general non-Haden population. It's not the same sort of social activity."

"It can be managed," I said.

"Of course," Powell allowed. "I didn't say it was nonexistent. Just not at the same level as the non-Haden population. That said, while I didn't find any evidence of casual drug or alcohol use, Mr. Chapman's work-up turned up a lot of pharmacological elements consistent with his status as a Haden and other known issues. He had an autoimmune disorder so drugs relating to that disorder are present in his system."

"Can we get a list of those?" I asked.

"It'll all be in my full report."

"Anything else?" Vann asked.

"You'd have to be more specific," Powell said.

"Chapman was a professional athlete. Anything in there that might have been performance enhancing?"

Powell frowned. "You're the third person to ask me that today."

"Who were the first two?" Vann asked.

"The first said he was a representative of

the sports league Mr. Chapman was involved in. A lawyer."

"Oliver Medina?" I asked.

Powell nodded. "That's right."

"Who was the other?"

"A reporter of some sort. Called me on my personal phone, which really kind of pissed me off. That number isn't public. Name escapes me at the moment. Started with a 'c' or 'k.'"

"Cary Wise," I said.

Powell blinked. "Do you know these people?"

"It's a small world, at least as far as the death of Duane Chapman is concerned," Vann said. "What did you tell them?"

"I told them both the same thing. That they could wait for my initial public report, which will be later this week."

"Is that what you're going to tell us, too?"

"I'm going to tell you that I don't know. I don't know what qualifies as performance enhancing for a Haden athlete. That's outside my normal experience." She turned to me. "No offense."

"None taken," I said. "I'm not much of an athlete anyway."

Powell smiled at this and turned back to Vann. "The work-up for recreational drug use is something we do a lot, and we know

158

Mr. Chapman's medical history so we know to look for those specific drugs as well. Everything else, all the stuff we don't know to expect, takes a little longer."

"So it'll take you a while, is what you're saying to me."

"What I'm saying to you is that if you know what I'm supposed to be looking for, then you can tell me, and I'll look for it."

"Do you know how much a threep costs these days, Agent Shane?" Lara Burgess, head of the Philadelphia FBI office, asked me. Vann and I were there for our requested meet-up, and for my scheduled dressing-down. Along with the three of us, another agent was in Burgess's office with us: Rachel Ramsey, whom Vann famously did not think much of.

"All too well, ma'am," I admitted. "I also know that the particular model threep I borrowed from your office runs about fifty thousand dollars."

"You understand that our current president and Congress aren't all that keen on expanding government agency budgets," Burgess said. "Fifty-thousand-dollar vehicles don't exactly grow on trees." Burgess pointed to Ramsey. "If Agent Ramsey here took a fifty-thousand-dollar car and rammed it into a tree, how do you think that would go over?"

"To be fair, Shane *did* rescue an unconscious woman from a burning building," Vann said.

"And then went back inside the building," Ramsey said. Vann shot her a look.

"To rescue a *cat,*" Burgess said. "Had Agent Shane destroyed a fifty-thousand-dollar vehicle rescuing an old lady, we wouldn't be having this conversation now. But I think we can all agree that as fond as we might be of our pets, very few are worth destroying fifty thousand dollars' worth of government property over. And in this case it wasn't even your cat, Agent Shane."

"Where is the cat?" Ramsey asked.

"It ran away," I said.

"Huh," Ramsey said.

"Did you follow up on the information I sent you?" Vann asked Ramsey.

"About the supplement bag?"

"The supplement bag and the box bar code Agent Shane found in the apartment."

"We sent an agent to retrieve the bag and ran the code from the box and from the bag." Ramsey said. "The bag was from a batch that Labram produced three weeks ago. The box in question was part of a shipment that was sent to the Boston Bays offices about two weeks ago."

"What about the contents of the bag?" Vann asked.

"We have the lab folks looking into it right now."

"So it's a reasonable assumption that the bag came out of that box."

"What's your point?" Burgess asked.

"My point is that in going back into the building and scanning that room, Agent Shane retrieved information relevant to the current investigation," Vann said. "It wasn't just a matter of rescuing a cat. We have two deaths under suspicious circumstances and this is a material piece of information."

Burgess looked at me, coolly. "And do you think a *box code* was worth my fifty-thousand-dollar vehicle, Agent Shane?"

"I couldn't say, ma'am," I said. "We're still investigating. But I will say that this opens up an interesting new avenue in the investigation."

"How so?"

"The supplement bag is a different brand than Chapman was supposed to be using." I was echoing what Tony was saying earlier in the day, but Burgess didn't know that, and I wasn't going to tell her. "The box was apparently originally shipped to the Boston Bays. That means it was probably meant for a player there. Chapman probably got the supplements from that player. We find out which Bays players have Labram IV supplement endorsement deals, and we likely have a connection to follow up on. Especially if your lab people find anything interesting in the contents of that bag. I don't know if the box code is worth a threep, but this lead could be."

Burgess looked at Ramsey, who gave a shrug. "We already had the bag," she said. "The information from the box code is useful but it doesn't tell us anything we probably wouldn't have figured out without it. Chapman was a player on the Bays. It would have made sense to look at the players there anyway."

"I agree," Burgess said. "It was reckless of you to go back into that building, Agent Shane. As a result this office doesn't have a threep and Agent Ramsey here" — Burgess nodded at her subordinate — "has to deal with a ridiculous amount of paperwork in order to explain how it burned up and why we should be able to requisition another one. It also means that until a new threep is approved, any Haden agent — including you, Agent Shane — who needs to work with our office has to rent one and jump through all the requisition hoops that requires. You know what a pain in the ass that is."

"Yes, ma'am," I said.

"I'm putting a disciplinary note in your record," Burgess said to me. "And I want to be clear that if you hadn't saved that old woman from the building, I'd be doing more than filing a disciplinary note. I'd have you fired. I don't care who you are or who your dad is, Agent Shane. Agents work for a living and we owe it to taxpayers not to waste their taxes on stunts like rescuing cats. Do you understand me?"

"I do, ma'am."

"Good. I'll send that note to the D.C. office today."

"I wouldn't do that," Vann said.

"Excuse me?" Burgess said, to Vann.

"You heard me," Vann said.

"I did hear you," Burgess agreed. "I'm just not sure why you thought you needed to offer an opinion, Agent Vann."

"I'm offering an opinion here because Shane might not know what you're up to, Director Burgess, but I do."

"And what am I doing, Vann?"

Vann jerked a thumb at Ramsey. "You're trying to cover her dumb ass."

"Oh, Christ, Vann," Ramsey said. "Don't be ridiculous."

Vann ignored Ramsey and kept looking at Burgess. "This idiot is the one responsible for the threep, yes? Because she's the Haden affairs desk here. And as soon as you file the disciplinary note, Director Burgess, Ramsey here is going to petition for the official responsibility for the condition of the threep to be put on Shane's head, not hers, and the cost of its replacement to come out of the D.C. office's budget, not yours."

"Shane *did* run back into a flaming building," Ramsey said. "This might seem like a trivial matter to you, but I think it might be considered relevant."

Vann turned to me. "Why did the threep burn up?"

"Because I ran out of power," I said.

"And why did you run out of power?"

"Because the threep was at about thirteen percent when I arrived," I said. "It was off its induction pad and the pad wasn't plugged in anyway."

"It's plugged in," Ramsey said.

"It is *now,*" I agreed. "Because I plugged it in when I got here."

"And you have a record of this," Vann prompted me.

"I was on duty," I said. "Of course I was recording."

Vann nodded and turned to Burgess. "If

Shane had been given a fully topped-off threep, as FBI regulations *specify,* I might add, none of us would be in this office right now having this little conversation."

"Agent Shane could have waited to charge sufficiently, but didn't. Likewise, Shane could have chosen not going back into the building and powering down while it was burning down, but again didn't. As a result, we *are* here in this office, having this conversation," Burgess said. "I see what you're trying to do, Agent Vann. It's admirable you're sticking up for your partner, but it doesn't change the facts."

"The facts," Vann said. "Okay, try this *fact* on for size. You try to pin this on Shane, and both you and Ramsey here are going to get hauled up for violating the ADA."

"What?" Ramsey said.

"The Americans with Disabilities Act," Vann said. "You may have heard of it."

"Of course I know what it is!" Ramsey said.

"Good, because in giving Shane an under-powered threep to work in, you engaged in discrimination." Vann looked back at Burgess. "And when you tried to railroad Shane into accepting discipline for Ramsey's fuckup, you engaged in discrimination, too."

"That's a stretch," Burgess said.

165

"It could be," Vann agreed. "But you said it yourself, budgets are stretched thin. You're about to try to suck fifty thousand dollars out of the D.C. office. I know my bosses. They will be *delighted* if Shane here punts up an ADA grievance to keep that money in our till. In the meantime, you two will look like assholes trying to pin Ramsey's incompetence on a Haden. A really *famous* Haden, since you went out of your way to bash Shane for that. And if you lose, well." Vann smiled at both of them. "Disciplinary notes in your files probably aren't going to cut it."

Burgess and Ramsey were both dead silent for a good fifteen seconds. Then Burgess turned to me. "And you'll go along with this stupidity, Agent Shane?"

"I mean, I *was* given a threep at thirteen percent power when I was working on an investigation where timeliness was critical," I said, and let that hang in the air.

"Christ," Burgess said.

"Well, now that that's settled," Vann said, and turned to Ramsey. "What do we know about the fire?"

Ramsey looked for a moment like she was going to tell Vann to cram her question up her ass but then sucked it up. "The fire department investigators think it was an electrical fire," she said, tightly. "The building's electrical system's old and not up to code. It's possible Chapman's apartment was drawing more power than the system could handle."

"Because of all the threeps in the place," Vann said.

Ramsey nodded. "There were several there. If they were all drawing power into the induction plates at the same time, there could have been an overload. Or enough of a strain that when anyone else drew power, it tipped the system over."

"This building didn't have circuit breakers?" I asked.

Ramsey shrugged. "Not up to code, remember."

"Has anyone talked to the old lady yet?" Vann asked.

"Shaniqa Miller," I said.

"She's still out of it," Ramsey said. "The hospital will call when she's conscious and able to talk to us. The fire department and the police want to talk to her too."

"What about the landlord or the property manager?"

"We can't find either," Ramsey said. "The landlord's apparently on vacation in Amalfi, wherever that is."

"Italy," I said. My family had vacationed

there before.

"Oh, that's nice," Ramsey replied, in a tone that suggested the opposite. "The manager, named Woody Poole, is also gone, although probably not to Italy. He told the police he was going to stay with his sister but didn't give an address or number. We'll find him."

"You impounded the threeps from the apartment?" I asked.

"We have them. Do you need them right now?"

"Just the serial numbers and VINs. For the moment."

"I'll send those to you."

"Thank you," I said.

"And now, unless we have anything else to discuss, I think we're done here," Burgess said, reasserting herself in the conversation. "And, Agent Shane?"

"Yes, ma'am?"

"From now on, when you visit this office, requisition a rental."

"We should be talking to Alton Ortiz now," I said to Vann.

"I wanted to see this first," Vann said. "It was on the way."

"Not really."

"It was on the way *enough,*" Vann

168

amended.

We were standing in front of the burned-out building where Chapman's love nest used to be. Debris from the fire littered the front of the building and the sidewalk.

Vann took out her cigarettes.

"Smoking at a fire wreck," I said. "That's nice."

"Everything that was going to burn already did," she said, and lit one up. She looked around. "This isn't a great neighborhood."

"I think the euphemism is 'gentrification ready,' " I said.

"Why do you think he would put a love nest here?" Vann asked. "Professional athletes aren't known for their financial prudence."

"Hey now," I said. "My dad lived in a tiny town house when he was making millions, because he was investing."

"I think we can agree your dad was an outlier in a number of ways, Chris." Vann took another drag on her cigarette.

"Chapman was a professional athlete but he wasn't a star," I said. "He was getting paid well but not a ridiculous amount like some of the league's franchise players. So maybe this was what he could afford."

"Or maybe this wasn't a groupie trap like

169

you assumed," Vann said.

"I can shoot you the map of the apartment again," I said. "It looked like it was designed for play."

"I didn't say it wasn't. But maybe just not for an endless parade of people." Vann took another puff and looked around. "This isn't the place you go to impress people with your star power. This is a place you go when you want to keep a secret."

"I think you might be reading too much into an address," I said.

"Maybe." Vann looked like she was going to say more but stopped.

"Wha—" I started to ask, but Vann held up a finger. I shut up and started to listen too. Then I heard it.

A meow.

"It's the *cat,*" I said, and walked toward the direction of the meow.

I needn't have bothered. A tuxedo cat burst out of the shadows of the trash cans two buildings over and ran up to me, meowing insistently and rubbing against me.

"It remembers you saved it," Vann said, watching the cat.

I knelt down to pet the cat and it jumped up on my back and shoulders. "No," I said. "It remembers its owner is a threep."

The cat jumped back down and looked

up at me, expectantly.

I looked at it and then looked up at Vann. "We can't leave the cat here," I said.

Vann registered a small smile. "Because the cat is a material witness?"

I picked up the cat and scratched its neck, the cat obligingly arching its neck back, showing the collar and the tag that dangled from it. A tag my threep identified as a small data vault.

"It might be," I said.

CHAPTER NINE

"Jesus," Vann said, as we drove to Alton Ortiz's town house. "You've had that cat for fifteen minutes and you're already spoiling it."

"I'm not spoiling it," I said, petting it as it sat contentedly in my lap, purring. The name on the tag said "Donut." I assumed it was the cat's name.

"You just fed it tuna. You made me stop so you could get tuna, and you fed it to the cat."

"That's not spoiling the cat. It's feeding it."

"Feeding it *tuna*. As opposed to cat food."

"It's had a rough day," I said, petting Donut.

"You don't understand," Vann said. "Once you feed a cat tuna, it doesn't go back to regular cat food. You try to feed that cat regular food now, it will just stare at you accusingly. And if you don't produce the tuna, the cat will go and shit in your shoes."

"Are we speaking from experience, here?"

"I might be."

"I'm in a threep. Threeps don't generally wear shoes."

"The cat will find something else to crap on."

"I will warn Marla Chapman about the tuna incident," I said.

Vann stared at me briefly, then put her eyes back on the road. "You're planning to leave the cat with Chapman's widow?"

"We don't need the cat," I said. "We'll take the data tag."

"And you think Marla Chapman will be happy to see the thing? 'Here's the cat your husband kept at the secret apartment where he was fucking other people, Mrs. Chapman. His name is *Donut.*' "

"It's possible I didn't think this one through entirely," I said after a minute.

"It's *possible,*" Vann agreed.

"You want a cat?" I asked Vann.

She glanced over for a second. "I'm not the one whose lap the thing is sitting in," she said.

"That's because you're driving. Put the car on autopilot and get some of this action."

"No."

"Is this because of past trauma involving tuna?"

Vann said nothing to this as we turned off of Cresson Street and onto Levering, where Ortiz lived.

"Look," I said, pointing. Alton Ortiz was walking up the street, in the same direction we were driving. He was carrying grocery bags. We passed him without him noticing and went up the street a few doors from where he lived.

We parked and settled the cat, who to be fair showed no interest in leaving the car. By the time we walked up to him he was on the small front deck of his apartment, standing by his door.

"Mr. Ortiz," I said, "I'm Agent Chris Shane of the FBI." I popped my badge up on my chest screen. "We talked yesterday."

"You were wearing a different threep then," Ortiz said.

"Yeah, I do that sometimes."

"What happened to the other one?"

"It burned up in a fire."

Ortiz smiled. "You've had an exciting twenty-four hours, Agent Shane," he said.

"I have," I said, and motioned to Vann. "This is my partner, Agent Vann. We have a couple of follow-up questions we'd like to ask you."

"About Duane?" Ortiz asked.

"Yes, and a couple of other things."

Ortiz nodded. "All right. Give me a couple of seconds to open this door." Ortiz set down his groceries and fiddled with his keys as Vann and I walked up onto his deck. When we were entirely on the deck Ortiz dropped his keys. He grabbed his deck railing and launched himself southward, toward his neighbor's porch landing. He was making a run for it.

Unfortunately Ortiz did not factor in his neighbor's door awning, which was at face height because Levering Street was at an incline. His neighbor's town house was slightly lower than his own. Ortiz caught a forehead full of awning, twisted weirdly, and missed his footing. He fell down his neighbor's concrete steps and collapsed into a heap on the sidewalk, moaning a little.

"I don't even know what to do with this," Vann said, after a moment.

I walked down from the deck and over to Ortiz, who by this time was sitting up, clutching his arm. "How are you?" I asked.

"I think I broke my arm," he said.

"That's because you were attempting to flee the two of us," I said. "Do you mind if I ask you why?"

"I'm not talking to you anymore without

175

a lawyer, Agent Shane," Ortiz said.

"You sure you want to do that?" Vann asked, from the deck. "We weren't coming to arrest you, Ortiz. We just had a couple of questions. Now you're on the sidewalk with a messed-up arm because you tried to run from us. That's some highly suspicious behavior. If you talk to us we can clear it up, easy. We can all agree you just accidentally fell, instead of trying to run from a couple of federal agents."

Ortiz looked up at her, still holding his arm. "Nice try," he said. He turned his attention back to me. "No more talking without a lawyer. Am I under arrest?"

I looked up at Vann. "Do we want to arrest him?"

"Well, he *is* technically a fugitive," Vann said. "He ran from us when we tried to question him."

"I don't think what he did counts as running," I said. "More 'jumping and falling.' "

"Your choice," Vann said, to me.

I looked at Ortiz, who looked back, cradling his injury. "Let's call him an ambulance and figure it out from there."

"You know what this means, don't you," Vann said.

"Tell me."

Vann pointed to Ortiz. "We're going to

have to come back up here tomorrow to question this asshole." She fished in her pocket for her smokes. "Christ. I hate this town."

Demarcus Hinson was the chief design officer of Van Diemen Concepts, and he was chatty and charming and determined to tell us everything about his work, which involved building threeps with simulated sexual organs.

"Some people are offended by what we do here," he said, as he gave us a tour of the factory floor. "Factory floor" was perhaps a grand term. Van Diemen's shop consisted of a dozen fabricators. The fabricators could run off the hard and soft parts of the threep with appropriate printers, and then join them together via robot arms. Somewhat bored-looking human workers stared at status monitors to make sure the construction process was going to specification. Two of the monitor stations appeared unattended but closer examination showed they were not. They were staffed by Hadens, working remotely.

"Because you give threeps genitals?" Vann asked.

"Yes, but not only that," Hinson said. "It's more that we give Hadens *sexuality.* Or more accurately, we make it clear that Hadens have sexuality. Obviously they had it before this." He waved at one of the fabricators, where a threep was being pieced together. "And of course it's not just about genitals either. Our models have full nerve sensitivity across their entire forms, like most threeps do, but with special emphasis on areas known to help contribute to sexual arousal. When you do that you make a few enemies."

"Why do people care?"

Hinson shrugged. "The usual. Some people have religious or so-called moral issues with sexuality. Other people are uncomfortable with people they see as being disabled having strong sexual drives and fulfilling erotic lives. We have some folks who see Hadens as sexless, in all senses of the term. They get upset when Hadens refuse to live down to their preconceptions. And then there's just the people who get weird about what they see as robots with dicks." Hinson laughed at his own joke. "So basically, we get all kinds."

"Do you ever get complaints from Hadens?" I asked.

Hinson pointed at me. "We do, actually," he said. "We get static from a few Haden purists, the ones that refuse to use threeps for anything. Those folks accuse us of trying to make Haden sexuality conform to non-Hadens' standards." Hinson shrugged again. "I don't see how that works, personally. We serve customers who want our threeps. If you don't want them, you don't have to use them. But even those who do use them don't have to use them in 'conventional' ways. Our threeps allow them to explore their sexuality in ways they might not otherwise get a chance to. And in some cases, in ways that are not actually possible with standard biological gender models."

"You mean your threeps with the ridges."

This got a furrowed brow. "I don't know how you know about those," Hinson said. "Those are still in beta. The testers all have to sign nondisclosure agreements."

I pulled up a picture of the threeps in Chapman's apartment and sent it to Hinson, who looked at it on his tablet. "I saw them personally," I said.

Hinson looked at the photo and then blinked. "Is . . . is this room on *fire*?"

"It is," I confirmed. "So these are all your threeps?"

"They certainly do look like our models," Hinson said. He pointed to the one with the penis. "This one is a 'Gable' model." He pointed to the one with a vulva. "This is

179

the 'Bette' model. We name the explicitly gendered models after golden age cinematic actors."

Vann nodded at the genitals. "Based on real life?"

"Oh, no. I mean, no, not of the actors specifically. Our base models are configured through statistical modeling of various populations. But we also do special orders. We can model your own genitalia, or you can choose from shapes we've licensed from adult performers and other notables. You're smiling, Agent Vann."

"It wouldn't have occurred to me to try on someone else's genitals," Vann said.

"Welcome to the future," Hinson said, smiling back.

I tapped Hinson's tablet. "What can you tell us about the other two?"

Hinson stopped smiling. "These two don't have an official title yet."

"No golden age actor these resemble?" Vann cracked.

"We're trying to get away from that particular branding identity," Hinson said. "Some of our clients asked us for models that would allow for full sensuality without any lingering issues surrounding gender roles. We tried several designs and this was the one that's worked the best, both aesthetically and functionally."

"Functionally?" I asked.

"Yes. Some earlier nongendered designs asked testers to move in ways they didn't find very sexy. The ridged design allows for conventional thrusting in a number of positions."

"Unconventional genitals for conventional sex," I said.

"Sure," Hinson said. "We pride ourselves in catering to our clients. But humans are still often creatures of habit, in a threep or in their own bodies. And while we can do custom work for clients, we do have the mass market to think about."

Vann looked at the factory floor. "How *mass* are you thinking?"

"We have a select clientele now but we have expansion plans for the future. Abrams-Kettering passing means that in a few years we'll have a new class of customers. Non-Hadens of all sorts. Some of them will want threeps for their sexual lives. Because their bodies are aging, or have a disability. Because they want to engage in fantasy play. Or just to try something new." He motioned to the tablet. "Some of them will want to try something new in a nongendered body. We're prepared for whatever they want, for whatever reason they want it."

"You think that many people will want sexbots," Vann said.

"We think we'll do fine," Hinson said. "But we're also realists." He motioned to the fabricators. "When we have downtime or low orders, we lease out the fabricators. Sometimes we subcontract for major manufacturers for specialized models. Sebring-Warner subcontracts to us for some of their Hilketa models, for example. And right now we're doing a tidy business subcontracting the production of basic threeps for a major manufacturer. It's for a new rental start-up."

"MobilOn?" I asked.

Hinson looked momentarily stunned, then recovered. "I probably shouldn't say," he said, which I took as a confirmation.

"Then let's get back to these," Vann said, pointing back to Hinson's tablet.

"What about them?"

"One of them activated while I was in this apartment," I said.

"You were in this apartment," Hinson said.

"Yes."

"While it was on *fire.*"

"Yes."

Hinson looked at my threep critically.

"Different threep," I said.

182

"I was going to say," he murmured. "Well, I'm not sure what you need me for, I'm afraid. I assume that if you were in the apartment at the time, then you know who our tester was."

"He was dead at the time," Vann said.

"Excuse me?"

"These are Duane Chapman's threeps. He died on Sunday. This threep was walking around in a burning apartment later that evening. We have a reasonable suspicion the threep might be involved with the apartment fire. At the very least we have questions."

"I see," Hinson said. "Because Chapman was testing these threeps for us, you want us to open his account for log-ins to see who else was accessing them."

"That's right."

Hinson spread his hands. "I'm afraid I can't do that without a warrant. Our clients expect privacy, for obvious reasons. And that privacy extends to those they invite to test our products with."

"Here's the thing about that," Vann said. "Duane Chapman bought those test units from your company and kept an account related to them on your servers, so you could get feedback on them. But it turns out he didn't buy them personally. He got them through his pass-through company. Which he co-owned with his wife. And as the owner of those threeps, she wants the information. She asked us to come get it for her."

Hinson looked at me. "Is this true?"

"We can call her if you like," I said. "Or you can call her lawyer, who will tell you the same thing." We had phoned Marla Chapman on the way to speak to Hinson.

Hinson looked at us both uncertainly. "I think I need to talk with legal about this."

"Hurry," Vann said. "We have a cat in the car."

"That's a cat," Tayla said, as I entered the house unsteadily with Donut, a cat box, kitty litter, and several cans of tuna.

"Your deductive powers as a scientist never cease to amaze me," I said. Donut wrestled out of my arms and plopped on the floor, and walked over, purring, to Tayla.

"I don't remember any house meeting about getting a cat," Tayla said.

"The cat's not permanent."

Tayla pointed to the cat box. "Your voice says one thing, and your purchases say another."

"The cat's a witness," I said. "In my case."

"A witness."

"That's right."

"You're kidding."

"Only sort of."

"And we are, what? A safe house for the cat?"

From the second floor there was noise and the door to the twins' room opened and their threep emerged. "There's a cat?!?" they squealed.

"Oh Lord," Tayla said.

"It's not a permanent resident," I said to the twins, as they stomped down the stairs.

"Why not?" they asked.

"It's a federal witness," Tayla told them.

"We have a witness protection cat?!?" The twins looked at Donut with obvious excitement. Donut gazed up at them.

"Let's all be calm, please."

"Can he stay in our room?" the twins asked.

"What's going on?" Tony yelled from his room.

"We have a fugitive cat!" the twins yelled back.

"What?"

"It's not a fugitive," I yelled.

"It's just a witness," Tayla said.

"It sounds ridiculous when you say it," I said to Tayla.

"Yes, well." Tayla reached down and

185

scritched Donut.

By this time Tony was making his way down the stairs. "We didn't have a meeting about a cat."

"He's not permanent," I said.

"He *could* be permanent," the twins said.

"Where's his owner?" Tony asked.

"He's dead. This is Duane Chapman's cat."

"The cat's widowed," the twins said.

"Stop it," I said.

"Why do *we* have it?" Tony asked.

I reached down and unlatched Donut's collar and gave it to Tony. "It's a data vault," he said.

"Yep," I said. "Do you think you can get into it?"

"Are you paying me to get into it?"

"Well, the FBI will be, yes."

"Then probably, eventually."

"And what about the cat?" Tayla asked.

I looked over to the twins and handed them the cat box, kitty litter, and tuna.

"Squeeee," they said.

"You actually said *squeee*," Tayla said to the twins, disbelievingly, but they were already walking up the stairs with their cat-related booty. She turned back to me. "This is on you," she said to me.

"I accept all blame," I replied.

186

"You know they're going to want to keep the cat."

"It's only temporary," I said again.

"Right," Tayla said. "Its owner is dead and the twins are acting like eight-year-olds over it. Sure it's temporary."

"Sorry."

"Just remember this when I ask for a dog. Because at a house meeting soon I'm going to ask for one."

"Seems fair."

"A *big* one."

"I like big dogs," I said.

"You better." Tayla walked off.

"I'm not a fan of dogs, personally," Tony said.

"Don't tell Tayla," I warned.

"Way ahead of you. Anything else interesting today, besides acquiring a widowed cat?"

I was about to say *Yes, but I can't tell you* when an internal ping told me I had a call. I looked at the caller ID.

And thought, *Well, that's certainly interesting.* I held my hand up to Tony, to tell him I had something going on, and took the call.

"Chris Shane."

"Hello, Agent Shane. It's Kim Silva. I'm a teammate of Duane's."

"Yes, I know. My condolences."

"Thank you. And I'm pretty sure by now

187

you've figured out that Duane and I were lovers."

"It had come to my attention, yes," I said. According to the information Hinson had given us, she had been logged in to the threeps in Duane Chapman's apartment multiple times in the last year.

"And I think you're also aware that was me piloting the threep you saw in the apartment when it was on fire."

"I did know that, yes. I have some questions for you about that, and some other things."

"I've talked to my legal team and with the Bays organization, and we've all decided that it's best if I cooperate fully with you. Would you be available to meet with me tomorrow? At eleven A.M. at the Bays' practice facility?"

"Yes, of course," I said.

"Thank you, Agent Shane." She hesitated for a moment.

"Is there something else, Ms. Silva?" I asked.

"This is kind of a strange question," Silva said.

"That's all right," I said. "Go ahead and ask it."

"When you were in Duane's apartment, did you happen to see my cat?"

CHAPTER TEN

I left Donut with the twins, headed to my room, laid my threep down on its induction lounge, and then opened up a passage to my cave.

It was not a real cave, of course. My "cave" was the personal space I had created for myself in the Agora, the network Hadens used to live their nonphysical lives in.

Every Haden defined their own personal space. Some Hadens, mostly the ones who contracted the disease later in life, created spaces that closely replicated their own houses or areas that were familiar to them in their non-Haden lives. Others, especially the ones who had contracted the disease early and whose main experience with life was the Agora, created personal spaces that were more abstract and often whimsical or even satirical to the idea of a "personal space." I had a friend in college who described his personal space as a "non-euclidean camel stomach." I can't vouch for the accuracy of that description, but it was as annoyingly pretentious as it was described.

My own personal space was somewhere in the middle — not a house, not a topological oddity, but a dark, quiet cave, based on the famous Waitomo Caves of New Zealand, only larger. Far above, simulated glow-worms twinkled at me. Below, a subterranean river flowed by, offering up the perfect level of ambient noise for relaxation and quiet contemplation.

Which I was about to completely ruin by opening up news about Duane Chapman's death.

To be clear, not just the news about Duane Chapman's death, since most of the pertinent information I was already aware of, or would be soon enough. I was also looking at commentary, opinion, speculation, and just plain old rumor-mongering.

I didn't have to look very far.

First, to *The Washington Post, The New York Times, The Boston Globe, Sports Illustrated,* ESPN, and other established media outlets, print, audio, and video. Their stories broke down into expected bins: straight reporting, follow-up reporting, feature stories for color, mournful opinion pieces, the occasional piece looking at how Chapman's death might impact the business of the NAHL. The straightforward pieces featured anodyne quotes from the FBI press spokesman saying nothing of any substance. He was good at that. The *Post* and other local media made note that Vann and I were on the case, and that my dad was considering taking part ownership in the NAHL's as-yet-unnamed future D.C. expansion team. No dark mutterings about what that might mean.

That was saved for the *Hilketa News* and some other second-tier outlets. Cary Wise in particular was trying to connect the dots between my involvement with the investigation and my dad's potential business dealings. They were coming up short because there wasn't anything scandalous there. I marked it as a potential issue anyway. Just because there was nothing to a story didn't mean there wouldn't be a story.

Which brought us to the less reputable sites, which were positively awash with written and spoken speculation from fans, wannabe journalists, and the occasional politically motivated screamers. I scrolled through these quickly, pulling out some of the charmers for later examination.

Among these:

That Chapman was killed because he knew too much about the NAHL's dirty business practices.

That he was murdered because he leaked the Boston Bays' playbook to other teams for money.

That he committed suicide to protest the commercialization of Hilketa, from its earlier, purer stance as a league run for the sheer bliss of the sport.

That he was killed so that there would be room on rosters for non-Haden players, and that his death would just be the first.

That he was dispatched by his wife because he was cheating on her. This one I put a star on not because I thought Marla Chapman had her husband killed but because I was curious just how widespread rumors of Chapman's infidelity might have been.

That Chapman had been killed for the league's insurance policy on him, because it was cash-short and needed the liquidity. I starred this one too, to remind myself to look up the league's and the Boston Bays' finances.

That Chapman's death was God's judgment for a Haden marrying a non-Haden.

That Chapman's death was God's judgment for the immorality of the North

192

American Hilketa League and the licentiousness of major league sports in general.

That Chapman's death was the work of terrorists trying to destroy the American way of life (and one assumed, tangentially, the Canadian and Mexican ways of life, as the NAHL had teams in both countries).

That Chapman's death was related to what caused Clemente Salcido to be dropped from the league. This was a theory put forward by a Mexico City Aztecs fan. I starred this one, too, and dropped a quick ping to Tony.

He picked it up immediately. "I haven't cracked the data vault yet," he said.

"I wasn't going to ask about that," I said. "Actually I was going to ask you what your final write-up on Duane Chapman's data feed was going to be."

"As it happens I was literally just about to send it to you and Vann," he said. And, like magic, a ping popped up letting me know he'd sent along an encrypted file containing the report. "My final determination is that the data feed wasn't tampered with in any way. It was just taken out of the public view. Also that it doesn't show anything that we didn't already know from this morning."

"Would there be any feeds that might show more than what we know now?"

"Sure. I told you this morning this data feed is mostly for entertainment purposes. But the league has more detailed feeds for bodily functions. Heart, brain, other systems. They keep them for examination to make sure there's no doping or other issues."

"We can get those?"

"Probably. You might need a warrant."

"Okay, I'll work on it. In the meantime, could you do something for me?"

"When?"

"Anytime."

"I'll do it now, since I'll get overtime. What is it?"

"Could you pull the public feed for Clemente Salcido's last game? He was with the Aztecs."

"I know who Salcido was," Tony said, chidingly. "What am I looking for?"

"Just look at it and if you see anything that pops out at you, let me know."

"Fine, be mysterious."

"It's not a problem, is it?"

"No, it'll just take longer. I'll pair it up with trying to crack this data vault."

"What's the holdup?"

" 'What's the holdup.' Anytime you want to dig into a heavily encrypted piece of hardware, Chris, you let me know." Tony dropped the connection. I went back to reading scurrilous rumors.

The point of reading the rumors and nonsense was not to give credence to any of them. It was to get an idea of the emotional lay of the land around the story of the first Hilketa player to die on the field.

A couple of hours of reading established that the story had captured the national imagination. Every major news outlet that covered sports had pieces on the story, and the chattering masses were actively and enthusiastically blabbing away on it. But so far nothing stood out as genuinely shocking or surprising. Even the wacky conspiracy theories were pretty normal, as far as conspiracy theories went.

Which was surprising to me. There were actual conspiracy-worthy things going on. For example: Alex Kaufmann's death, so quickly after Duane Chapman's. It was no secret we were investigating Kaufmann's death along with Chapman's. But aside from the *Post* and the *Globe,* and an Associated Press report, few outlets were following up on his death, outside of printing the AP story. The *Post* had the most extensive story, a feature-y write-up titled "Alex Kaufmann's Death Could Have Been Big News. Then Duane Chapman Died." I thought that was a little on the nose and basically the *Post* admitting Chapman's death was the sexier story so they weren't going to do much with Kaufmann's.

It also meant that the NAHL's press people were doing a very fine job keeping the spotlight off Kaufmann, an actual league executive. The Chapman story wasn't a *better* story for them — a player death story is not a best-case scenario in any formulation — but it meant they really had to manage only one story.

Well, so far, anyway. We had the forensics on Kaufmann's hotel bed and the information on the neighboring room coming in the morning. We'd see what happened then.

I let the video and audio and comment posts babble on for a bit, taking in the takes, and then wiped them simultaneously, muting them all so quickly that the resulting silence was almost physical. Then I pulled up a single screen, to an all-purpose fan-run information site on the sport, called, appropriately enough, Hilketapedia.

I accessed Duane Chapman's page. His avatar, based on his physical body, popped up, along with a photo of him piloting his game threep in a match against New York in his first season, vaulting over New York's Marcello Gibbons. That was one of his better games, and an early one, when it looked like he might break out and become a star. It never happened for him. He was good enough to stay on the roster of the Boston Bays, but not good enough to make the team nervous that his free agency was coming up on the horizon.

That would be Kim Silva, his teammate and now, apparently, lover. Her Hilketa-pedia page scrolled for quite a while, listing her accomplishments, records, awards, and various career achievements. Chapman was a player for a franchise. Silva was the franchise player, the one around whom the rest of the team was built.

As well she should have been. She had basically dragged a mediocre Bays team to the championship last season over Los Angeles, which had a better record and a far more balanced set of talents. With her, the Bays were an elite team. Without her, they were middling at best.

Silva's dominance of the league had paid off well for her. In addition to a record-breaking contract, she had scores of product endorsements, some relating to Hilketa and some not. She endorsed Pepsi, as an example, a drink whose particular charms would mostly be lost on a Haden. We could ingest soda. Most of us did not. Silva had gotten

Haden's early enough that she probably didn't have a residual fondness for the stuff. But I guess if Pepsi wanted to have her as a spokesperson, that was their business, and hers.

The Hilketapedia page had a full list of her product endorsements, with a rough idea of the value of each annually. Like a fair number of elite athletes, Silva's league salary was worth less than the yearly endorsement take. I scrolled through the list, counting up the dollars in my head.

And stopped when I saw that Silva had an endorsement deal with Labram for their IV supplements. The same specific brand, in fact, that Chapman was using the day he died.

"Well, *that's* interesting," I said out loud, to no one in particular. We had our people looking at the supplement bag for anything out of the usual. If they found anything, and Silva was indeed sharing her stash with Chapman, then this could have some pretty substantial implications for her. This among everything else might have been why she was suddenly so interested in speaking with us.

I wiped the Hilketapedia from the air and called up images of everyone we'd had contact with during the investigation to date. Duane Chapman. His wife, Marla. His assistant, Alton Ortiz. Alex Kaufmann. MacKenzie Stodden, Oliver Medina, and Coretta Barber, apparatchiks of the North American Hilketa League. Wendell Gordon, the NAHL commissioner. Reluctantly I put my parents up as well. This point of the lineup here wasn't to list suspects or people who were engaging in suspicious activity but to try to see all the connections between them. To see in the connections something that I or Vann might otherwise have missed so far.

I definitely felt like we were missing things. The word I would use for our investigation so far was "frustrating." Two suspicious deaths, one apartment fire, a yanked data stream, an interviewee bolting, a cat with a data vault for a collar, and kinky threeps galore. And yet, at the moment, nothing solid to show that Duane Chapman died of anything other than natural causes. The most we had right now was the NAHL data stream showing Chapman's brain activity ramping up. But it didn't mean anything if we couldn't connect it to an outside cause.

I stared up at the faces, drawing lines of connections between them. Something about the lineup was bothering me.

I'm missing someone, I realized. I was about to add another face when I got a ping.

"Chris," the voice on the other end said. "It's Amelie Parker. We met earlier today at your parents' place."

"I remember," I said.

"Good," she said. "I was wondering if you were busy at the moment."

"Just looking through some pictures." I floated up an image of her into my lineup. "Why do you ask?"

"I'd like to invite you over for a discussion," she said.

"Now?"

"If you're willing, yes."

"Is this concerning our investigation?"

"No. I'm not going to go anywhere near that."

"Then what is it about?"

"It's about the future. Mine, and, perhaps, yours."

CHAPTER ELEVEN

A white brightness, the impression of autumn air against my face, and then I was in the back seat of a 1940 Chrysler Newport Phaeton, cruising down an estate road, headed for an impressively large mansion, the sort you have if you're the descendant of an earl or a robber baron.

I looked toward the side, at the trees, mostly maple, lining the road, bursting with the reds and oranges of fall foliage color. Each leaf was individually drawn and reacting to the gentle wind that wafted through them, carrying away their scent as it did. Then I turned forward and saw the chauffeur driving the Phaeton, or the back of him, anyway. The cut and weave of his suit fabric was exquisite, as was the detail of his skin, down to the individual short hairs of the back of his neck. The red leather of his seat back was richly grained and I was certain that if I leaned forward and sniffed,

I would smell cow.

I get it, Parker, I thought to myself. *You spent a lot of money on your personal space.*

The Phaeton wasn't real, nor was the chauffeur, or his uniform or the road or the trees or the woody smell of the breeze, or the breeze, for that matter. Nor the impressively large mansion I was currently wending toward. It was a simulation created in Amelie Parker's personal space, just like my outsized Waitomo Cave.

What was different was the amount of processing power it took to generate Parker's living space. Parker wasn't generating just a room, or a house, or a single cave. She was generating hectares of land and modeling everything in it to an exhaustive degree. Not just trees but individual leaves. Not just individual leaves but the smell those leaves would create. Not just the smell but the wind that would take it to me, or anyone else, as we sped on by in a simulated car from the 1940s, complete with accurate thrum and crunch from the wheels connecting with fine gravel.

It's a level of detail for a personal space that's possible only with money. It's not difficult to create a room full of realistic detail. It's not even difficult to create a passable large area if you know how to cut processing corners, by offering close detail only in a sphere that corresponds to someone's field of awareness, with everything else generic shapes and patterns until you're actively looking at it. My own cave is large but dark and self-contained. The only real detail in it is the platform I have over the river. Everything else — the cave, the river, the glowworms far above — is generated with *just enough* detail.

But if you want more than just enough, if you want literally billions of leaves and blades of grass and gravel pebbles, then you have to pay for them all. And not only do you have to pay for them, you have to pay for their upkeep. You're not paying just for their generation. When I was done with my cave, it collapsed into a waiting state. As I looked around Amelie Parker's estate grounds, I strongly suspected she kept it running when she wasn't in it.

You pay for persistence.

And every Haden knows you're paying for it, too. In a community where everything is possible and anything imagined can be made real *enough,* persistence on a very large scale of detail is one of the few possible displays of actual wealth in a virtual world.

Which is why, ironically, relatively few

genuinely wealthy Hadens did it — or, more accurately, few did it in front of people who weren't very close friends. Most wealthy Hadens created well-appointed but processorily modest areas to meet with business associates and acquaintances. It wasn't until after they got to know you that they'd take you to the entire planet they'd modeled from the tectonic forces upward.

Amelie Parker inviting me to this richly detailed personal space of hers suggested one of two things. Either she considered me a very good friend already, on the basis of a single meeting, or she was nouveau riche and didn't know how Hadens with money did things.

The Phaeton circled around the fountain in front of the mansion and parked at the steps. The chauffeur, who I saw now bore more than a passing resemblance to 1960s-era Robert Redford, opened the passenger door for me and tipped his cap as I exited the Phaeton. He drove off as I walked up the steps toward Parker, waiting for me on the marble landing at the top of the stairs.

"Thank you for coming, Chris," she said, extending her hand.

I took it. "You asked, I came," I said. "Although I didn't expect to arrive by chauffeur."

Parker smiled. "Only the best for you. You like the place?" She motioned at the mansion.

"It's very impressive." I could still hear the Phaeton receding into the distance.

"You mean it's a bit gauche, don't you. Showing off an estate-sized personal space on a first meeting."

"It's not really our first meeting," I reminded her.

"No, it's not," Parker agreed. "Also I think the thing rich Hadens do is hypocritical. You know I have money. I know you have money." She motioned around her again. "We both can do this. There's no point in pretending to you or anyone else that this is not how we live."

"You'll scandalize the old money," I said.

"Fuck 'em." Parker motioned toward the mansion. "Shall we?"

The mansion continued the idle-rich vibe, with slightly more ostentation than was necessary but not enough to be entirely garish, but we didn't stay in it long enough for me to peer into the details. We walked through to the back portion of the yard, which abutted a lake and a pier. Tied to the pier was a large sailboat.

"Are we going out on that?" I asked.

"I thought it would be nice. Unless you

have a problem being on the water."

I shrugged. "It's not like I can drown."

Parker laughed at this and waved me onto the sailboat. When we were safely on, the sailboat unmoored itself and headed into the lake.

"I should tell you this space is still relatively new to me," Parker said, as we sailed.

"Is it," I said.

"I grew up like you, Chris. A rich kid. But unlike you my parents never fully accepted the Haden part of my identity. They kept me focused on the material world. Kept me in my threep most of the time and let me have only a basic connection to the Agora."

"That doesn't sound great."

"They didn't mean any harm in it. But of course not meaning harm isn't the same as not doing harm. I missed out on a lot that my Haden contemporaries took for granted. And the irony is that my parents' company has done very well catering to the Haden market along with everything else it does. But Mom and Dad were both definitely of the 'we don't like what we don't understand' stripe, you know? Very conservative that way. They thought the Agora was somewhere I'd get taken advantage of, or where I'd get radical, heretical ideas."

"To be fair, both can happen there," I said.

"The Agora is home to millions of people," Parker pointed out. "Of course it could happen there. But it could happen in the so-called real world, too. In that respect the two are not that different from each other."

I glanced around the lake. "So when did you get this?"

"A couple of years ago. After the first company I founded went public, and I could afford to build something like this without family money. It's persistent, you know."

"I guessed."

Parker nodded. "So you know what that's about. It did it on my own, so Mom and Dad couldn't complain about it. Well, that's not true, they *did* complain about it. We compromised by me never inviting them here."

I laughed at this. "Seems fair."

"And now you know why I was fine flouting the rules about showing off *this* place to you, Chris. It's not about trying to impress you. I know you're not going to be impressed by it. It's me showing you who I am. My declaration of independence, if you want. And maybe you'll be impressed by *that*."

"Why do you want to impress me?"

"I have my reasons. I'll get to them in a

moment."

I didn't press it. Instead I motioned to the simulation. "And how do *you* like your declaration?" I asked.

"Well, to be honest it's kind of a pain in the ass," Parker admitted, laughing. "Persistence is expensive. There's code rot, which means there are places all over the map that need maintenance. Last week the code that governs wind messed up and everything froze for two days until I could get the programmers to figure out what was going on. Leaves and birds, frozen in the air. And even when it's running at full capacity I had to cut some corners." She pointed to the lake. "Go further down than three meters in the lake and you'll clip out of the simulation. You'll fall right out and be punted from it entirely."

"That's no good."

"I have to warn people if they go swimming, otherwise they get very confused."

"You could always downsize."

"I could but I don't want to. It's a pain in the ass, but it's *my* pain in the ass, you know?"

I nodded at this and we spent a few moments silently, enjoying Parker's pain-in-the-ass simulation.

"As much as I'm enjoying this, this isn't

why you asked me here," I said, eventually.

"It's not," Parker said.

"What's up?"

"Do you like working for the FBI, Chris?" Parker asked.

"I like it just fine," I said. "It has its ups and downs like any job, but most of the time it's interesting, and I like the people I work with."

"It's not especially glamorous."

"That's a feature, not a bug. I got tired of being the poster child for an entire people."

"But you know you didn't *stop* being that, right?" Parker said. "I know you've spent the last few years pulling away from the public eye, but even as a lowly FBI investigator you're still in the spotlight. You and your partner have a way of making waves with your investigations. That thing with Lucas Hubbard last year. Sending the most famous Haden in the world to jail isn't exactly laying low. And now investigating Duane Chapman's death. That's headlines for days."

"We didn't choose the cases," I said. "We take them as they come."

"Right, but the ones that come to you keep putting you back into the spotlight," Parker said. "So, you know my company. MobilOn."

"The one you want Dad to invest in," I said. "The one we talked about earlier today. With the rental threeps."

"That's right. On-demand threeps, yes. When we were starting up we thought about who we wanted to partner with. Not just in terms of funding, although obviously that's important. Also in terms of who we wanted to associate with our brand, as endorsers or even possibly spokespeople. So we paid Ginsberg Associates to make a poll for us a few months ago of the most admired Hadens in the United States."

"I didn't hear of this poll."

"It was an internal poll, not for the public. Would you like to know where you showed up on the poll?"

"Since you brought me here to talk about it, I'm guessing pretty high."

"Leaving out Hilketa players, who really are their own category, you're the fourth most admired Haden in the United States, Chris. Specifically you're tied for fourth among Hadens, and you're third among non-Hadens. Which is pretty amazing."

"It's residual goodwill from being a kid," I said.

Parker shook her head. "We thought that too," she said. "But we followed up. Turns out your current job feeds into your ranking. Ironically people like that you're spending your adult life having an actual job, rather than floating on your unearned wealth. Turns out arresting bad people and sending them to prison makes you look really good."

My brain suddenly flashed back to the reporter in the hotel lobby, telling me I was still famous. "There are other Haden FBI officers," I said, to Parker.

"Sure. But none of them are you. Which is my point. Your fame persists. And it's even growing. You're still you, Chris. As far as celebrity is concerned."

"Okay, and?"

"And, I'm wondering how you like your current job."

"It appears to be making me famous."

Parker smiled. "I think we can do better."

"Ah. Now we're coming to it."

"MobilOn is a great company, Chris. It's going to be serving a market that needs it now, and it's going to be growing into a market that doesn't exist yet, but will. It's also a market where being first to the field matters. First not only with having product, but with having awareness."

"You're capitalizing off of people being too broke to afford their own threeps," I said.

Parker shook her head again. "I know you think that. It was obvious from our conversation this morning. But let me say it again: I didn't pass Abrams-Kettering, Chris," she said. "Congress did. So now we're in a situation where Hadens have a choice of having to spend more than they can afford for a threep, or staying completely within the Agora." She motioned to her lake. "And that's not a problem for some of us. But you made the point yourself that most Hadens still have to take part in the physical world. MobilOn will let them keep doing that."

"And you want to hire me to make people feel good about downsizing their lives."

"I would say I'd want you to help people realize that there are other options between mortgaging their lives or being shut in again."

"We're saying the same thing."

"I don't think so," Parker said. "And anyway, that would only be part of it. The other part, when non-Hadens start using threeps, as we both know they will, very soon now, is to be someone they trust, holding their hands while they try the technology for the first time."

"Ah," I said. "And that's your *real* market."

"Of course it is." Parker looked mildly testy now. "Chris, let me put it this way. This market is going to be served. The technology that's been Haden-only is going to be available to everyone. Threeps are going to be used by everyone. Now, who do you want to see profiting from it? A company run and operated by Hadens? Or by non-Hadens who will waste no time marginalizing us because there's money to be made? *We* deserve to be here, Chris. *We* deserve to be the ones at the front of this particular line."

"We deserve to get rich first."

"Yes! Well, richer." Parker paused for a moment, looking off. Then, "I get it, Chris, you know. You have ethical issues here. Things about MobilOn that bother you. But that's one of the reasons I want you on our team. To keep us in line. And to let others know you're keeping us in line. That's good for us, internally and with messaging."

"And it will help you with Dad," I said.

"How do you mean?"

"I mean Dad hasn't decided to invest in you yet."

"That's not it," Parker said, and then held up her hand. "I mean, yes, obviously, if you're on the team, that helps. I'm not going to insult your intelligence by suggesting otherwise. But this is independent of that. Whether or not your dad invests, I want you on the team."

"I'm really not in the endorsement market right now. It's against the FBI rules."

"Again, that's why I'm asking whether you're happy with your job."

"Happy enough not to want to leave it for endorsement money."

"How about for endorsement money and equity?" Parker asked. "Two and a half percent. We're projecting that when we take MobilOn public a few years down the road, a market capitalization of a hundred billion dollars is not outside the realm of possibility. You'd be your own billionaire, Chris. Not just a trust funder."

"Two and a half percent for being your celebrity endorser."

"Well, no. For *that* large of a pie slice, we'd get to own you. You have other uses too. We'd have you lobby congresspeople. Write op-eds. Basically go where we tell you. You'd work, not just smile and wave. But the payoff would be worth it."

"If you succeed."

Parker smiled. "Like I said, this market is going to happen. *Is* happening. Right now it's a matter of who gets there first. We're well-placed. If you're part of it we're better off."

"And how do I explain running off with someone who is hoping to be an owner in a league I'm currently investigating?"

"Well, how do you explain investigating a league your father is currently thinking about being an owner in? If you can square one, I think you can square the other. I want to be clear, Chris, that this offer has nothing to do with your investigation. My Hilketa ownership stake comes out of an entirely different pool of money. Family money. And it's not like your investigation wouldn't continue without you. Agent Vann is on top of things, isn't she?"

"This tells me you want an answer soon," I said.

"I have a series of meetings next Monday with potential investors. I would love to be able to tell them you are on board."

"I can't quit in a week."

"No, but you can give notice. That'd work for my purposes."

"So you want an answer by next Monday."

"I'd love an answer *now.*"

"That's a little rushed for me."

"Then I will take Sunday afternoon. Even better would be by Friday evening. I'll be at the Boston Bays' season opener then. But

I'd take your call."

"You said you ran that poll of yours a few months back," I said.

"Yes," Parker said.

"So, why get hold of me only now? When I'm in the middle of an investigation that you're at the very least adjacent to? Why not a couple of months ago, when none of this ever happened?"

"Do you want the truth?"

"Of course I do."

"You're the fourth most trusted Haden in the United States. We went after numbers one through three first."

I smiled at this. "Well, that's fair."

"Sorry," Parker said.

"I said I wanted the truth."

"Yes you did," Parker agreed. "And now you know. Hopefully that will convince you I'm not up to anything sinister with the timing."

"It helps."

"You sure you don't want to give me an answer now?"

"I'm sure," I said. I stood up on the deck of the sailboat. "Three meters down?"

"What? Oh. Yes. Or you can wait for me to turn the boat around."

"I think this will work." It was impolite in Haden personal spaces to magically appear

216

or disappear. Most of us used doors for people to walk in or out of. Parker used a car on the road. That seemed drawn out to me.

"Suit yourself," Parker said. "Let me know your answer as soon as you can, Chris. I don't want to say I have a lot of money and planning riding on your answer, but I do."

I nodded and dove over the side, pushing down into the water in now wet clothes. The water looked clear and I could see farther down than three meters, to a dark and indistinct bottom several meters below that. There didn't seem to be any reason why I couldn't make it all the way down.

Except for the fact that at three meters I clipped out of the lake into a featureless gray space. The bottom was an illusion, just like the rest of the space. I began to fall out of the bottom of the lake and turned my simulated body upward, to look at the water and the sailboat, rippling from the underside, farther and farther above me until suddenly I was standing in my cave, not falling, or doing anything else. I'd been unceremoniously booted out of Parker's space and back into mine.

That's some bad coding, I thought.

There was a ping in my awarenesss. Someone had been trying to call me. It was Vann.

"Where have you been?" she asked when I connected with her.

"I was fielding a job offer," I said.

"What?"

"It's a long story."

"Who was it with?"

"Amelie Parker. She's an entrepreneur. She's trying to get my dad to invest in her company."

"Amelie Parker," Vann repeated.

"Yes. You know her?"

"In a way," Vann said. "Forensics got back to me about Kaufmann's bed. Turns out there was another person in it. Want to guess who it was?"

"It wasn't Amelie Parker," I said. "She's a Haden."

"It wasn't Amelie Parker," Vann agreed. "It was someone named Lena Fowler."

"She's an Integrator," I said.

"Why, yes, she is," Vann said. "And guess who one of her primary clients is."

"If you say Amelie Parker I'm going to feel very uncomfortable."

"Start feeling uncomfortable. But that's not the interesting part."

"What's the interesting part?"

"I got a preliminary report from the D.C. medical examiner about Alex Kaufmann."

"And?"

"And someone might not be a suicide anymore."

"And someone might not be a suicide anymore."

CHAPTER TWELVE

I popped the image up in my view. "Okay, I see an X-ray of Alex Kaufmann's neck," I said. "What am I supposed to be seeing here?"

"You're looking at the C4 vertebra," Vann said. She was driving us to Lena Fowler's home in Arlington. It was now Tuesday morning, and we were betting we would have just enough time to talk to her before I had to go to Boston to interview Kim Silva. We were against traffic this time of day, so we had that going for us.

"Which one is that?"

"It's the fourth one down, strangely enough."

"You're helpful," I said. "I've located it. What am I looking for?"

"There's damage to it."

"Right," I said. "From Kaufmann's body weight and the belt."

Vann shook her head. "It might be from

220

that. But the medical examiner also said it was possible that it was damaged from something else, and then exacerbated by the hanging."

"And do we have an idea what that something else is?" I asked.

"It could be blunt force. Like someone whacking him on the back of the neck."

"But there wasn't any sign of a struggle."

"No," Vann agreed. "Whoever did it would have had to knock Kaufmann out or at least daze him enough to get the belt around his neck."

I flipped to a picture of Kaufmann on the morgue slab. "And they would have had to do it fast," I said. "If there was any time between the first neck injury and the injuries caused by the belt, there would be evidence of it."

"Yes," Vann said. "Which is why I said the blow to his neck knocked him out rather than killed him. If it had killed him, there would be forensics evidence of two separate events by the way the body bruised and the blood pooled. There's not."

"So why do we think someone snapped him across the neck first?" I asked.

"The ME said the damage to the vertebra looked like it could be more extensive than might happen with just a hanging, especially one like Kaufmann suffered. It wasn't a long fall with a sharp snap. He hung himself in the shower with no real drop. Kaufmann would basically have choked himself along with crushing his neck."

"So slower but with less bone damage."

"That's what the ME said."

"But he's not sure."

"No. He said the damage could have happened if Kaufmann put some force into it, as long as the hotel piping held. He also said that if Kaufmann had previous damage to his neck or bone disease affecting his neck or spine, it might be consistent with that. He's going to look into those for us."

"So in fact he probably was a suicide," I said.

"Except for the fact that Fowler was in his bed just minutes before he killed himself," Vann said.

"You think Fowler did it, then?"

"I think I want to hear how she denies it, at least."

Fowler's house was in the Arlington Views neighborhood, just off Columbia Pike, a comfortable but unimpressive brick suburban home surrounded by other comfortable but unimpressive suburban homes, across the street from an elementary school. Just the place for a growing family, which Fowler, whose Integrator profile listed her as single, didn't have.

"Ever want a place in the suburbs?" I asked Vann, as we walked up to Fowler's door.

"It's not compatible with my preferred lifestyle," she said.

"I'm sure there's a bar around somewhere," I said.

"Nice," Vann said. "I grew up in the suburbs. That was enough for one lifetime." She knocked on the door.

Lena Fowler came to the door, saw who it was, and looked back for a second into her home. Then she turned back to us with a sour expression on her face. "I'm with a client," she said. Which meant that as we spoke, there was another person watching us from inside her body.

"Right now?" I said.

"Yes."

"At your home?" Vann said.

"We were about to head out."

Vann glanced at me at this. While it wasn't out of the question for an Integrator's client to connect with an Integrator at a home base, theirs or an Integrator's, in most cases the integration happened at or near a destination. Integrators charged by the hour. No one wanted to waste a large sum of money for time in transit.

"We don't mind talking to you in front of your client if you don't," Vann said.

Fowler made a face at this. We had already put her in a wildly awkward position by making her surface during a session with a client. That was a breach of all sorts of protocols. Questioning her in front of a client would be unheard of.

Which, I suspect, is why Vann suggested it. She was happy to keep Fowler off balance for as long as she could.

"Excuse me for a moment," Fowler said, and closed her door. Vann and I looked at each other and then waited for about a minute. Then Fowler came through the door and closed it behind her.

"Whatever this is about, it better be good, Agent Vann, Agent Shane."

"You remember us," Vann said.

Fowler pointed at me. "I saw this one yesterday," she said. Then she pointed at Vann. "You I remember from the depositions and the trial of my client."

"It's nice to be memorable."

"Not really," Fowler said. "What do you want?"

"We'd like to ask you a few questions about Alex Kaufmann," I said. I gestured to her door. "May we come in?"

"No, you may not," Fowler said.

"Why not?" Vann asked.

"Because I said so, Agent Vann."

"You knew Alex Kaufmann," Vann continued, content to question Fowler on her landing.

"Obviously I did, otherwise you wouldn't be here."

"Then you know he's dead."

"I'd heard."

"You're taking his death very well, considering you were in his bed just prior to his suicide." Vann paused. "Unless you were in his bed on behalf of a client."

"If I were, you know perfectly well I couldn't talk to you about it," Fowler said. Integrators let Hadens borrow their bodies by syncing up the neural networks in their heads. The connections weren't perfect, however, so the Integrator was always present and conscious to assist the Haden using their body. Because of the intimate nature of the work, there was a legal veil of privilege over the relationship, similar to doctor-patient or attorney-client privilege.

"And if you weren't acting on behalf of a client?" I asked.

Fowler turned to me. "Then you may assume that whatever relationship Alex and I had was not something I'm going to tell you about without a lawyer," she said.

"We don't need a lawyer to see you're not exactly broken up," Vann observed.

"I don't peg you as an expert on how people process bad news, Agent Vann," Fowler said.

"You don't deny seeing him just prior to his death."

"Of course not. I'm sure by now you have physical evidence of my presence there, and of my being in the next room as well."

"The additional room paid for by Kaufmann."

"Yes, it was."

"Why did he pay for the extra room? You lived in the area."

"You'd have to ask him, Agent Vann."

"That's difficult, Ms. Fowler."

"I suppose it is."

"Did Kaufmann seem upset or agitated to you?" I asked.

"You mean, before he hung himself in the bathroom with his belt?" Fowler asked, mildly incredulously.

"So, yes."

"I'm not going to speculate on his state of mind," Fowler said. "The only thing I will say was that he was alive when I left him."

"That's not especially helpful," I said.

"Then you can assume that's my intention, Agent Shane. Aside from my general belief in the sanctity of the Integrator-client privilege, as a general rule I don't talk to law enforcement about anything other than generalities."

"Why is that?" Vann asked.

"Call it my libertarian tendencies," Fowler said.

"I thought it might have something to do with your general client list," Vann said. "I went through our records last night. You integrate with a lot of shady people, Fowler. And not just here in D.C. When you were in Denver your private client list featured people who are now spending time as guests of the government."

"It also featured tech CEOs, artists, and other perfectly normal people," Fowler said. "I know about you, too, Agent Vann, through that client of mine you put away. You were an Integrator once, too. I suppose you still are, even if you don't have a practice anymore. If we went through *your* former clients, would all of them be saints? I'm pretty sure they wouldn't."

Vann grimaced at this. She had stopped being a professional Integrator after one of her clients tried to throw Vann's body in front of a Metro train. The client wanted to experience death without the inconvenience of dying herself. Vann's death would have been close enough for her. Fortunately the attempt was not successful.

"Are we done here?" Fowler asked, looking at both of us. "I have a client to get back to."

"Before you were an Integrator in Denver, you were in the military," Vann said, to Fowler.

"Yes," Fowler said. "So?"

"In fact, the army paid for your schooling and integration training."

"Yes, they did. I did ROTC at University of Texas and then was stationed at Fort Benning, where I assisted army officers with Haden's. As I'm sure you know."

"In fact you were assigned to assist at the Western Hemisphere Institute for Security Cooperation."

Fowler smiled. "Is this where you are going to get paranoid on me, Agent Vann?" she said. "Just because it used to be the School of the Americas during the Cold War doesn't mean anything now. Those days were a long time ago."

"I'm sure," Vann said. "But I imagine that as part of your skill set, and to better serve those you were integrating with, you had a certain amount of specialized training. Hand-to-hand combat. Close-up killing.

That sort of thing."

"What a *vivid* imagination you have, Agent Vann," Fowler said. "My service record is public information. You're free to look it up. Otherwise, from this point forward, if you want to talk to me, you can set up an interview through my lawyers. Unless you are planning to arrest me right now?"

"No," Vann said. "Not right now."

"Good. Then get off my porch." Fowler stepped back in without looking back at us.

"The Western Hemisphere Institute of what?" I said to Vann, when Fowler had gone back in.

"The Western Hemisphere Institute for Security Cooperation," Vann said. She stepped off Fowler's porch. I followed. "It's where we teach other countries in the Americas how to kill people they find inconvenient."

"I didn't think we still did a lot of that."

"We never stopped," Vann said. "We're just quieter about it."

"And you think Lena Fowler is an actual assassin?" I asked.

"I wouldn't be surprised if she has a certain set of skills that she doesn't use much anymore."

"And she pulled them out to murder Alex Kaufmann? Why? He wasn't exactly an enemy of the state."

"I think it's pretty clear from Fowler's client list she stopped being a flag-waving patriot a while ago."

"You seriously think she killed him. That she went in and snapped his neck."

"I think she knows why he died, at the very least."

"If you think any of that, you couldn't have thought she was going to admit it to us on her front porch."

"Of course not," Vann said. "I knew she wouldn't say anything useful."

"Then why did we come out here at all?"

"Because I want to see what she does next."

"I don't actually understand you sometimes," I said to Vann.

"It's not complicated," Vann said. She reached into her jacket pocket for her cigarettes. "Whatever happened with Kaufmann, she was in the room for it, or close enough that it works for us. She's not going to talk to us, and never was. But who she talks to *next* will tell us something."

"You'll need to get warrants on her phones."

"I got them last night after I spoke to you. Judge Kuznia owed me a favor."

"You have to figure she assumes you have

those warrants now. She strikes me as the suspicious type."

Vann nodded. "I'm working on the assumption that she thought we might be bugging her from the moment Kaufmann died, and forensics placed her on the scene. Which is another reason to be here right now." She motioned back to Fowler's house with her head. "You saw how she looked back into the house when she came to the door."

"Yes."

"She's got people in there, I'm guessing. Having a meeting. The client is a participant."

"Which means anything said in the meeting is protected under privilege."

"Unless they're planning a criminal enterprise," Vann said. "Which maybe they are, but it's hard to prove." She fished out her lighter and lit her cigarette.

"So what are you going to do?"

"What I'm going to do is drive the car a couple of blocks away and then I'm going to walk back here, hide in some bushes, and see who comes out."

"And if she's not actually meeting with anyone?"

"Then I guess I get some fresh air in the morning."

"What about me?"

"What about you?" Vann asked. "You're going to Boston."

"Yeah, but my threep is staying here," I said. "I thought we were heading back to the office."

"Surprise."

"It's not going to look conspicuous or anything, a car with an inactive threep in it."

"That's a good point," Vann said.

"So what are we going to do about it?"

Vann took a long draw of her cigarette. "I suppose there's always the trunk," she said, finally.

CHAPTER THIRTEEN

My threep did not go into the trunk. Instead I called a car and headed to my parents' place. Along the way I pinged Tony. "Any luck with that data vault on Donut's collar?" I asked.

"Not at all," Tony said. "I'm running some of my standard cracking tools on it and they're bouncing right off. I can see there's something on it and I can tell you how large the file is, but I can't actually get it to open up."

"What's the problem?"

"Encryption's the problem. It needs an encryption key to unlock, which is common enough, but it's how it's asking for the encryption key that's the problem. It needs another particular device to give it the key, and we don't have that."

"A particular device."

"Sure. Some device that will connect to the vault through near field communication.

233

You put the two within two meters of each other and the vault will unlock."

"Is that a normal thing?" I asked.

"It's not that unusual. Phone manufacturers have been doing something like this for decades, where a phone will unlock if it's near a trusted device like a home computing device or known wireless network. It's not something I would advise, from a security point of view, because a lot of those times those 'trusted devices' are horribly insecure. But in this case it's working out because whatever the trusted device was, we don't have it. Unless you salvaged anything from that fire."

"We have the charred remains of threeps."

"How charred?"

"Anything that wasn't metal is burned down into ash."

"Yeah, that's probably no good, then."

"I can still have them shipped down if you want to try."

"You mean, if *you* want to try, Chris. This is on your dime."

"Keep at it some more and see if you can find another way into the data vault."

"Will do. Don't get your hopes up."

"I'll try to contain my upcoming disappointment."

"That's the spirit. That said, I do have

234

some good news for you. Well, good news in a particular context."

"That sounds exciting," I joked.

"You asked me to look at Clemente Salcido's data feed from his last game and see how it compared to Duane Chapman's. I looked."

"And?"

"Long version or short version?"

"Start short."

"There are some similarities."

"Okay. Now go longer."

"There was the same sort of ramping up of brain activity that we saw with Chapman. Not as much and not with the same severity, but it was there and led right into his seizure."

"And no one noticed this before?"

"You'd have to ask the medical people who dealt with him. But even if they did, there's not much there that looks so out of the ordinary that it'd get tagged. Or maybe it's better to say that it's possible someone looked at the data, went, 'Yup, that's what it looks like when you're about to have a seizure,' and didn't think about it after that. I mean, I noticed it specifically because you asked me to go looking for it."

"I didn't tell you what to look for," I reminded Tony.

"No, but you *did* tell me to look. Which was enough for me to be paying close attention. I doubt that anyone else is looking at Salcido's data with the same eyes we are."

"I think I'm going to need to talk to Salcido."

"I would if I were you," Tony agreed.

"Keep at the data vault," I said.

"I will," Tony said. "When are you going to be back home?"

"Probably tonight. Why?"

"We're going to have to have a house meeting about Donut. The twins are totally hogging him for themselves."

I chuckled at that.

"Amelie Parker did what?" Mom asked.

We were in my bedroom at my parents', and Mom, as was her inclination, was trimming my hair. Although I was presenting mostly threep forward, I could still feel her hands moving over my hair, picking it out before working the trimmer. Mom always felt it was practical to keep my hair short, and I was inclined to agree. Some Hadens didn't worry too much about appearances — their bodies typically weren't going anywhere — but I didn't see any reason not to look decent in all my iterations.

Besides that, I liked when Mom trimmed

me up. She could obviously have someone else do it for me. We had two full-time caretakers for me, and my mother and father both had a stylist who would come to the house on an on-call basis. Any one of them could keep me in my basic trim without too much of a problem. But it was something Mom chose to do.

Hadens sometimes suffered a deficit of human touch. When your body is immobile and you use a threep to get around in the world, people sometimes forget you're still actually in your body, and that immobile or not, you can still sense and feel. Haden bodies respond to touch. Hadens need touch like anyone else.

My mother cutting my hair was one way she kept in touch with me, literally and figuratively. There were others, of course. But this one was special in its way, precisely because it was such a simple, mundane task, one mothers do for their children all over the world.

And fathers too, of course, let's not be sexist about it.

That said, my father tried to trim my hair once. It ended . . . poorly.

"She offered me a job," I said. "Celebrity spokesperson for MobilOn. Salary plus equity. Told me I could be a billionaire in my own right."

Dad, sitting on the couch in my room, snorted. "She's ambitious, I'll give her that."

"You don't think it's going to be a hundred-billion-dollar business right out of the gate?" I asked Dad, mock shocked.

"I think she's underselling the competition to you," Dad said. "Several of the major threep manufacturers are already working on their own subscription threep services. Unlike MobilOn, they already have the infrastructure in place to get their threeps to the public quickly. It's going to take Amelie at least eighteen months to get her production output at the level she needs."

"She's subcontracting to some specialty threep makers," I said. "I was at Van Diemen yesterday and one of their people let slip they had a contract with her."

"The sex threep people?" Dad said.

"Marcus," Mom said.

"I didn't say there was anything *wrong* with sex threeps," Dad said, holding up a hand. "But I also know they don't have near the capacity Amelie would need, either short-term or when non-Hadens start finally using threeps."

"Which is why we suggested to her that she try to partner with one of the threep manufacturers directly when she came to us for funding," Mom said.

Dad nodded. "She said she didn't want to do that. She thinks they're going to crater and then she can get better deals from them to complement the threep stock she'll manufacture in-house."

"Which is *optimistic*," Mom said, working the trimmer. I felt the buzz through my head.

Dad motioned at Mom. "What she said."

"Why is it optimistic?"

"It's optimistic because all the major consolidation in the field's already happened," Dad said. "It was happening before Abrams-Kettering passed into law, and it finished up within a few months of its passing. Some of the mergers are still in process because of regulatory issues, but they'll get done soon enough."

"And in the meantime the market's already priced the downturn in the sector into share price," Mom said. "The remaining companies have also pared down in terms of workers and production."

"Which I take it means there's no crater coming," I said.

"No *new* crater, no," Mom said. "Which means Parker is making a bad gamble not pairing with an existing manufacturer."

"So I shouldn't count on being a billionaire, is what you're saying."

"You weren't planning on it anyway, were you?" Mom looked up at me, which meant that she looked away from me, since she turned her attention from my physical head to my threep. Well, the threep I was currently in, since my other threep was sitting on its induction chair in the corner. Having multiple bodies could be confusing until you got used to it. "I thought you liked your job."

"And you're not exactly hurting for money," Dad added.

"I do like my job," I said. "And I agree I'm fine with what I have. But I have to admit she knew which buttons to press. When I was visiting her personal space she was talking about how she built it with her money that she made from her first company, not family money."

"Did she," Mom murmured, returning her focus to my head.

"What does that mean?"

"It means that Amelie might have been minimizing the fact that her first company's primary investor was the family business," Dad said.

"And then it bought it from her a couple of years later, at a very comfortable premium for her," Mom continued.

"Entirely legal, possibly defensible from a business standpoint, and definitely nepotism at its finest," Dad finished.

"What's the family business?" I asked.

"Labram Industries," Dad said.

"I know them," I said. "They're doing business with the NAHL."

Dad nodded. "Creches and some other specialized hardware. Not just for the NAHL. They have an entire 'active lifestyle' hardware line devoted to Hadens. It's a sideline to their primary business, which is heavy equipment for shipping and construction. But after Amelie was born a Haden the company moved into that market."

"So where do their sports supplements fit in?" I asked, remembering the IV bag in Chapman's house. "That's not exactly hardware."

"That's Amelie's previous business," Mom said. "When Labram brought it in-house the argument was that it was complementary to their sports hardware." She shrugged. "It might even be true."

"What did the investors think?"

"They don't think anything," Mom said. "Labram's a private company. Family owned."

"If they bought her previous company, they might buy this one, too," I said. "Once she's drawn it out long enough."

Dad chuckled at this. "If they do, it won't be for a hundred billion dollars, Chris. I'd love to get a look at their books."

"Why?" I asked.

"Because I want to know more about them before we do any potential business with them."

"I didn't know you had anything planned with them," I said.

"It's to do with the Hilketa league."

"I knew Amelie Parker was looking to be a partner in the Washington franchise."

"That's a little different," Mom said. "That's out of her own money. But Labram itself is about to make a big investment in the NAHL expansion plans into Asia and Europe."

"It's a defensive move," Dad said. "They want to make sure they stay a preferred supplier for player creches, and they want their supplements as the default in the foreign leagues."

"It's pay for play," Mom said. She was done with my hair. She put the trimmers down and began brushing off my neck. An automated vacuum would show up soon to clean the hair off the floor.

"Why do you care about the foreign leagues?" I asked Dad. "The Washington franchise would be in the North American league."

Dad nodded. "Yes it would. But the corporate structure is built so the actual leagues are subsidiaries of the NAHL corporation. All the money from franchising and merchandising and everything else goes into the parent corporation. All the leagues' profits go into the same pot."

"Which the league needs right now," Mom noted.

"I thought you told me the league's finances were fine," I said to her.

"I said they were marginal. Over the last couple of days I've gotten a closer look at the books."

"And?"

"And the league is marginal *today*. In the next couple of years it's going to go over a financial cliff."

"A *big* ol' cliff," Dad chimed in.

"Okay," I said. "Why?"

"Because of real estate and taxes, for one," Mom said. "And because of Abrams-Kettering, for another."

I looked at Mom and then Dad. "I'll bite," I said. "What does one have to do with the other?"

Dad smiled and looked at Mom. "Educate our offspring, my dear," he said.

243

"The league doesn't own any of the stadiums or arenas it plays in, Chris," Mom said. "It's been leasing them either from local governments or other sports franchises. And it's been doing it that way because prior to the passage of Abrams-Kettering, the federal government had an incentive package for organizations that promoted, quote, the health and welfare of Haden citizens, unquote. Which Hilketa technically does. So it got tax breaks and credits and even some direct funding for the sport by Uncle Sam."

"And that wouldn't cover arenas or stadiums?"

Mom shook her head. "Real estate investments or construction was only covered if the resulting business was only used by and for Haden-related purposes."

"So you could build a stadium for Hilketa, but you could only ever use it for that," I said. "No revenue from other uses."

"Right," Dad said. "But if you rented or leased an arena, you'd get a tax break on what you paid for the rental."

"Not only that," Mom said, "but the entity the league was leasing from got incentives if they gave the league a break on the cost. If it was a state or local government it was reimbursed by the federal government. If it was a private entity it got a tax credit. So it was in the interest of the league to rent, not build, and in the interest of stadium owners to give the league low rental fees."

"That . . . kind of seems like an abuse of what the federal government meant for a program like that to do," I said. "I'm guessing it was meant for things like summer enrichment programs for Haden kids, not an actual moneymaking professional league."

Dad nodded at this. "And now you understand why Abrams-Kettering got traction in Congress. For every program that was quietly beneficial to Hadens, you had a boondoggle like this."

I turned back to Mom. "And now that Abrams-Kettering's passed, all those rents are going up."

"Yes." She looked down at my neck, frowned, and picked a stray curl of hair she found there. I felt her nails delicately tweeze it away. "Most of the league's stadium contracts are up at the end of this season. And when they're renegotiated they'll go up by anywhere from two hundred to one thousand percent."

I let out a low whistle. It's not a natural thing for one to do in a threep body, but it seemed appropriate.

"That's just the tip of the iceberg," Dad

said, and then looked at Mom. "Tell Chris about salaries."

"They had tax breaks for salaries, too?" I asked.

"They had tax breaks for *everything*," Mom said. "Salaries. Support staff. Medical and caretaking supplies. Training facilities. Transportation of the threeps to and from games."

"The tax credit for Haden view is my favorite," Dad said. "Because it was created to help Hadens experience the game, the cost of developing it and then implementing it on a game-by-game basis was credited to the league. Then it turned around and sold access to it. Every cent of that was pure profit."

"And all of it is going away in the next fiscal year," Mom said. "The league has never been profitable in itself. It was profitable because it was an engine for tax avoidance, and even then it was only marginally so, as I said. That party's over now. The Canadian and Mexican teams are still getting breaks. But most of the league is in the U.S. It's going to get swamped."

I was quiet for a moment. Then I turned to Dad. "And you still want to become an investor in this thing?"

"You think it's a bad idea," Dad said.

"I'm suddenly very concerned for my trust fund," I said. Dad laughed.

I turned to Mom. "Well?" I said.

"I'm not very happy with it, no," she said. "And I'm not very pleased that the league is trying to soft-shoe around it. I confronted that odious twerp MacKenzie Stodden about it yesterday afternoon, and he tried to give me a runaround."

I recalled Stodden, the investor relations suit who was stunned to discover I was not on the catering staff. "What did he say?"

"He tried to say that all of that was accounted for moving forward, which it isn't, and then punted me upstairs to talk to the league's general counsel."

"Oliver Medina," I said.

"That's the one. He's a piece of work. First he reminded me that our negotiations with the league are covered by a nondisclosure agreement — I think he was telling me about that because of *you*, Chris — and then he suggested that what the league's done here to this point they'll be able to do in the rest of the world."

"What? Scam tax breaks and government subsidies?"

"It checks out," Dad said. "If you look at the countries the league is looking at expanding into, it's the ones who still have strong Haden-related programs and tax incentives."

"The league plan will be to shuffle costs around so that the hit they take in the U.S. is absorbed elsewhere," Mom added. "But to do that they have to survive until they get the Asian and European leagues up and running."

"How are they going to do that?" I asked.

"You've noticed they're expanding the league," Dad said. "For investors in the Washington team, it's a minimum of ten million dollars, all up front. For the foreign investors, it's one hundred million minimum, with half of that up front."

"And you two think this will work."

"If the league meets its domestic and foreign funding goals in the next few weeks, it might keep the league afloat for a couple of years. *Might.* After that, it depends on whether other countries put the equivalent of Abrams-Kettering on their books. And if they do, how long it will take them to do it."

"Mind you, the league *could* look into how to make itself profitable *without* relying on government breaks," Mom said.

"If they did, they'd be the first pro league to do so," Dad reminded Mom. She rolled her eyes. He turned to me. "I'm not a fan of the league business model, either. I don't see it ever being a money spinner. I also don't want to lose money. But I'd be fine with it being a long-term, breakeven investment. I'd like to see a team in the area. I think it'll be good for D.C., and I think it'll be good for the Hadens here, too."

"For as long as *that* lasts," Mom said.

"What does that mean?" I asked.

"She means that part of the league's long-term growth is to start more aggressively developing non-Haden players here in the U.S.," Dad said. "They already have what they call developmental leagues that anyone can join. But now they say they intend to actually use them. Like they've been saying they've been using them all along."

"Once non-Hadens start playing in the NAHL, the league thinks the developmental leagues will really take off in participation and attendance. Another potential profit center there," Mom said.

"You said you wanted them to do something besides rely on government breaks," Dad said to Mom.

"I'm allowed to be conflicted," Mom said. She turned to me. "Sorry, Chris. I'm not sure you were expecting a business conference while I was giving you a haircut."

"It's not usual barbershop chatter," I

admitted. "But inasmuch as I'm about to head to Boston to talk to Kim Silva, surrounded by league officials, it might be useful context. Don't worry, I won't tell them you broke your NDA to talk to me."

"I didn't," Mom said. "You're a nonvoting member of the board of the family business. We can talk to you all we want."

"I'm still not going to tell them I talked to you."

"A pity. But wise." She motioned to my head. "Is the haircut all right?"

"It always is."

Mom smiled at this and kissed the top of my head.

CHAPTER FOURTEEN

I blinked into the guest threep the Boston Bays had set aside for me at their administrative and practice facility in Allston and was surprised to find it was an actual Hilketa-ready scout model.

"Whoa," I said, holding up my hands to look at them. Then I noticed another threep waiting for me. Her information popped up: Kim Silva.

"Welcome, Agent Shane," she said. Her threep wasn't a player model, but a fashionably discreet high-end Sebring-Warner. "You look like you're surprised by your threep."

"I am," I said. "Is this . . . is this a real game threep? I mean, has it seen *actual* play?"

"Sort of," Silva said. "It's one of the ones our practice squad uses. It's seen practice play."

"That's really cool," I said.

251

"We thought you would like it," Silva said. She held out her hand. "It's nice to meet you, Agent Shane."

I took her hand. "And you, Ms. Silva. I should tell you that all my flatmates are dead jealous I get to meet you."

"Well, you can tell them that some of my teammates are dead jealous I get to meet you. I used to have the picture of you on my wall. You know, the one with the pope."

"Oh, that," I said. When I was a kid my dad took a picture of me in my kid-sized threep offering a flower to the pope. It went out on the news and became one of the most iconic Haden-related pictures ever. Dad liked to joke it paid for my college tuition.

"I'm just sorry we have to meet under these circumstances," Silva said.

"Yes," I agreed. "My condolences to you."

"Thanks," Silva said, and paused a moment. "It's complicated, you know."

"I know."

"I'm not really supposed to be talking to you yet," Silva said. "About Duane or any of the rest of it. Medina would kill me."

"He's not wrong," I said. "I'm happy to wait for that until we formally start the interview. Are you here to get me for that?"

"Sort of," Silva said. "I was sent to tell

you there's going to be a delay. Medina and Bob Kreisberg had a meeting prior to ours. It's going long."

"I hope there are no problems," I said. Bob Kreisberg was the owner of the Boston Bays franchise.

"There's a lot of yelling going on, so I'm guessing there are problems."

"Anything in particular?"

"I wasn't listening that closely. I was just in Bob's waiting area long enough for his assistant to tell me there could be a delay and to say Medina asked me to keep you company in the meantime."

"I could have just sat in the lobby."

"I have a feeling Medina thinks you'll get in trouble if you're left alone. Sorry. I'm a spy."

"That's fine," I said. This reminded me to run a quick diagnostic on my borrowed threep to make sure that it had a secure channel to me. It did. "I'm sure we can find a way to make pleasant, inconsequential chatter until they're ready for us."

"Would you like a tour?" Silva asked. "I can show you the practice field. That's where I usually am when I'm here."

"That would be great," I said.

As we walked I took note of the surroundings. "Do you know what this building was

253

used for before the Bays took it over?" I asked.

"It used to be part of Boston University. Or Harvard, one of the two. They're both nearby. Actually I think it's still part of whichever of the two it is. I think the league's leased the building."

"That would make sense," I said, remembering my parents' discussion of the league's tax situation.

"In which case it's probably Boston University. Bob's an alum there. He's kind of obnoxious about it."

"That will happen."

"I don't get it. But then I didn't go to college. I went right into Hilketa after high school."

"You're not worried about having a marketable skill?" I joked.

Silva looked over. "You know, I think I'll be okay." The tone in her voice told me she got the joke.

"That's good," I said.

"I don't have as much as some," she ventured, seeing if I could take a joke as well.

"But you made what you have on your own."

Silva shrugged. "It's a game, right?" She motioned to the halls, which featured photos of the Bays in action. "We're not exactly solving world hunger, here."

"It's a game but that doesn't mean it's not important," I said. "Hilketa means a lot to a lot of Hadens. I'd say you mean a lot to a lot of us. You're a legitimate sports star."

Silva laughed. "I just like beating the crap out of people. This way it's legal and I get paid for it."

"A lot of rage?" I joked.

"You have no idea," Silva said. We went into the part of the building holding the practice field.

"Where is everybody?" I asked, after a minute of taking it in. The practice field was a repurposed baseball diamond, enclosed in a rectangular warehouse-like siding. It was aggressively industrial and unromantic.

"Practice isn't until two today. Pena is giving us a couple of light days because he knows we're all still dealing with Duane's death."

"It makes sense," I said.

Silva shook her head. "It's stupid. We have a short practice week as it is and giving everyone time to get into our heads about Duane means we're going to be distracted and unhappy. Me most of all. We're going to get the shit kicked out of us on Friday. We should be having double practices." She stopped. "That doesn't count as talking about Duane, does it?" she asked.

"Probably not," I said.

"Good." She pointed at me and motioned to the field. "You should go run on it."

"Excuse me?"

"You're wearing a scout threep. Those things are really fast. More than most threeps. Try it out."

"I don't think I should."

"You totally should," Silva said. "You're not going to ruin the field. That's what it's there for. And you're probably not going to get another chance to be in an actual scout threep, short of joining the league. You might as well." She pointed at the far wall, past the goalposts with the netting in them. "See how quickly you can get over there. Try it."

I looked at her for a moment, shrugged, and sprinted off as fast as I could to the far wall.

Four seconds later, my threep's face planted firmly in the ground, I heard Silva laughing.

"I don't see why this is so funny," I said, with mock gravity.

"I'm sorry," Silva said, walking up to me. "Actually, I'm not sorry."

"I know you're not, since I'm guessing you

knew this would happen." I picked myself up off the field.

"It's not just you," Silva said. "*Everyone* falls over in a scout threep the first time they try to run in one. You're used to running at one speed. The scout operates at an entirely different speed. You have no idea where your center of gravity is."

"And then you face-plant," I said.

"Yes. You and literally everyone else. People think the tank threeps are the hardest ones to control in the game, because the tank is so big and powerful." She pointed to my threep. "It's the scouts. They're a real pain in the ass."

"And in the face."

Silva nodded. "Scout control is a real skill. I mean, *I* can't do it. There's a reason I stick to the general model, or sub in with the tank. Your brain has to run fast to handle the scout."

I thought about it for a moment. "Did you have them put me in the scout model just so you could bring me down here to watch me fall on my face?" I asked.

"I will neither confirm nor deny that," Silva said. "I will say we often put visitors in scout threeps. And we often bring them here and invite them to go for a run."

"And here I thought I was special," I said.

"Well, if you want to feel special, hold on." Silva's threep suddenly snapped into a neutral resting position.

"Hello?" I waved a hand in front of her threep and got nothing.

"Over here," Silva said, and came out of a side room, which I quickly understood was a threep storage area, in a tank threep.

She lumbered over to me, faster than I would have thought a tank threep could move, and held up the two weapons she was holding, one in each massive fist. "War hammer or sword," she said. "Pick one."

"What?"

"War hammer or sword," Silva repeated.

"Sword?" I ventured.

"Good choice," Silva said, and handed the sword to me. I took it, hesitantly. "Okay. Ready?"

"Ready for what?" I asked, and suddenly on my threep's neck red lights began blinking. I looked up at Silva's tank, and a red ring of lights was flashing on her neck as well.

"On the count of three, try taking off my head," Silva said.

"Are you serious?" I asked.

"One."

"You are serious!"

"Two."

258

I grabbed my sword with both hands and held it out in front of me like, well, like a sword, I guess.

"Three," Silva said, and then my entire line of sight was filled with a tank threep rushing at me, war hammer in hand.

"Oh, *shit*," I said, and turned to run, just in time to get a hammer blow in the side. My threep magically transported sideways by about three meters and my sword flew out of my hands. I rolled on the field and jumped up just in time for another hammer blow in the chest. I lifted into the air and tumbled backward. I scrambled to the side just barely fast enough to miss a hammer blow that would have broken a human spine, and, I suspect, whatever support truss this threep had as well.

From my scramble I managed to get up on my feet and run over to where my sword had fallen. Silva watched me as I grabbed it and squared off.

"Having fun, right?" she said.

" 'Fun' isn't exactly the word I would use," I said.

"Oh, come on," she said. "The pain isn't even turned on in that threep. You're fine."

She was right. I was being knocked around but I wasn't feeling any pain. "That's not regulation," I said, to Silva.

"You can turn it on if you want," she said, and then rushed me. I disobeyed my amygdala's frantic request to run away and sprinted toward Silva, sword up. The plan was to run past her on the side not holding the hammer and take a swing at her neck as I flashed by.

It was a really excellent plan except for the part when she saw immediately what I was planning, spun as she ran toward me, and then suddenly there was the hammer in my chest, and there was me, flying sideways again.

At least this time I held on to the sword. I stumbled and almost fell from the hit, but kept upright and moving.

"Now you're learning!" Silva said, and seemed about to say something else, so I rushed her to catch her off guard and was then deeply disoriented as the room went spinning.

Oh, I see, I thought as I realized I was now getting a rotating bird's-eye view of the field. *She* absolutely *just hammered my head off my body.*

And then the field was rushing toward me, or at least my head, at an alarming speed.

A second later I saw the tank's feet out of the corner of the one eye that was not directly in the field's artificial turf. "Rushing right at me while I had a war hammer," Silva said. "That was a bold strategy, Agent Shane."

"I was hoping for the element of surprise," I muttered into the turf.

"If you're hoping for the element of surprise, it helps to be surprising."

"That's a good tip," I said. "I'm going to remember that for next time."

Silva laughed and then my head was lifted up and pointed in the direction of my threep's body. "That was such a clean hit that your body remained upright," she said. "That almost never happens."

"Yay?" I said.

Silva laughed again and reattached my threep's head to its body. I could hear the attachment mechanisms shift into place, locking it down and returning control of the threep body to me.

"Well, that was a new experience for me," I said to the tank threep.

"I'm back over here," Silva said, from her nongame threep. I walked over. "I'm betting that was the first time you've had your head knocked off," she said to me.

"Actually, no."

"Really."

"I was hit by a truck when I was eight. My head went flying. This is the first time someone did it *intentionally,* though."

"What did you think?"

"I think I'm glad I had my pain sensitivity turned all the way down."

"You're not wrong about that." Silva reached out and touched my arm. "Thank you, Agent Shane."

"What for?" I asked.

"For letting me beat the crap out of you. After everything in the last few days, I needed that. And I didn't know I needed it until I was doing it. That was really . . . cathartic."

"You're welcome. Although I think you should know that I'm never doing that again. At least not with a scout against a tank."

"Oh, no. Scouts are the best against tanks."

"My experience here makes me sincerely doubt that."

"I'll give you a tip. Tanks are top-heavy. Once they're down they're really hard to get back up. Run behind them, go low, and topple them. Then just hammer their legs until they fall off. Scouts are really good for pushing tanks over. All that speed turns into momentum."

"You could have told me that earlier."

"I could have," Silva agreed. "But where's

the fun in that?"

I was about to respond to that when Silva held up a hand. I waited.

"That was Sandra, Bob's assistant," she said, after a minute. "They're ready for us."

I looked around at the weapons and the tank threep. Silva followed my gaze. "We can leave them," she said. "Someone else will come and deal with them."

"Okay," I said.

"Agent Shane, I'm glad we got to do this," Silva said. "Before we have our formal interview, I mean. We got to be friendly with each other. Now we have to go and be not so friendly, I think."

CHAPTER FIFTEEN

"We'd like to begin by stating for the record that Ms. Silva voluntarily offered to meet with you today to answer questions," Oliver Medina said, as he, Silva, and Boston Bays manager David Pena sat down at the conference room table with me.

"All right," I said, sitting down myself.

"And that at any time Ms. Silva may choose not to answer questions if she or I feel it is not in her best interest to do so."

"Are you formally representing Kim Silva at this interview, Mr. Medina?" I asked. "I ask because I know your title is general counsel for the North American Hilketa League. I want to be sure that you're here for her, not for the league."

"I don't believe there's a material conflict between the two," Medina said.

"I don't doubt that you believe that," I said. "But maybe we should ask Ms. Silva."

Medina looked over to Silva, who looked

over to me. "I asked Oliver to be here today," she said. "Actually, when I told David and Oliver I wanted to talk to you, they both offered to be here with me, and I accepted the offer."

"You were at Duane Chapman's apartment on Sunday night," I said.

"Yes."

"Is this an apartment you shared with Mr. Chapman?"

"No. It was his apartment. Or, as I understand it now, his company's apartment, the company he co-owned with his wife. Which for obvious reasons is now very awkward. But I kept certain things there and used it as a mail drop from time to time."

"Including," I prompted.

"Including a threep, some personal objects, and a cat."

"Why the cat?"

"Because I'm allergic to cats and I can't keep one at my own home. The allergic reaction is unusually severe thanks to complications from my Haden's. So I kept Donut at Duane's apartment."

"Since you kept a cat there it's fair to say you were in the apartment frequently."

"I wasn't in the apartment frequently because of Donut. I was in it frequently because Duane and I were lovers. And because of that, I was there frequently enough to keep a cat."

"A consensual relationship between two people isn't grounds for a federal inquiry, Agent Shane," Medina said.

"It's useful for me to establish she and Mr. Chapman knew each other well," I said.

"Of course they knew each other well. They were teammates."

"In your knowledge of Mr. Chapman, as a friend and . . . *teammate*, Ms. Silva" — I nodded to Medina — "were you aware of any physical impairment that might have caused him to collapse on Sunday?"

"No," Silva said. "Duane had some Haden-related health issues, but we all do. None of them ever affected him like this. He was always healthy for games, and for everything else."

"Why did you come to the apartment after Mr. Chapman's death?"

"Because I needed to get Donut and my personal effects. I mean, it wasn't *my* apartment. And to be honest I didn't want Marla to know about my relationship with Duane. She never liked me, even before Duane and I started our relationship, and she and Duane have been on the rocks for a while."

"Did he ever explain why to you?"

"I know she accused him of infidelity,"

Silva said. "Which was true. But there were other issues, too. I think Marla felt cheated that he wasn't a bigger star, and took it out on him. She wanted a bigger lifestyle than she had. I think she felt he was her way into riches. Duane told me at one point he had started to feel like it was one of the reasons she was with him at all. She didn't have any positive feelings about Hadens in general, I can tell you that much."

"So your plan was to get your cat and your effects."

"Yes."

"And then what?"

"I had ordered a car. I was going to put Donut and my things in it and have it drive up to here in Boston. I was going to meet it outside of town and take delivery. Donut would go to my mother's house. Everything else I would take home."

"That's a long drive from Boston."

"I can afford it."

"I meant, why didn't you have a friend do it for you?"

"Because no one knew Duane and I were more than teammates."

I turned to David Pena. "Is that accurate? That no one knew?"

"*I* didn't know," Pena said. "I don't encourage players to screw around with their

267

teammates. When they break up it makes things awkward. It still happens. But I didn't know about these two and as far as I know none of their teammates knew, either."

"And this car you hired?" I asked Silva.

"I got it from an app. It took a while to match me with someone willing to make the drive. But I paid well."

"And to be clear," I said, "did you, accidentally or on purpose, set the apartment on fire?"

"No, of course not," Silva said. "It was on fire when I got there. As you know, you were already there."

"And when you came to the apartment to get your things, you had no idea it was on fire."

"No idea," Silva said.

"Can you think of a reason why someone would want to burn down the building Duane's apartment was in?"

"Are you suggesting there was arson involved, Agent Shane?" Medina asked.

"I'm following up on all possibilities," I said.

"Nothing comes to mind," Silva said. "Other than Marla being angry enough to do it."

"Do you think that's possible?"

"Duane told me stories of her temper. But

268

I don't think she would do that. It's one thing to be angry at your husband. It's another thing to burn down an entire building and endanger the lives of other people."

"What can you tell me about the box of your IV supplements that were in the apartment at the time it went up?"

"I had it shipped to the apartment once it arrived here at the Bays headquarters."

"Why did you do that?"

"Because Duane asked me to. He wanted to try my supplements."

"Why would he do that?" I asked. "My understanding is that he could get in trouble with the league for using different IV supplements."

"That's not accurate," Medina said. "He wouldn't be in trouble with the league directly. Tigertone, our general IV supplement supplier, could argue breach of contract if it became known he was using a different supplement supplier, and we would then pay a contractual penalty to them. It would be up to the Bays organization to then fine or reprimand Chapman."

I turned to Pena. "Would you have fined him?"

"Probably," Pena said. "The league wants us to take endorsements seriously. I've fined other players for it."

"How much?"

"The last time I did it, it was five thousand dollars. First offense."

"Five thousand dollars wasn't trivial for a player like Mr. Chapman," I said. "He wasn't a franchise player, and wasn't getting paid like one." I turned back to Silva. "So my original question still stands. Why would he risk it?"

"Because he wanted to have a good game," Silva said.

"It was just a pre-season game."

"No, it wasn't *just* a pre-season game," Silva said, and I could hear some annoyance in her voice. "This was the game the league was using to woo potential new owners and investors. This was the game where your father and other important people, Agent Shane, might see him have a great night and decide to make him a key part of their new team in the expansion draft. Duane wasn't a fool. He knew he was never going to be anything but a role player here in Boston. So he wanted an edge."

"How would your supplements give him an edge?"

"They wouldn't, and I told him so when he asked. When you're endorsing a product you're supposed to pretend that it's better than everything else. But come on. There's

270

no real difference between the supplement mix Labram uses and the one Tigertone uses. Everyone knows that. *Duane* knew that."

"So why did he ask?"

Silva laughed. "You understand that athletes are superstitious, right? We'll try anything if we think it's going to give us an edge. Even if we know logically it won't. Duane knew there was no difference in our supplements. He also knew I was the one of us with a multimillion-dollar deal and he wasn't. And if he felt like borrowing a bag or two of my supplements would give him an edge, you know what? Maybe it would."

"A placebo effect," I said.

Silva nodded. "Placebo, psychological projection, superstition. Call it what you want. So I took a box of my supplements, shipped it to the apartment, and he used a bag of it on Sunday."

"Are you saying that you think there was something in the supplements that triggered a reaction?" Medina asked.

"I can't say anything about it," I said. "The Philadelphia office of the Bureau has it in their labs and will let us know if they find anything."

"What about the rest of the box?"

"The damage at the apartment was pretty

271

substantial," I said.

"Agent Shane, when I called you yesterday I asked about Donut," Silva said. "You said he was all right."

"He *is* all right," I said. "He's at my home at the moment. He's very popular."

"That's nice. I want to know when I can get him back, please."

"I'd say probably in a few days, although it might take longer."

"What's the holdup?" Medina asked.

"He's relevant to our investigation," I said.

"How? It's a *cat,* for Christ's sake."

"I'm aware how it sounds," I admitted. I turned to Silva. "Be that as it may, we need him a little longer. As soon as we can, we'll release him to you."

"I'm worried about his well-being," Silva said.

"He's being fed tuna."

"See, now, that's no good," Silva said. "It doesn't have all the nutrients a cat needs. And if you feed him too much, he can get mercury poisoning."

"And if it's raw tuna it will disrupt his ability to absorb B vitamins," Pena said. We all turned to him. He suddenly looked defensive. "My mother was a vet."

Silva turned back to me. "Now I'm very concerned about my cat. I'd like him back."

"I promise I will pick up proper cat food today," I reassured her. She appeared unconvinced. "Now. Did you know Alex Kaufmann?"

"Commissioner Kaufmann? I knew him, sure. Him and most of the people in the commissioner's office. I wouldn't say that I knew him particularly well. I know I've talked to him from time to time but I can't say we ever talked about anything I can remember."

"Do you know if there was any relationship between him and Duane Chapman?"

"They weren't friends, no," Silva said. "Commissioner Kaufmann was a kind of a climber, Agent Shane. I mean, in terms of status. He'd be happy to be seen with me, but he wouldn't have wasted his time with someone like Duane."

"This bothered you?"

"There's a reason I don't have any conversations with Kaufmann that I particularly remember. Why? Do you think Kaufmann's death has something to do with Duane's?"

"It happened right after Mr. Chapman's, and right after Mr. Kaufmann ordered his data feed pulled from the public."

"I don't know why he did that," Silva said. "It wouldn't have been because they were close, if that's what you're asking."

"What do you think it might be?"

"You're the FBI agent," Silva said. "You tell me."

"Agent Shane, if I may," Medina said, raising a hand. "It's very important to us that these discussions remain confidential. I'm sure you're aware Duane's death and your investigation are national news, and it's not escaped the notice of the press that you and your partner are the Bureau's leads on this. We have a concern that if news of Duane and Kim's relationship gets to the press, it's going to be an untenable situation for everyone. It will make your job harder. It will make our job harder too."

"It's our policy not to discuss active investigations," I said.

"And yet they leak."

"Not from me. I've done my time in the press. I know how to handle them."

"What about your partner?"

"You've met her, Mr. Medina. I don't think you can tell me she's the sort to buddy up with a reporter. You recall you threatened her about going to the press when you released Mr. Chapman's data feed to us. It didn't leak."

"We just don't need the distraction," Pena said. "This has been a difficult enough week for everyone here with the Bays. Duane wasn't our star player, but he was admired by everyone here. A lot of us lost a friend on Sunday, Agent Shane. We're barely keeping it together. And we have a game on Friday."

"I can't tell you there aren't going to be leaks," I said. "There are a lot of moving parts to this investigation. All I can tell you is that the leaks won't be coming from me, or from Agent Vann. That much I can guarantee."

Medina nodded at this. "Then are we done here, Agent Shane?"

"For now," I said. "If I have any follow-up questions for Ms. Silva, I will let her know."

"You'll let *me* know," Medina said. I looked over at Silva, who nodded her agreement.

"As long as you're here, would you like a tour of the facility?" Pena asked. "We can show you the practice field, at least."

"Thank you," I said to Pena, and then looked over to Silva. "I've already seen it." I stood. Silva and Pena stood when I did. Medina did not.

"Agent Shane, if I may have a word with you alone," he said.

"What is it?" I asked when Silva and Pena were gone.

"I understand you and your partner have

275

plans to question Alton Ortiz today in Philadelphia."

"In fact, as soon as I get back from here, she and I are driving up to talk to him."

"Well, you do keep yourself busy, Agent Shane."

"You have no idea," I said.

"Well, allow me to save you a trip," Medina said. "Speaking for his lawyer, we're not going to offer him up to speak to you today."

"Speaking *for* his lawyer?" I repeated.

"Mr. Ortiz couldn't afford adequate representation and didn't want to risk the public defender, so an associate of mine out of the league's counsel office offered to represent him pro bono. She knew I would see you today at this meeting and asked me to speak to you on her behalf. I'll send you all her information."

"And when do you plan to make Mr. Ortiz available for questions?"

"I don't know that we will. At the very least, my associate will have to meet with him first. She has her first meeting scheduled for tomorrow afternoon."

"That's not great for our schedule."

"I sympathize, Agent Shane. But as a matter of legal responsibility, we're not interested in your schedule."

"I don't understand why you made Silva available and not Ortiz," I said.

"Obviously, I made Silva available because I didn't think there was any risk in making her available to you," Medina said. "She's not guilty of anything other than choosing an ill-advised man to have an affair with. But we don't know what's going on with Ortiz. And until we know, you can't talk to him. And when we do know, you still might not be able to talk to him. That's how these things work, Agent Shane. Surely you knew that."

CHAPTER SIXTEEN

"Who am I looking at?" I asked Vann as she had lunch at a storefront pho shop in Sterling, and I watched her eat. Vann had picked me up at my parents' once I came back from Boston. She offered to let me into the trunk but I declined. When we were seated she sent over photos.

"Those two gentlemen are Martin Lau and Yegevney Kuznetsov."

"You photographed them coming out of Fowler's house."

"Yes."

"Did they see you?"

"No. I lurked."

I pictured Vann lurking in my mind and enjoyed the image. "What about Fowler?"

"She didn't come back out before I left."

I nodded. "So who are these gentlemen?"

"Lau works for Richu Enterprises out of Singapore, and Kuznetsov is an associate of Egor Semenov, an oligarch type from St.

Petersburg. The one in Russia, not Florida."

"Are they bad people?"

Vann shrugged and poked at her pho with her chopsticks. "It depends on what you consider 'bad.' I ran both of them through our system and Interpol's and they both come up clean in themselves. But who they work for aren't great. Richu is a conglomerate with some ethically shaky business in their recent past, and Semenov is a real piece of work. He's the sort of person who politely asks the Russian government to arrest journalists snooping around his business."

"And the journalists are arrested."

"No, they are not," Vann said. "But they do show up dead a week later, having been conveniently mugged. Having that happen once is a tragic coincidence. Having it happen three times to date is a pattern."

"Got it."

Vann pointed at my head, where she assumed the photos she sent me were floating around, and she wasn't wrong. "Both Lau and Kuznetsov are lawyers. They're not musclemen. They're not the sort to have criminal records. They're the sort to keep others from having criminal records. Or civil judgments against their companies and bosses, take your pick."

"So what do Richu and Semenov have in common that they need to send lawyers to a suburban tract home in Virginia for?"

"They don't," Vann said. She took a drink of her Vietnamese coffee. "On the legitimate side of things Richu and Semenov have no business with each other, going back a decade at least."

"How do we know that?"

Vann looked at me levelly. "I repeat: They're not great."

"Meaning they've been on our investigative radar for shady business for years now," I said.

"Yes. I called in a favor with an analyst friend of mine at the CIA. It took her all of fifteen seconds to send me a pile of documents."

"Got it."

"So legitimately they have no business with each other," Vann continued. "But *illegitimately,* they don't really have much to do with each other either. Their spheres of influence and interest are almost entirely separate. Semenov keeps his interests largely in Russia and the Baltics, and Richu is almost exclusively in Singapore, Malaysia, and Indonesia. Other than tangentially, they have almost nothing to do with each other."

"So it's not what they have in common

with each other, but someone else they have in common."

Vann, who had a mouth full of noodles, nodded.

"Which is someone Fowler has in common with them, too. Unless *she's* the one they have in common."

Van swallowed. "Well, she does have a history."

"You mean with that Western Hemisphere Institute thing."

"I'm thinking afterward. Her client history has a larger-than-average percentage of shitty people in it, no matter what she says about it."

"Well, not to take her part —"

"Oh, Jesus," Vann said, and reached for her coffee again.

"— but she had a point when she asked you whether all the clients you had when you were an Integrator were on the up-and-up all the time. Hadens aren't any more ethical or law-abiding than any other group of people. That's why the two of us have jobs."

Vann set down her glass. "I can't say what any of my clients were doing in their personal lives because that wasn't any of my business. I can say when they were with me they didn't do anything illegal. Integrators are like lawyers. Our so-called client-Integrator privilege stops if we help our clients participate in a crime. Integrators remain active when we're with a client because we have to help them move around in our bodies. Anything *they* do with our bodies, *we* do, too. And I wasn't going to risk going to jail for a client."

"So you never did anything illegal for a client," I pressed.

"I made it clear to clients before we integrated that if they tried to use my body for anything outside the law, I'd disconnect them and immediately put a note in their record. Integrators don't want to deal with clients who are a pain in the ass. Someone who wants you to break the law is a pain in the ass."

"I can't help but notice that you didn't actually answer the question."

"Then you can assume I'm not going to," Vann said.

"Oh, come on," I said. "The statute of limitations is probably expired by now."

"It's *definitely* expired by now."

"Vann."

Vann actually looked around and then leaned in. "Fine. I did some coke with a client."

"Actual cocaine," I said.

"Yes, you jackass. I'm not talking about soda." Vann leaned back.

"Why?"

"Because the client was curious and because back in the day I liked cocaine. So when the client offered me an extra grand because she was curious, I took it."

"And then you went and bought some coke."

"Well, no. I just went to my stash. You think I was going to score some off the street? That shit's mostly baby powder and fentanyl. It'll kill you."

"I like that I'm still learning things about you, Vann," I said, after a minute.

"Oh, don't act shocked," Vann said. "You know my past. The irony is, the client hated it. Made her paranoid as hell."

"That's no good."

"I wasn't surprised. Cocaine makes you who you are, only more so." She dug into her noodles. "And I had a point a long time ago, which was that if you're an Integrator, it doesn't matter if your clients are criminal or shitty people. It only matters if you let them be criminals or shitty people when they're with you. I never did. I kind of doubt Fowler can say the same."

"You think she's aiding in criminality."

"I think there's a reason she doesn't like

283

to talk to law enforcement, and it's not because of her libertarian political leanings."

"Did you find any connection between her and her two guests?"

"No. But I did find a connection between one of her clients and her guests. I'll give you a hint. It's someone you know."

"Amelie Parker?"

Vann pointed at me with her chopsticks. "Bingo," she said. "More accurately, between Labram Industries and Richu and Semenov."

"What's the connection?"

"Labram does extensive business with both, mostly in shipping and construction. But, Richu and Semenov also have investment arms, and both invested substantially in Amelie Parker's start-up a few years back."

"The one that Labram bought from her," I said.

"You know about that?" Vann asked.

"I talked to my parents about it today."

Vann nodded. "They would know. The Richu and Semenov investment arms are also putting money into Parker's new start-up, and into the NAHL overseas expansion."

"Labram is too," I said. "The overseas expansion, I mean."

"Your dad's about to do some business

284

with some interesting folks," Vann said. "Not *only* them, there are a lot of people investing in the NAHL and this MobilOn thing. But you should make them aware of it, too."

"They know."

Vann nodded again. "They're smart people, your parents."

"Thanks, I like them," I said, and then was quiet.

"What is it?" Vann asked, eventually.

"This still doesn't help us," I said. "Maybe Fowler was integrated with Parker and having a meeting with these guys, but so what if she was? She has legitimate reasons for doing so. It doesn't tell us anything about what Fowler was doing in Alex Kaufmann's bed, and whether she murdered him, or if he hung himself."

"If Fowler murdered Kaufmann, it's possible she did it because Parker wanted her to," Vann said.

"Or that Parker was a witness, at least," I said. "We would need to find out if she was integrated with her at the time. We could get a warrant for Parker's client log."

Vann shook her head. "I already asked Judge Kuznia for her phone log. I'd need more evidence for a client log."

"So let's bring Parker in," I said.

"I have news for you, Chris," Vann said. "If Parker's not already lawyered up to her armpits, she's about to be. If she was integrated with Fowler when we came to visit, then she knows we had questions for her Integrator. She's not stupid. She'll put two and two together. But maybe there's another way to talk to her without her lawyers around."

"How?"

"Well," Vann said. "Rumor is, she's looking to hire you for a job."

"Sneaky," I said.

"We're the FBI. That's what we do. You should set up a meeting with her today. We have a hole in our schedule where talking with Alton Ortiz used to be."

I shook my head. "I already filled it."

"With what?"

"With someone who by the sound of his response to my request for an interview, is going to be very, very happy to see me."

"I am *delighted* to see you, Agent Shane," Clemente Salcido said to me, as I stepped through into his personal space. It was clean, neat, sunny, uncluttered, and entirely off-the-rack. I recognized it as a basic hacienda model from PositiveSpace, a company that designed mass-produced

286

personal spaces for Hadens with not a whole lot of money to throw around. It was the equivalent of tract housing.

Or maybe something a little less than that. I looked over to one of the walls and the picture framed there. It was a cliffside with a threep posed just so right at the edge, looking out to a shore with gentle waves flowing in and out. And in the corner, words: *The Metro Vista 3. Imagine where it will take you.*

Salcido's wall art was an advertisement. Chances were almost all the art on his walls were advertisements. The advertisements were how Salcido, along with hundreds of thousands of other Hadens, lowered the cost of having a private space of their own within the Agora.

As I watched, the cliffside advertisement faded into something new, this with sunflowers.

Salcido followed my gaze to the wall art. "Not what you were expecting from a former Hilketa player, right?"

"You're the first former Hilketa player I've ever met," I said, truthfully. "I have no idea what to expect."

"I like that answer," Salcido said, and laughed. Then he motioned to the advertising. "It's not so bad, really. If something offends you, they'll remove it and put something else up. After the first few days it learned to give me landscapes. I can live with landscapes."

"Landscapes are nice," I agreed.

"Let's go sit in the courtyard, Agent Shane. There is much less advertising there."

As promised, the courtyard was advertising-free. We sat on patio furniture while a creditable sun burned above us, and realistic-enough birds flitted among perfectly acceptable trees and shrubs.

"I had a nicer personal space when I was with the Aztecs," Salcido said, easing into his chair. "It was an actual hacienda. I mean an estate, not just a house. Much more realistic, overlooking a simulation of the Bahía de Banderas. My family is from Jalisco. I'd ride horses."

"It sounds nice."

"It *was* nice. But then I was cut and I had no more income and I had to decide whether I was going to spend my remaining money riding fake horses on a fake bluff over a fake ocean, or give my parents and family a nice house in the real world." He opened his arms to motion about. "And as you can see, I made my decision."

"Do you regret it?"

Salcido smiled. "I miss the horses. I don't regret my mother and father and sister having a house. Now, Agent Shane. You are here to ask me about my seizure, yes?"

"I am."

"What do you want to know about it?"

"I'm curious about what brought it on."

"So am I!" Salcido said, laughing. "In all my life, before I had Haden's or after it, I had never had a seizure. Suddenly during a game I have one. And since then I have never had one again."

"You were examined by doctors?"

"Lots of doctors. By the Aztecs' team doctor right after. By a raft of doctors at the City of Hope right afterward. Test after test. By the doctors the Aztecs and league's insurance carriers made me go to, just after they dropped me. And by the doctors my lawyers hired after I sued the NAHL and the Aztecs for dropping me as a player."

"No one could explain it?"

"There was nothing to explain. No aberrant brain activity, no physical changes to the structure of my brain, no new physical ailments. For a Haden I was as heathy as any of us ever are. The seizure came out of nowhere and went back there just as quickly. I was healthy. *Am* healthy." He raised his arms again to encompass the prefab hacienda. "And this is where it got me."

"So the league doesn't want to have anything to do with you anymore."

"No," Salcido said. "They wouldn't have anything to do with me after their insurers decided I was a risk. Technically I was cut because of persistent health issues, but there weren't any of those. Persistent, I mean. Which is why I sued. Now they won't have anything to do with me because I'm suing. I've been blackballed."

"You've been told that."

"Of course not," Salcido snorted. "They never tell you that. But no one will hire me, either. I'm twenty-eight, I'm healthy, I was a solid player, and my health isn't an issue. I played five seasons for the Aztecs. I could have played another five, easily. I was popular because on the Aztecs because I was a Mexican when most of the players were from the U.S. There's no reason I shouldn't be playing. Except the one seizure and the fact I'm suing."

"And how is the suit going?"

Another motion to the hacienda. "It's not just my parents' house that keeps me in this sort of personal space, Agent Shane. Lawyers are expensive. I've filed suits in Mexico and the U.S. Both the team and the league are stringing everything out as long as they can. They're trying to bankrupt me to get me to drop the suit."

"If you don't mind me asking, how are you making money now?"

"I do some convention appearances," Salcido said. "I can't appear in a Hilketa threep — they're licensed by the league — and I can't post any pictures of myself with league or Aztec symbols. But I can still sign photographs and pose for pictures."

"And that pays well?"

Salcido shrugged. "It would be better if I could be in my Hilketa threep, like I used to be able to do. If you're just showing up in a rental threep they don't always believe you're you. They don't always want to pay for a photo. I also sell autographs and memorabilia online. I make enough for my family and my lawyers. Just not much more after that. I'd like to play Hilketa again."

"So, Mr. Salcido, you never had a seizure before or after that one game. You say doctors haven't been able to find any reason for your seizure. But in your own mind, why do you think it was?"

Salcido looked at me intently for a moment. Then, "This is about Duane Chapman, yes?"

"I'm investigating his death, yes."

Salcido waggled a finger at me. "No, no.

291

There's something specific about his death that brought you here to me. Something similar to what happened to me. Otherwise you wouldn't be here now. I know. I tried to get the FBI involved before. My lawyers couldn't get past the door."

"I don't know anything about that."

"Of course you don't. That's my point." Salcido waved his hand in dismissal. "So you don't have to tell me. But I will tell you, because whatever you find I think will help me. And what I think was that I was drugged."

"How?"

"Something in my supplements, is my guess."

"How would that work?"

"How do you think it would work? Somewhere between the bag coming out of the box and it hitting my bloodstream, someone added something to it."

"Is this something you've told your lawyers or the league?"

"Of course."

"What was their response?"

"The league said there was nothing to it. They tested the bag and they tested my blood and urine and didn't find anything they said was unusual. The lawyers went back to the manufacturer a few months later to find out if there were any remaining samples of the batch the bag was from. They found a box and tested it."

"So why do you think it was something in your supplements?"

"What else could it be?" Salcido asked. "Nothing else had changed."

"What do you mean by that?"

"I mean I'd switched supplements about a month before. I had gotten an endorsement deal from Labram. We hadn't announced it yet because they wanted to make a big deal out of it. I was their first player from the Aztecs and their first Mexican national. They were planning a campaign around me. Then the seizure happened and I was put on the injured list and then I was dropped. When I was dropped, Labram dropped me too."

"You just said you were using the supplements for a month without any ill effect."

"Maybe it took that long to take effect," Salcido said. "What I'm telling you is that before I used Labram, I wasn't having any problems. After, I had a seizure. It's the only thing that changed." He read my face, and smiled. "Ah, there it is."

"There what is?" I asked.

"The look I get when I go on my supplement conspiracy theory. That is literally what the league's fucking lawyer said to the judge when he tried to get my suit dismissed."

"Oliver Medina?"

"You've met him!" Salcido said. "I'd like to feed him to sharks but they wouldn't eat him."

"Professional courtesy," I said.

Salcido nodded. "You've heard the joke. The more I know of Medina the less amusing I find it. Fortunately the judge didn't dismiss the case. Agent Shane, I know how my supplement theory sounds, believe me. You're not the first person to give me that look. I just don't have any other explanation."

"Okay," I said. "Let's say for the sake of argument Labram did dope your supplement bag —"

"Then why did they do it?" Salcido finished for me. I nodded. "And for that I don't have any answer for you. It doesn't make any sort of sense. It goes against the integrity of their product and against the integrity of the sport, and both of those are very bad for Labram. And it didn't make sense to do it to me or the Aztecs. I wasn't one of the team's star players and the Aztecs weren't in contention for the playoffs."

"As you say, it doesn't make sense for

Labram to do that."

"So maybe *they* didn't. Maybe someone else did. Maybe gamblers who had bet on the match. Maybe someone who doesn't like me."

"Does anyone not like you, Mr. Salcido?"

Salcido grinned. "There might be a few angry spouses. And a few league lawyers at this point. Otherwise, no."

"So, no offense, it doesn't really make sense for anyone to mess with your supplements."

"No. And yet I never had a seizure before that game, and I haven't had a seizure since."

"Maybe it's just bad luck."

"Perhaps," Salcido said, and leaned in. "And perhaps Duane Chapman's death was just bad luck as well. Perhaps we were both just very unlucky." He leaned back. "But then, here you are, Agent Shane. I don't think you'd be here if you thought all that happened to me, and all that happened to Duane Chapman, was bad luck. Everything looks like bad luck, until it doesn't."

"It might still end up being just bad luck," I said.

"If it does, then my parents still have their house," Salcido said. "But if it isn't just bad luck, and it is something else, let me know.

Especially if it makes the league settle my case. I would like my fake horses back."

I popped back into my threep at the office and turned to Vann, who was sitting at her desk across from mine. "So, we should really get those results from the Labram supplements back from the Philly FBI lab," I said to her.

"Oh, good, you're back," she said. "You ready?"

"Ready for what?"

"One: Report from the Philadelphia Fire Department investigators about Chapman's apartment building fire. Definitely electrical, possibly arson."

"Possibly?"

"Yes, because, two: The last company to work on the wiring, this last week, was a firm called AAACE Electrical and Wiring, owned by a Pedro Ortiz, who is —"

"The brother of Alton, right?"

"Let me finish."

"Sorry."

"The *cousin* of Alton, who does all the electrical work on all the properties owned by the landlord."

"That's a hell of a coincidence."

"Pretty sure it's not a coincidence. I've asked the Philly PD to do us a favor and pick him up for questioning."

"Why not the Philly Bureau branch?"

"I'm not there yet. You're interrupting again."

"By all means continue."

"So that's the good news."

I waited.

"That was a prompt," Vann said.

"You have me very confused about what I'm supposed to do here," I said.

"Now you ask me what the bad news is."

"Uh-oh," I said. "What *is* the bad news?"

"The bad news, and the reason I'm not asking the Philly Bureau branch to do another goddamned thing for us, is that they fucked up the testing of the Labram IV bag. Their lab technician apparently contaminated the sample. It's useless to us now for anything but standing as testament to how the entire Philadelphia branch of the FBI should be burned to the ground."

"All right, that actually is bad news," I said.

"Yes it is," Vann agreed. "Now ask me what the possibly even worse news is."

"There's worse news?" I asked.

"Possibly," Vann repeated. "Somehow that reporter from the *Hilketa News* found out that Chapman and Kim Silva were boinking each other and put it up on their site."

"That's not great, but that's not horrible, either."

"That lawyer from the NAHL has called the director. They were classmates at Yale. Apparently he thinks you leaked."

"Okay, that's definitely worse," I admitted.

"So you and I have a meeting with the director in ten minutes. Oh, and one other thing."

"Oh, Jesus," I said.

"Marla Chapman has gone missing."

CHAPTER SEVENTEEN

"Hey, did you know that Kim Silva and Duane Chapman were totally having sex?" the twins asked when I came home in the evening. They ran up to me excitedly as I came through the door.

"I'm pretty sure Chris knows that," Tayla said from the front room. She and Tony were playing a card game of some sort.

"Did you leak that to the press?" the twins asked.

"Of course I didn't," I said.

"Because all the discussion forums say it was you."

"I've seen your discussion groups. They also say NASA found the face of Jesus on the moon."

"Only some of them say that," the twins protested. "Not the ones that say you leaked."

"Well, if it makes you feel better the NAHL also thinks I or Vann leaked. I spent twenty minutes in the FBI director's office being yelled at for it."

"So it was you!" the twins said.

"No," I said. "I was able to account for every second of my time. That's one of the nice things about being a Haden. When you need it, you can produce documentation of your whole life."

"Any idea who might have?" Tony asked, slapping a card down in front of Tayla.

"I might, but I can't say."

"So professional," Tayla murmured, and then countered Tony's card.

"Kim Silva wants her cat back," I said to the twins as I moved past them.

"It's Duane Chapman's cat," they said.

I shook my head. "Lived in Chapman's illicit apartment. But is Silva's."

"Well, he likes it here," they protested. "You can ask him."

"He's still her cat," I pointed out. "I'm going to have to give him back soon."

"But Tony isn't done with that data vault!"

"Thanks for ratting me out, guys," Tony said to the twins.

"You can't give the cat back before then."

"I have Kim Silva and her entire league mad at me for no reason of my own," I said. "I suspect returning the cat will help."

"Hmph," the twins said, and then stomped

up the stairs, presumably to spend more time with their purloined cat.

"I told you that cat was trouble," Tony said.

"Actually it was Tayla who said the cat was trouble," I reminded him. "You were the one who complained we had not had a house meeting about the cat."

"I stand by that," Tony said. "And also my complaint about the twins hogging the cat."

"It's a cat," I said. "If Donut wants to spend time with you he'll show up in your room and sit on your important things."

"That's my point. I keep trying to lure Donut in and then the twins scoop him up and take him back to their room."

"It's delightful how childishly petulant you've become about it," Tayla said.

"I just feel cats are a community resource." Tony laid down another card.

"Uh-huh." Tayla dropped a card of her own. "Just remember what I said about how I still get a dog out of this."

"That's another house meeting," Tony said to her.

"I already have the votes."

"So, Tony, I hear from the grapevine that you have made no progress with the data vault," I said, changing the subject.

"Guilty," Tony said. "But then I told you

it was unlikely unless you found me the physical token that unlocks it. So I don't feel too bad about it." He pointed to Tayla. "She, on the other hand, may have found something useful to you."

"Oh?" I turned my attention to Tayla.

"So you remember you asked me if there were any drugs for Hadens that are intentionally designed to increase pain," she said.

"I do."

"Two things about that. First, I hate you for putting that idea in my brain, because for the last couple of days all my downtime has been spent going down the rabbit hole of Haden-specific pharmaceutical therapies. It's like you activated a nexus of my obsessive-compulsive disorder, my professional interests, and my love of weird trivia."

"Uh . . . sorry?"

Tayla waved off the apology. "Second, I didn't find any specific drug or therapy that is designed to increase pain in Hadens. But if you dig through the journals you can find references to experimental therapies that do a lot of weird shit. And I think I might have found something on point for you."

"Tell me."

"About fifteen years ago Neuracel developed a drug they called Attentex, which was designed for the general population to help kids with attention deficits to focus. It didn't work very well with non-Hadens but it showed some promise with us, especially when paired with mild electrical stimulation of the inferior frontal junction of the brain. Without the stimulation it was inert. It didn't have any effect. With it, some of the study subjects snapped to attention."

"And of course we Hadens have neural networks in our brains, which can be used to transmit targeted electrical stimulation," Tony said. He slapped down another card. "It takes a little bit of programming but it can be done."

"I assume there's a reason why I haven't heard of Attentex before this," I said to Tayla.

"There is," she said. "The side effects in the test subjects included intense nausea, vertigo, sensitivity to sound and light, and seizures."

"So your attention would be focused," Tony said. "But it would be focused on how sick you were feeling."

"Basically," Tayla said. She laid down her own card and Tony swore. Clearly this card game was not going very well for him. "And the problem for Neuracel, according to the paper I was reading, was that the side ef-

303

fects increased with the electrical stimulation."

"This is the part where my ears perked up," Tony said, then motioned to Tayla. "Tell Chris about the plateaus."

"Plateaus?" I asked.

"So, when the electrical stimulation was applied in conjunction with Attentex, stress reactions went up and were very slow to come back down, even when the electrical stimulation was withdrawn. So when electrical stimulation was provided again —"

"It made the side effects even worse," I finished. "Interesting."

"I assume this has some relevance to your investigation," Tayla said, and motioned to Tony. "The soon-to-be loser of this round here wouldn't tell me anything."

"You know we're doing two out of three," Tony said.

"*You* might be," Tayla said. "But I know when I've won."

"This information about Attentex is out in the public?" I asked Tayla.

"Yes," she said. "Well, sort of. Once Neuracel discovered it might have use for Hadens it applied to have its research costs funded by the National Institutes of Health, which meant that under the Haden Research Initiative Act it had to publish all the findings, including the side effects, into the government research database. So it's out there. But you really have to go looking for it. The database is immense. Literally millions of pages of research data. I found it by accident, just clicking through to something else. I'm probably the first person to read it since it was put into the database. Almost certainly the first since Neuracel went under."

"It went under because of this?"

"No," Tayla said. "The research on Attentex was subsidized by the government and then they probably took a tax credit on the rest of their research when it didn't pan out. This failure didn't hurt them."

"This is why when any company before Abrams-Kettering found themselves blowing a wad of cash on something stupid, they'd find a late-stage application to Hadens for it," Tony said. "It was a well-known, well-loved tax hedge. Which is one reason why Abrams-Kettering passed." He put down his last card.

Tayla slapped a card over his and then raised her arms in victory. Then she turned her attention back to me. "No, I looked it up. A few years ago a new CEO tried to move Neuracel away from pharmaceutical development and into consumer goods like sports drinks and supplements based on their already existing products. It went very poorly. The stock crashed, Neuracel went bankrupt, and it was sold for parts. The CEO walked away with a fifty-million-dollar golden parachute, so that was nice for him." She turned to Tony. "You're paying for the movie tomorrow."

"So unfair," Tony said.

"If by 'unfair' you mean 'lost entirely fairly because you suck,' then yes. Otherwise, no."

Tony turned to me. "Want to play cards?"

"I'll play with Tayla," I said. "She seems better at them."

"Oh, good, soon I'll have two free movies," Tayla said, then kicked Tony lightly to get him out of his chair. "Have a seat, friend."

"Is . . . that a *tank threep*?" the twins asked, looking out the house's windows into the street, and the rest of us had roughly a second to look up from our game before the tank threep tore through the windows and into the house, spraying glass everywhere.

The twin's threep put up its arms and was punched aside by the tank, who then dropped something on the floor and moved quickly away.

"Fire!" Tayla yelled. What the tank had dropped was an incendiary device of some sort. It set fire to the floor and rug and the flames were moving quickly toward the couch. Tayla unfreezed and ran to the fire extinguisher on the living room wall. There were fire extinguishers in nearly every room of the house. When you're a Haden, you have fire extinguishers everywhere in your living space. It's hard to move an immobile body.

Tony ran to the twins, who were struggling to get up off the floor. The hit had damaged their threep. I looked as the tank lumbered, quicker than expected, toward the stairs.

Toward the stairs that would take it upstairs to where our bodies were.

"Oh, shit," I said, and ran to block it from the stairs, running straight into it, center mass.

I had no illusions that I was going to be able to defeat or damage the tank on my own. What I wanted was to keep it on the ground floor until one of the other flatmates could help me.

I hit the tank and shoved hard. It wobbled slightly and then punched me directly in the head. I heard and felt something in the neck of my threep give way at that and suddenly couldn't turn my head to the left anymore. The tank punched again and this time I avoided the punch and wrapped my arms around its neck to drag it to the floor.

It didn't follow me. Instead it turned, picked a wall, and drove me into it, shoving me deep into the drywall. I lost my grip and fell. The tank turned to head toward the stairs —

— and was clocked in the head by Tayla with the fire extinguisher. She had put out the fire and was now swinging freely. Tony by this time had stopped bothering with the twins and was looking around for something to hit the tank with.

Tony! Upstairs! I sent to him on the house's local communication channel. We set it up to talk to each other when some of us were watching movies or playing games on the downstairs monitors, or needed to talk to each other at night when we'd already retired. Easier than yelling and in this case also more secure.

Tony got what I was saying to him. He raced to the stairs while I jumped into the kitchen and grabbed the fire extinguisher there.

I came back out just in time to see the tank duck Tayla's wide swing with the fire extinguisher and then absolutely hammer

308

her threep, lifting it up and hurling it all the way across the room.

Shit — Tayla sent, and then her threep collapsed onto the floor.

The tank turned again, and I raised my arms to swing my fire extinguisher. The tank moved to block the blow, which was when I let it have it in the head with the contents of the extinguisher. The dry chemical in the extinguisher generously coated the tank's head, blocking its vision. It tried to wipe the chemicals off its head and discovered the tank's hands were not great for the purpose. I went in and started swinging hard at its arms.

What are you doing? Tayla sent to me. She was back up.

It's a Hilketa threep, I sent back. *When they take damage parts fall off.*

She got it immediately. She picked up her fire extinguisher and ran over, squirting it in the face to put a new layer of blinding chemical on, and then swinging at the tank's nearest leg. The three of us danced around for a few seconds, the sound of my and Tayla's extinguishers beating out the time.

Then Donut the cat came out of the twins' room and meowed down the stairs, as if to say, *What the actual fuck, humans?*

The tank threep lashed out, knocking me

and Tayla off balance, and lurched up the stairs toward Donut. Donut took one look at the rampaging tank and bolted, running in the direction of my room at the far end of the upstairs. I righted myself and took off up the stairs after the tank, grabbing at its legs.

Call the cops, I sent on the house channel.

Already did, the twins answered, and then I got a head full of tank fist, dislodging me from the leg.

The tank crested the stairs, and then immediately flew back simultaneous to a very loud bang. It came from Tony's shotgun, which he kept in the house for home defense. The pellets struck the tank in the shoulder, spinning it counterclockwise and detaching its left arm from its body, which flew into the wall and then tumbled down the stairs past me.

Tony's shotgun was a single-shot and before he could reload the tank was up and barreling toward him, shoving him into the wall and knocking the shotgun out of his hands. Then the tank was past him, running toward my room.

"What the hell?" Tony said out loud, picking himself up as I crawled up the stairs to him.

The crashing sounds from my room were

immense and I suspected very expensive for me. The door slammed shut but refused to close. It was a sticky doorknob that I kept meaning to fix but hadn't gotten around to, because inasmuch as my body wasn't in the room, there was no great concern about privacy. The door rebounded back and out of the open crack Donut fled, running into the next room over, Tony's room.

The door swung open and the tank's bulk showed in it, looking directly at us. Behind the tank were my room's best feature, the bay windows, looking out onto the street.

"Run at it," I told Tony.

"What?" he said.

"Hit low. Keep going." And then I ran at the tank as fast as I could. A millisecond later Tony followed, yelling as he did.

We twisted to get through the doorframe together and hit the tank simultaneously, low on the chest. The tank lifted and our momentum carried all three of us back to the bay windows and the little reading nook there, and then through both, utterly wrecking the prime selling feature of my room.

We three fell all the way down to the street, tank on the bottom. It hit with the force of its own impact and the force of the two threeps on top of it. It hit so hard that all its remaining limbs popped right off, skittering across the asphalt.

The tank twisted its head back and forth, trying to inch away from me and Tony. It wasn't getting very far.

And then it stopped. Whoever was piloting it was gone.

"How are you?" I asked Tony.

"I think you owe me a new threep," he said. He was pulling himself upright and it was clear he'd taken damage. He looked over at me. "And I think you owe yourself a new threep, too."

"That wouldn't surprise me," I said. I slowly sat up and could hear various things grinding. Maintenance alerts were beginning to populate my field of view.

Tayla came out, her threep cracked. "What just happened?" she asked.

"We jumped out of a window, tank first," I said.

"No, I mean, what just happened?" She made arm movements to encapsulate the entire incident.

"I think someone was trying to kill Chris," Tony said. He was standing up but his threep was wobbly.

I shook my head. "Not me," I said.

"They ran into your room," Tony said. "They trashed it. If your body had been there like the rest of ours, it could have killed you."

I shook my head again. "They weren't looking for me."

"Then who? Me? Tayla? The twins? Elsie?"

"Someone else."

"There is no one else," Tayla said.

I shook my head and looked at Tayla. "There's someone else currently living in the house," I said.

It took her a moment. "Oh, you have *got* to be fucking kidding me," she said, figuring out who I was talking about.

I turned to Tony. "Donut went into your room," I said. "Do me a favor and go check if he's there. And if he's there keep him there, please."

"The cat?" Tony said. "You think they were coming for the fucking *cat*?"

"Go, please," I said. Tony got up and limped away. I looked back over at Tayla. "You okay?"

"It's never a dull moment around you, Chris," she said.

"I know. I'm sorry." By this time other people on the street were coming around to see what the fuss was about. The Metro police would be along presently, I knew.

"You think they were really after that cat?" Tayla asked.

"The tank went after Donut as soon as he

313

meowed," I said. "You were there."

Tayla laughed. "I don't know if you realize it, Chris, but in the moment I wasn't really paying attention to the cat. I was trying to beat the crap out of a monster threep."

"Fair point."

"The thing is, if you're right, then whoever this asshole is, they would have been happy to kill all of us to get at that cat. They set our house on fire."

"I think that was meant to be a diversion," I said.

"I know what it was meant to be," Tayla said. "I also know that if we didn't have extinguishers in every room, we'd all be dead now. Including that stupid cat. I almost got murdered over a pet, Chris."

"I didn't mean to put any of you in danger," I said. "I'll take the cat out of here tonight."

She laughed again and then motioned to the house, with its fire damage and wrecked windows. "I mean, we're *all* out of here for a while, don't you think?"

"We have insurance, right?" I joked.

"I think the real question is whether the insurance covers rampaging threeps."

Hey, Chris, I think you should get in here, Tony sent to me, directly.

Everything okay? I sent.

Relative to the last ten minutes, yes. And the cat is fine, if pissed off. But you want to get in here. I have something to show you that you're gonna want to see.

"Tony wants to see me," I said to Tayla.

She nodded. "Go on in. I'll wait for the police."

I pointed to the threep torso and head. "Don't let them impound this," I said. "It's official FBI evidence."

"I'm sure they'll listen to me when I say that," Tayla said.

I got up slowly and hobbled into the house, through the wreckage, and up the stairs. I stopped briefly at the twins' room. "You two okay?"

We're fine, one of them answered, and again the weirdness of the two of them deciding to share a communication channel struck me. *Our threep is trashed, though.*

"Sorry about that."

It's kind of cool, actually, they sent. *Like being in a movie. Now that it's over, anyway. How is Donut?*

"He's fine. He's in Tony's room."

If Tony wanted Donut to visit all he had to do was ask, they said. *The rest of this wasn't necessary.*

"I'll tell him you said so."

Chris?

"Yeah?"

Is this going to be a regular sort of thing?

"I really, really hope not," I said, and then hobbled over to Tony's room.

"Don't let the cat out," he said as I opened the door, which was smart of him, as Donut was at the door, ready to bolt. Tony walked over and picked up the cat, who protested loudly. I came through the door and closed it behind me. Tony sat Donut back down. The cat immediately went back to the door and stood by it, looking at us. *Let me out, you assholes,* was clearly the message.

"You wanted to show me a pissed-off cat?" I asked, looking at the cat.

"No," Tony said. "I want to show you what the pissed-off cat unlocked."

I turned back to Tony. "What?"

"Come into my office," Tony said, and sent me an invite to his personal space. I went in, and his room in our house, filled with him and an annoyed cat, disappeared, replaced by a neon-themed cavernous space.

"Look," Tony said, and pointed to a monitor window he'd pulled up. On it was an index of files.

"The data vault," I said.

"Bingo," Tony said. "Turns out that what

316

we needed to unlock the data vault on the cat's collar was the actual cat. Donut's got an implanted key transmitting in him somewhere, probably powered by his own body heat. But again, he has to be within a couple of meters of the data vault for it to unlock. If you'd kept the collar with the cat, we would have unlocked it days ago."

I pointed at the files. "So what are these?"

"Well, some of them are spreadsheets and some of them are emails and some of them look like transaction records, and from what little I know about them, all of them look like what you really want to do is get stacks of forensics accountants in here to dig into them, fast, because no one locks all this stuff on a data vault hanging on a cat collar just for the fun of it."

"Can you copy any of this?"

Tony shook his head. "Not a file. It's all tied to the vault. I can try to make visual captures of the information but I will bet you there's a shielding program on it that will register any capping effort and deny it." He pointed to the data. "I'm guessing this can only be opened someplace like a personal space, too. Try to open it up on a standard monitor and it won't port in. I mean, I've done that before, on proprietary information I don't want others to see."

"I assume there's a way around that."

"There's a way around everything, Chris. But it takes time. Easier to bring the accountants here."

"Or not," I said.

"What are you thinking?" Tony asked.

"I'm thinking that whoever came here came to kill the cat."

"Right."

"Which means that they know Donut's only good to us alive."

"Yes."

"So I think what I'm going to do right now is go back down and tell the Metro police that aside from the damage to our house and our threeps, some asshole in a tank threep made our cat run out into the street, where it got hit by a car."

"Our poor cat," Tony said, dryly.

"Right. And then I want you to *very quietly* take our furry friend over to the FBI building and get to work with those accountants you're talking about."

"Got it. Overnight rates apply, by the way."

"I'm glad that you can still think about money," I told Tony. "And before you go, talk to the twins about it. They've had a long day already."

Out in the street I got with the Metro

318

police, told my dead cat story while privately messaging Tayla to go along with it, and finished up just as Vann pulled up in her car.

"We've had an exciting night here," I told her as she walked up.

Vann looked up, saw the carnage, and seemed about to comment on it, but stopped. "Your night is about to get more exciting," she said. "Or at least longer."

"What's going on?" I said.

"You haven't looked at the news tonight," Vann said.

I motioned to the wreckage of the house and of the tank threep. "We've been kind of busy on our own," I said.

"They found Marla Chapman," Vann said.

"Where?"

"Outside Kim Silva's house. She's dead, Chris. And it looks like she tried to take Silva with her."

"So we're going to Boston, is what I'm hearing."

Vann shook her head. "I'm going to Boston. And then Brookline, which is where Silva's house is."

"Why aren't I going?" I asked.

"One, look at your threep. You've wrecked another one."

"I didn't wreck it alone," I said, defensively. "I had help."

"Two, you don't need to go to Boston. You need to speak to Kim Silva."

"I thought you said Marla Chapman tried to kill her."

"She tried. She didn't succeed. She's in Brigham and Women's Hospital's ICU unit, but she's alive and she's conscious, and she wants to talk. She said the only person she wants to talk to is you."

CHAPTER EIGHTEEN

"I don't recognize this place," I said to Kim Silva, after I entered her private space and looked around. It was a beach, and a lush, green woods came straight up to the sand.

"That's because it doesn't exist," she said. "Well. Doesn't exist like this now. It's Dauphin Island. It's in Alabama."

"Does it not exist anymore?" I asked.

"There used to be more of it," she said. "It's a barrier island that's getting eaten away by the ocean. But we used to go to Dauphin Island when I was a kid. Before I got Haden's. My mother's family was from the area and we'd go and visit my great-aunt every summer for a couple of weeks. We'd run around the beaches and chase birds. After I got Haden's I didn't go again. I missed it."

"It's nice," I said.

"Thank you. When I signed with the Bays, one of the very first things I did was upgrade my personal space. I had my designer look at maps from the island from the twentieth century, so I could have the whole island back. And then I took out every bit of human existence, except for my great-aunt's beach house." Silva pointed east, down the beach. "It's down there a ways."

I nodded to the bit of beach we were on. "So this is your public entrance," I said.

"Actually you're only the second person I've ever had here," Silva said. "The first was Duane. I had him come in from here because I liked walking down the beach with him."

We had a nice moment watching the smallish waves come in from the simulated Gulf of Mexico, while pelicans glided down and dipped their beaks into the water.

"How are you feeling?" I asked Silva, after a minute.

"I'm not feeling anything right now," she said. "I've got a bullet wound in my abdomen and some glass shards from where that bitch shot out my windows, but they gave me a nerve block right below my neck. I'm in worse shape than I feel. If I suddenly zone out on you, or disappear, that's why."

"I understand."

"I'm tempted to get my tank threep, find Marla, and punch her into next week."

"Marla Chapman's dead," I told Silva. "They found her body in your yard."

Silva took this in. "A suicide?"

"Everything points to one."

"But you don't think so."

"I don't know," I said. "I'm curious what you think. And why you decided that I was the only one you wanted to talk to."

Let's walk," she said, and started walking down the beach of Dauphin Island, away, I noted, from where she said her house there was.

"You met Marla?" Silva asked me, as we walked.

"After Duane died," I said.

"Did she strike you as the suicidal type?"

"It's hard to say after one meeting," I said. "Especially one in a situation like that. She was distraught, definitely. And angry."

"Angry is her thing," Silva said. "At least that's how Duane explained it. I knew her, of course. Everyone on the teams knows everyone else's partners. There's nothing about her that makes me think she would kill herself."

"Her husband died and she discovered he was having an affair," I pointed out.

"That would make her want to kill *me*," Silva said. "That's the part I don't have any problem believing. Normally, anyway."

"Ms. Silva."

"Go ahead and call me Kim," Silva said. "You're here in my personal space. That counts as being on a first-name basis."

"Kim. I think there's something you want to tell me, and I think all things considered it's probably something we should get right to."

Silva stopped and looked at me. "First. Did you go to the press about Duane and me having an affair? Please don't lie to me."

"No, I didn't," I said.

Silva held up her hand, pinky up. "Pinky swear."

I smiled at this despite myself. "Really?"

"Really. Chris — I'm going to call you Chris, okay?"

"If I'm calling you Kim, that seems fair."

"Chris, right now my body is in a fucking hospital with a gunshot wound. And while I'm making chitchat with you on the beach at the moment, what I really want to do is run screaming and never stop running."

"You'd run out of beach eventually," I said.

"It's an island."

"Fair."

Silva waggled her hand. "I'm asking you for a pinky swear because I'm shot, the man I loved is dead and so is his wife, I'm tired

324

and I'm hurt and I don't know who to trust at this point, but I need to trust someone. I want you to be it, Chris. I kind of need you to be it."

I hooked my pinky into hers. "Pinky swear," I said. "I didn't go to the press. I didn't go to anyone. I told my partner. She would rather push a reporter down a stairwell than talk to one."

"That sounds vaguely totalitarian."

"It's not. She's just cranky. Reporters are just one group on the list."

"I've been blackmailing the league," Silva said.

"How?"

"It's complicated."

"Give it to me as simply as you can."

"The league is funded by bad people, and they're setting up their upcoming foreign leagues to launder a shitload of money."

"You have evidence of this?"

Silva nodded. "Lots of it."

"How did you get it?"

"I have a fan in St. Petersburg who is very good at getting into confidential files. He asked if he could trade them for some signed merchandise."

"You didn't ask for them?"

"It wouldn't have occurred to me to ask for them. Once I *had* them, though, I decided I was going to put them to use."

"Your contract," I said.

"What? No," Silva said, scornfully. "I earned that thing on my own. I don't know if you noticed but I dragged the Bays to the championship last year."

I smiled. "So I heard. But then what?"

"A place for Duane in one of the international leagues."

"I thought he was going to try to be in the expansion draft for the new teams in the NAHL," I said.

Silva shook her head. "He was eligible but he'd never have been a franchise player in the NAHL. I loved him, but I also played with him every week and practiced with him every day. He wasn't at that level. Not here in North America, at least. But he could have been a star in Europe or Asia. He could have helped the league develop talent there as a player and then as a manager. It would have given him what he wanted. It would have made him happy. Then *we* would have been happy."

"May I ask an indelicate question?"

"What is it?"

"Couldn't you have just asked? You're one of the sport's biggest stars. They have a vested interest in keeping you happy. You wouldn't be the first celebrity to get a sweetheart deal for a sweetheart."

"I *did* ask. I was told that wasn't how it worked. Then I asked again, and I was told I shouldn't ask again. So I said, fine, and told them I had the receipts and if they wanted them to go away they should do what I tell them."

"I imagine that didn't go over well."

Silva smiled. "No, it didn't. But it did escalate me upwards. Before I was just talking to Pena and Kreisberg," she said, naming the Boston Bays' coach and owner. "After I made my threat I was dealing with Alex Kaufmann."

"Why Kaufmann?" I asked.

"Because he was the league's point man for developing the foreign leagues. Also, he was the league's go-to guy for driving hard bargains and dealing with difficult partners. You know. An asshole."

"And he went along with your plan."

"We were still negotiating it."

"Then Duane died."

"Yes. And then so did Alex. And then you found the apartment and our threeps, which implicated me. That's when Medina told me to talk to you, with him and Pena in the room. He wanted to make sure I didn't talk to you about the foreign leagues."

"Medina knows you tried to blackmail the

league."

"He's its general counsel, of course he knew."

"And he also knew about the plan to launder money through these foreign leagues."

Silva looked at me. "He's the general counsel," she repeated.

"A lot can happen in the lower ranks without the people in the upper ranks knowing," I said. "Or at least without them having a direct link to it."

"Come on," Silva said. "If he knew what I was doing, he knew what else was going on."

"Medina didn't want you to tell me about the foreign leagues. But you're telling me now. Without counsel of any kind, I should add, which isn't necessarily smart from a legal point of view. I feel obliged to tell you that because we pinky swore."

"Thank you." Silva reached down and picked up a shell on the beach, examined it for a moment, and then set it back down. "Duane's dead. Marla's dead. Alex Kaufmann's dead, for some reason I just can't figure out. I'm not dead, but it's pretty obvious someone wants me to be. That's why the news about me and Duane leaked in the first place. To give a reason for Marla to take a shot at me. I'm Haden. It's hard for me to run and hide, Chris. At this point, possibly being hauled up on blackmail charges is the least of my problems."

"You still have this evidence," I said. "Of the money laundering in the foreign leagues."

Silva looked away. "Yes."

"And you're willing to give it to us."

"Yes."

"And it's reliable."

Silva looked back at me. "I have a bullet hole in me, Chris. It's not there because the information I have is bullshit. That's why we're talking right now."

"Because the information isn't bullshit?"

"Because I'm in the hospital with a bullet hole. Medina isn't a Haden. He forgets I can talk to you without him seeing me do it. And no one is going to think that I'll do it right before surgery."

"And what are you going to do if someone asks if you've talked to me or Agent Vann?"

"I'm going to lie my ass off, is what I'm going to do."

I smiled at this. "Seems reasonable."

"Just one thing, Chris," Silva said.

"Yes, Kim?"

"Whatever you're going to do, do it soon. I don't think they're done with me. I'd like not to die."

■ ■ ■

"Imagine being worth eighty million dollars and still being afraid for your life," Vann said, after I had caught her up. "On second thought that might not be a stretch for you."

"Thanks," I said, dryly. I was standing in my personal space while she, in Boston, ported in through the use of her glasses. She was represented by a relatively rudimentary avatar. She looked like herself but in a lazy, computer-animation-from-the-turn-of-the-century way. Tony was also there, looking like himself. It was past midnight by this point. "That said, her fear at this point is entirely reasonable."

"And entirely her own fault," Vann said.

"That's not entirely accurate," I said.

"All right, let me ask you: You've been sent a stack of documents suggesting your employer is in bed with the mafia in Europe and Asia. Is your first impulse to say to yourself, 'How *excellent,* now I will blackmail my employer with these incriminating documents to get favors for my boy toy, surely neither my employer nor the mafia will mind in the slightest'?"

"She's not wrong," Tony observed.

"I wouldn't have put it that way," I said.

"Of course you wouldn't, you did that dumbass 'pinky swear' thing with her," Vann said. "You're best friends forever now."

"You saw Marla Chapman's body," I said to her. "Was it a suicide?"

"It looks like a suicide. Single shot to the head, with the same handgun used to shoot up Silva's house in Brookline. The shots went through a bedroom window. Silva used her home threep to shield her body once the shooting started. We have it on video because of Silva's home-monitoring equipment."

"Anything of the shooter?"

Vann shook her head. "Nothing useful."

"So it could have been someone else," I said. "If it was meant to be a pro hit, they would have made more of an effort than just shooting through a window with a handgun."

"Silva *was* shot," Vann pointed out. "You didn't get this because you were walking beaches with a virtual version of her, but she was seriously injured. If that bullet had carved a slightly different path in her torso, she'd be dead. It's luck she survived, not luck that she was hit. She's not playing in Friday's opener, that's for sure."

"Do *you* think it was a suicide?" I pressed Vann.

"I can't say," she said. "I *am* curious how Chapman got to Boston. She left her car at home."

"Hired car to the train station or airport," Tony said.

"No purchase information on her credit accounts or purchases from Amtrak or the airlines. She definitely didn't walk through airport security in Philly. I made those assholes from the Philly branch check."

"It's six hours from Philly to Boston by car or train," I said.

Vann nodded again. "For the timing of this to work, Marla Chapman would have had to start going to Boston pretty much the minute the news about the affair broke. It's that tight."

"So, no. We don't think it was a suicide," I concluded.

"We don't. You and I. Brookline's police think so because they have Marla Chapman's dead body in Silva's side yard with a gun and a bullet hole in her head. But given the fact that the Brookline police's major crime investigation experience involves trying to find who is stealing FedEx packages from apartment foyers, I've had the Bureau's Boston branch step in and take over the investigation."

"And how do we feel about Boston's

FBI?" I asked.

"They're better than Philly's, at least." She turned to Tony. "Tell us what you have."

"Well, first," Tony said, "the tank threep that destroyed our house and tried to kill an innocent cat has no official owner. The VIN pops up nothing in the vehicle database, but it does pop up a manufacturer, which is a certain boutique operation out of Baltimore."

"Van Diemen," I said.

"Bingo," Tony said, pointing at me. "This is not the first time they've popped up in your investigation, so if I were you the next time I visited them I'd be going in there with warrants and firearms."

"Not very subtle."

"My house is wrecked and I'm sitting in an FBI conference room with a cat and three forensics accountants. I'm not into subtle at the moment."

"Fair."

"What else?" Vann asked.

"Speaking of forensics accountants, ours here found some very interesting things. Chris, you said that Silva said her information showed the league was laundering money."

"That's right," I said.

"Well, she's not one hundred percent accurate with her police work. There's nothing here that shows the league laundering money directly."

" 'Directly'?"

"You caught the qualifier there. Good. So, what's happening is that a lot of what looks to be dirty money is coming into a third-party company, and that third party is the one who is investing heavily into the international leagues."

"Let me guess," I said. "It's Labram."

"Another bingo," Tony said. "And from what these accountants here are telling me, it looks like they're doing it reasonably cleverly. Labram works with these shady companies on legitimate enterprises and charges them a premium on standard rates. Like a third or so. Enough to soak up some ill-gotten money, but not enough that it looks like anything other than your basic capitalistic taking advantage of a client thing. Labram gives the companies the option of paying in cryptocurrency, so they get paid in one that is relatively cheap to buy into, and then they manipulate the market to drive up the price."

"How easy is that to do?" Vann asked.

"*Super* easy," Tony said. "There are a lot of chumps out there who think they're financial geniuses. You don't even have to do anything illegal to do it, just trigger the greed of the underinformed. The secret is selling before it all crashes, which it will."

"So Labram overcharges and then speculates," I said. "Where's the laundering?"

"The laundering comes with Labram's investments in the foreign leagues. They're not making an investment in the league directly. They're creating these limited liability companies as investment vehicles, taking a controlling partnership in the LLCs, and then inviting the shady companies they do business with to become minority partners in them."

"So then the foreign Hilketa leagues start play and a year or two later the minority partners sells their shares back to Labram, who buys them for a ridiculously inflated price," Vann said.

"A ridiculously inflated price that corresponds to the premium they paid for Labram's services plus some percentage of the run-up on the cryptocurrency," Tony said. "The dirty money's clean, everyone's happy, and everyone's richer, except for the dumbasses who came in too late on the cryptocurrency."

"Seems a little straightforward for world-class money laundering," Vann said.

"I'm giving you the condensed version,"

Tony assured her. "The accounting geeks tell me the actual setup is really very clever in some deeply questionable ways. And it's not even the first time Labram's done it."

"When did they do it before?"

"When Amelie Parker went and created that sports supplement company. A fair chunk of the angel investors just happened to be either the shadyish companies Labram does business with, or their owners taking a personal flier. They invest, Amelie Parker's company putters around for a few years, doing just well enough not to fail, and then Labram comes in and buys it up at a premium."

"Everyone makes money, everyone's happy," Vann said. She turned to me. "And I'm guessing they're going to do it again with that MobilOn thing. The one she wants you as a spokesperson for."

"The one she's going to pay me in equity for," I said.

"I would *definitely* do that if I were you," Tony said. "That's as close to a guaranteed payout as you're ever going to get."

"But she doesn't *need* me," I said. "If all of this is a money-laundering scam, a celebrity spokesperson is beside the point. Or outside investors like my parents."

"No, that's the genius of it," Tony said.

336

"Get enough publicity and enough legitimate outside investment to camouflage the money-laundering parts."

"I feel so used," I said, and I was only half-joking about it.

"Now you know what your celebrity is good for," Vann said.

"So the North American Hilketa League is completely out of the loop on this," I said to Tony, getting back to the conversation at hand.

"Sure," Tony said. "Let's go with that."

"I sense skepticism."

"Your pinky pal tries to blackmail the league with this information and her lover turns up dead shortly thereafter. Then the league official responsible for the foreign deals. Then the dead player's wife, who allegedly tries to murder her rival. Oh, and let's not forget that our house got destroyed trying to kill a fucking cat. Yes, I am skeptical the league is not in on this somehow."

"You didn't tell Silva we got into her data vault," Vann said.

I shook my head. "No. And for that matter she didn't tell me about it. She wants me to think she still has the information."

"Your pinky promises sit on a throne of lies," Tony said.

"She feels like she's bargaining for her

life," I reminded him.

"We have people with her," Vann said. "And the hospital has her on a private floor to keep the journalists and fans away. Unless ninjas come for her, she'll be fine."

"Is there anything in the data vault implicating the league?" I asked Tony.

"Your people are still looking through it. There's a lot of stuff here."

"What about Labram itself?" I asked. "Chapman died with Labram supplements in his system. Parker's Integrator was with Kaufmann just before he died. And she had the lawyers of some of Labram's shadier partners in her home this morning."

"It's all circumstantial at this point," Vann said. "If we had the supplements we could test them but the fucking Philly branch screwed that up. Chapman's autopsy didn't find anything. Kaufmann's autopsy is inconclusive. And there's no law against having shady lawyers in your home."

"It's a *lot* of circumstance," I pointed out.

"And it's still not enough. We're not actually investigating money laundering or blackmail or morally compromised Integrators. We're investigating the deaths of Duane Chapman and Alex Kaufmann. Right now, there's still no evidence that they didn't die of cardiac arrest for one and suicide for the other. The circumstances around it are damning as hell. But we still have to connect them."

"What do you want to do?" I asked. "We have Silva, but everyone else is either lawyered up or a lawyer."

"We start small," Vann said.

"No one in this is small. Or has small lawyers."

"No. We've got a few."

"What are you going to do?"

"Scare the shit out of them, is my current plan."

CHAPTER NINETEEN

"I flew down from Boston today and my colleague here drove up from Washington, D.C., Mr. Ortiz," Vann said, leaning forward on the Philadelphia police interrogation room table. "I tell you this so you can appreciate how magnificently fucked you are, that you have federal agents coming from across the Eastern Seaboard to talk to you."

Pedro Ortiz, cousin of Alton Ortiz, looked as deeply confused as only someone who had spent the night in the city jail on charges he didn't comprehend could. Sitting next to him was his attorney, a young kid in a bad suit who was clearly out of his element.

"And you," Vann said, turning her attention to him. "Public defender or junior associate?"

"I happen to —" the (I assumed) public defender began, but Vann cut him off, and then pointed to him.

"This one is not good enough for the shit you're in right now," Vann said to Pedro.

"I went to Penn," the lawyer said, defensively.

"Do you know what shit you're in right now?" Vann asked Pedro, ignoring the lawyer.

Pedro looked at Vann, and then me, and then his lawyer. "When I was arrested they said arson, but —"

"Tell him what else he's won, Agent Shane," Vann said to me.

"So, there's the arson charge, which you already know about," I said. "Also, destruction of property, multiple charges, attempted murder, multiple charges, voluntary and involuntary manslaughter, also multiple charges, conspiracy to commit arson, conspiracy to commit murder, and animal cruelty."

"Animal cruelty?" Pedro said.

"There was a cat in that apartment when you set it on fire," Vann said.

"I didn't know about any cat," Pedro said. His lawyer groaned and slid down a little in his chair.

"Basically a whole raft of local, state, and federal charges that you'll be charged with, not to mention the civil suits that will be filed by the landlord and every single tenant you burned out of a home. Do you have insurance, Mr. Ortiz?"

"Not *that* much," he said.

"I didn't think so. So," Vann said, and folded her hands together on the table. "You can talk to us, or take your chances with Clarence Darrow over here. But before you answer, let me be honest with you: We don't want you. We don't even want your cousin, who is why you're here in the first place. So if you work with us and tell us useful things, we'll work with you. But if you don't —"

"We don't want you but we'll be happy to take you," I finished. "It'll give closure to the people you burned out of their homes."

"Give me a second with my client," the lawyer said, and then leaned over to whisper in Pedro's ear. Pedro listened for a few seconds then screwed up his face and looked at his lawyer. "No shit, genius," he said, and then turned to Vann. "This one here thinks I should make a deal with you."

"He's very wise," Vann said.

"I want immunity for my client," the lawyer said.

"I'm sure you do." Vann looked to Pedro. "Let's hear what you got."

"A couple years back Alton tells me that he's got a friend who is looking for an apartment," Pedro said. "Nothing fancy or too expensive, just someplace he can use as an office. He knows I do a lot of electrical work for landlords and property managers so I might know someplace and maybe get him a good deal. So I find him that place on Natrona. It's only an okay building, but the area is gentrifying. It's fine. Alton slips me a hundred in appreciation, and that's it. I see him sometimes at family things.

"Then about two months ago he comes back to me and wants a favor. Turns out his friend is using the apartment to screw around and the wife wants to come in and take pictures and gather evidence for the divorce proceeding. And I say, okay, so what does that have to do with me? And he asks me to cut the power to the apartment so she can get in. So I ask what's wrong with a goddamned key and he says the dude doesn't know his wife knows about the apartment so it has to be a secret, and the dude has all sorts of security because he has expensive threeps in there. And then Alton offers me a bribe."

"How much?" Vann asked.

"Two thousand dollars. So, okay, I have a kid in college. Fine. He tells me what day his girlfriend wants to get into the apartment, and then the next time I'm checking the system I program in a routine that turns off the power in the apartment for thirty minutes. It's a kludge and I have to turn off some safeguards for the building to make it work, but it's for thirty minutes so I don't think it's a big deal. I tell Alton the time, and set a note for myself to revert the system the next time I go to run maintenance to purge out the kludge. The next thing I know the place has burned down."

"What do you think happened?" Vann asked.

"I don't know," Pedro said. "The electrical system was old and even with the software to manage it there were always problems and shorts. Someone probably just plugged one too many things into an old shitty power strip."

"You'll affirm all of this in writing."

"Give me a pen. Whatever this is, I don't want any part of it. I love my cousin, but this is out of 'do for family' territory."

"This was all through your cousin," Vann asked. "No one else involved."

"Not with me," Pedro said.

"Did you know Duane Chapman at all?" I asked.

"The guy who rented the apartment? No. But I didn't know any of the renters that well. I'm not on site all the time. I contract out for a lot of buildings. Occasionally I go into the apartments if I have to do work. The manager lets me in if they're not home. I was never in that guy's apartment after the first week he rented it and he needed the high-capacity outlets for his threep pads."

"How about Marla Chapman?"

"No, I never met her."

"You called her Alton's girlfriend," Vann said.

"Yeah."

"Why did you do that?"

"Because she was."

"Are you sure?"

"That's what he told me when I asked him why he gave a shit."

"And you're sure they're sexually engaged with each other."

"I don't have *pictures,*" Pedro said. "But, yeah, I'm sure. Ma'am, I don't want to be sexist, but the only reason a man sells out his friend is if he's screwing his wife."

"Did you go to Penn Law?" Vann asked the next lawyer we saw, two hours later, this one in another part of town, in a hotel conference room the NAHL rented for the occasion.

"No, I went to Georgetown," said the lawyer, who had introduced herself as

345

Keshia Sanborn. "Why do you ask?"

"No particular reason," Vann said. She turned to Alton Ortiz, who sat there in his suit. "And you're sure that you want to be represented by the NAHL and Ms. Sanborn here?"

"Yes," Ortiz said, and then looked over to Sanborn, confused.

"Is there some reason you're choosing to start this entirely voluntary session by attacking me, Agent Vann?" Sanborn asked. "Because I have to say that it doesn't incline me to allow my client to continue."

"I just want to make sure Mr. Ortiz is aware that at some point, his interests and the interests of the NAHL diverge. And while it's all very well that you've taken his case pro bono out of the goodness of your heart, Ms. Sanborn, I think it's fair for Mr. Ortiz to ask himself how much of the advice he gets from you is for his benefit, and how much is for your usual employer."

"What does that mean?" Ortiz asked.

"It means we know about you and Marla Chapman," I said.

Ortiz looked shocked.

"Your cousin told us all about it, Mr. Ortiz," Vann said. "Told us how Marla Chapman decided that if her husband was seeing people on the side, it was only fair that she was extended the same privileges."

I pushed forward a manila folder to Sanborn. "Texts and messages between Mr. Ortiz and Marla Chapman," I said. "We got a warrant for her phone as part of the investigation into her death." I turned to Ortiz. "My condolences to you, Mr. Ortiz."

"Thank you," Ortiz said, in a dazed tone of voice.

"Here's the thing, Mr. Ortiz," Vann said, stepping on my condolences. "We know you and Marla Chapman were an item. We have a sworn affidavit from your cousin attesting that you approached him to fiddle with the wiring in Duane Chapman's love nest, which led to the entire building burning down." At this I slid another folder over to Sanborn, with Pedro Ortiz's statement inside. "And you ran from us when we came to talk to you the other day, which we don't usually consider the action of someone with a clear conscience."

"What are you accusing my client of, Agent Vann?" Sanborn asked.

"It's not what I'm accusing him of that's important here, it's what *your* interest is here, Ms. Sanborn." Vann looked at Sanborn. "Yours and the NAHL's. But since you've asked, we're going to accuse your client of first-degree murder. He had the means, motive, and opportunity to kill Duane Chapman, and there's evidence to suggest he'd been planning this for a while. For as long as he and Marla Chapman were an item, at the very least." Vann turned her attention back to Ortiz. "You decided you'd had enough of Chapman and you didn't want to have to keep sneaking around with Marla. You doped his supplement IV with something you thought could get past the usual sorts of tests, he had his seizure and died, and you and Marla Chapman live comfortably ever after on the insurance and league benefits. And you might have gotten away with it too if it weren't for the apartment fire and your cousin giving you up."

Ortiz gaped. "That's *nuts,*" he said, finally.

"We're happy to hear an alternate theory of the case," I said.

"I didn't dope that supplement bag! Test it yourself!"

"We can't," I said. "The lab contaminated their test sample. It's unusable for legal purposes."

"There was an autopsy," Ortiz protested.

"Nothing conclusive at this point." This was true as far as it went.

"So in fact you have nothing on Mr. Ortiz," Sanborn said.

"We have his cousin's testimony and his

348

tweets and, as I said before, means, motive, and opportunity."

"All of which will be destroyed in court if you're stupid enough to charge my client."

"Possibly," Vann said. "If you take it to court at all." She turned to Ortiz. "See, this is where I make the point that I think the NAHL, Ms. Sanborn's boss, will be *delighted* to have you make a plea bargain, Mr. Ortiz. When we're gone she's going to make the case to you — the correct case — that if this goes to trial, it's going to be essentially our word against yours, and our word is better. So she'll want to see if you'll go along with a plea for a lesser charge, which the prosecutors will go along with because it saves the government money. Then the problem will be solved. No one will snoop around any further. The NAHL can get back to its very important business of expanding into Asia and Europe, which this little investigation of ours is complicating."

Ortiz was now looking at Sanborn with a pissed-off expression on his face.

"I think maybe she already brought up the idea of a plea to him," I said to Vann.

"Wow," Vann said. "I think you're right. Even Pedro's public defender didn't open with a plea."

Ortiz turned his attention back to us. "I didn't murder Duane. He was my friend."

"A friend whose wife you were fucking," Vann observed. "I'm guessing he wouldn't have thought that was very friendly."

Ortiz put his face in his hands. Sanborn cleared her throat to say something. Ortiz put a hand up to her, as if to say, *Don't you even.*

"We do have another theory of the crime," I ventured.

"And what is that, precisely?" Sanborn asked.

"One that also hinges on a supplement bag," Vann said.

"You said the supplement bag was contaminated."

"Not *the* supplement bag, *a* supplement bag."

"The supplement bag that was contaminated was part of a particular shipment. One that was meant for Kim Silva and shipped to Duane Chapman's apartment," I said.

"Yes," Ortiz said. "I went to the apartment and got the supplements for the game."

"Unfortunately, Mr. Ortiz, the box of supplements your bag came from burned up in the fire."

"What if there were another bag from that box?" Ortiz asked.

"Then depending on what we find, it would go a very long way to clearing you of the murder charge," Vann said.

"That's good to know," said Ortiz, "because I took two bags with me when I left the apartment. The other one's still in Duane's town house."

"And you can get into Chapman's town house?"

"I still have the door code."

"Fine." Vann looked up at the clock on the conference room wall. "It's twelve thirty. Shane and I have an interview up in Trenton. That's going to take a couple of hours. Let's meet at the town house at four thirty. Then you can take us in."

"So you're not going to charge me for murder?"

"That depends on whether those supplements are where you say they are, Mr. Ortiz."

"Why Trenton?" I asked, as we waited in the car, several addresses down from the Chapman town house.

"I said that an hour ago and you're asking me about it now?" Vann said. She was sipping coffee from behind the wheel. A hand with a cigarette was held outside the driver's-side window.

"I've been thinking about it since then."

"It's close enough to be a plausible trip and far enough away to take a lot of time. That's it."

"So, no special memories of Trenton."

Vann looked over. "No one has special memories of Trenton, Chris."

I was going to comment on that but then noticed down the street someone heading up the Chapman steps. The person punched in an access code on the door and then let themselves in.

"Jesus, I really do owe you a dollar," I said to Vann. "I didn't think they'd actually send someone through the front door." When we made the bet, I'd put a small camera on the rear entrance and garage of the town house, which I had been monitoring. It was picking up nothing but stray cats.

"These are arrogant people," Vann said. "And we said we would be out of town. Why would we lie?"

"But which arrogant people are they?"

"Let's go find out," Vann said, and got out of the car.

We came up to the town house just as the interloper was coming out. They came out looking away from us as they closed the door, and didn't see us until they were down the entrance steps entirely.

It was Rachel Ramsey, of the Philadelphia branch of the FBI, clutching a plastic bag.

She seemed surprised to see us. "What are you doing here?" she asked, stupidly.

"We just got back from Trenton," I said.

"What are *you* doing here, Ramsey?" Vann asked.

"I . . ." Ramsey began, and there was an infinitesimal pause before she continued. "I was following up on an investigative tip about Marla Chapman's death."

Vann nodded at the bag. "And you put whatever it is in a plastic Wawa bag?" she said. "We're not being exactly *rigorous* in our chain of evidence, are we, Agent Ramsey?"

"Look, Vann," Ramsey began.

"Oh, let's *not,*" Vann said, shutting her down. "Here's the deal. You're going to give that bag in your hand to Agent Shane. If it's anything but a bag of IV supplements, then I'll apologize to you, we'll have a big laugh about our misunderstanding, and then you'll give us everything you have on Marla Chapman's death because as you know we are the lead investigators and you really should have told us what you were up to in the first place, and you didn't. Did she,

Agent Shane?"

"I don't have anything from her in my mail queue," I said.

"But if it *is* a bag of IV supplements, Ramsey, and it *is,* then you're going to tell us everything, starting with who told you to come get the bag."

"Or what?" Ramsey said.

Vann rolled her eyes at Ramsey. "Oh, for fuck's sake. What do you want me to say, Ramsey, that I'll shoot you?"

"She might in fact shoot you," I said, to Ramsey.

"But I'm *not* going to because I don't have time for the paperwork," Vann said. "I don't have time for any of this shit. I don't have time for *you.* I don't give a shit *about* you, Ramsey. We've spent an entire day working up a chain of people we don't give a shit about so we can get to the ones we do. You're just the next link. But as I told another one of you earlier today, if you *want* to make it about you, I'll be happy to give you my *undivided* attention."

"You might prefer being shot," I said to Ramsey.

"You might," agreed Vann. "Ramsey, if you didn't have the IV bag in your hands, you would have passed that bag over to Shane by now. So why don't we stop fucking around and get to it."

I watched Ramsey through all of this. Her poker face wasn't very good, and Vann had been having a day of running over people in order to not give them enough time to think. Ramsey didn't even have a lawyer around to help handle the steamrolling. She knew she had been caught, that her career was about to go up in flames, that she might be headed for prison, and believed Vann would cackle while it happened.

And Vann would, if it came to that.

But it didn't have to come to that. It was time for me to play good cop.

"Ramsey, there's a way out of this for you," I said. "Tell us what we want to know, right now, and work with us moving forward. Do that, and if anyone asks —"

"And they will," Vann said.

"— we'll say you've been working with us all this time. Quietly, so you wouldn't spook whoever approached you. Work with us now, and you can still turn this around."

"Or don't and we burn you," Vann said. "All the way to the ground."

Ramsey looked at me. "You'll say I was in on it."

"Right from the beginning," I said.

"You're serious about that."

I almost said *Pinky swear* but stopped in

time. "Yes. Ramsey, we could use your help. And we could use it right now. Before whoever you're breaking the law for realizes you've been found out."

"Yes," Vann said. "Clock is running."

Ramsey looked at us both, sighed, and handed over the Wawa bag. I opened it. The second bag of supplements was in it.

"Talk," Vann said. "Fast. To the point."

"I've been on thin ice at work," Ramsey said. "Bad performance reviews. Too many days out because I have to deal with my mother. She has Haden's-related dementia, and her care costs are too much, especially now."

"Since Abrams-Kettering," I said.

Ramsey nodded, and then motioned to me with her head. "The thing with the threep you borrowed from us was the last straw. It was on me, and that on top of my reviews . . . well. I'm pretty much screwed. Then the other night I go home and there's an envelope on the door. Inside is an inactive cryptocurrency card and a note with a phone number. I call the number and a computerized voice picks up. Tells me the card has enough currency on it to pay for my mother's care for six months. One month was accessible on it already. For the rest of it, I just had to get rid of Duane

356

Chapman's IV sample."

"So you did it," I said.

"I was pissed at you anyway," Ramsey admitted. "You were going to get me fired from the agency." She pointed at Vann. "And she's the asshole that didn't let me shift the cost of the burned-up threep to D.C. So, sure. It wasn't difficult to mess with the sample and make it look like a routine screwup. I sent evidence of it and then the rest of the card unlocked."

"You weren't worried that this was some sort of setup?" I asked.

Ramsey looked at me with a tired expression on her face. "Agent Shane, I can barely afford my mother's care. Forgive me for not looking this sudden and unexpected gift horse in the mouth."

Vann pointed to the current IV bag. "And this?"

"Text on my personal phone less than a half hour ago. Told me what to look for, gave me the door code, promised a quarter of a million dollars in another cryptocurrency card when I delivered." She shrugged.

"What have you done with that first installment of currency?" I asked.

"Nothing," Ramsey said. "No time."

"You can't keep it," Vann said.

Ramsey gave her a look. "No, of course not."

"You're supposed to deliver the IV bag?" I asked.

"Yes."

"When?"

"I don't know. I need to send a photo showing I have it in my possession, including the bar code, and we'll set up the exchange."

Vann and I looked at each other. "And you think this is a *wise* thing to do," Vann said.

"I'm not going to meet them in an isolated parking lot at midnight, for Christ's sake," Ramsey said. "I may not be a great FBI agent but I'm not entirely stupid. We'll make the exchange in broad daylight somewhere busy."

"When are you going to contact them?" I asked.

"Actually, I should have already sent them a picture of the bag."

"Do it," Vann said.

Ninety seconds later: "The George Washington statue at Independence Hall," Ramsey said. "One hour."

I turned to Vann. "What do you want to do?" I asked.

358

She looked me up and down. "Get you a rental threep," she said.

CHAPTER TWENTY

The rental threep was a Sebring-Warner Pallas, one of their more affordable models, and also the only one the rental place on Chestnut Street had in their inventory. I paid an extortionate amount for the last-minute pickup, ported in, and immediately walked out of the parking garage, heading east toward Independence Hall.

"I'm in the rental," I said to Vann, over the internal phone.

"Good," she said. She was at the Hotel Monaco, in the lobby, out of sight. My personal threep was in the car I borrowed from my parents to drive to Philadelphia, in the hotel's valet parking. The valet was weirded out by having to drive a threep along with the car, but Vann tipped up front. "Are you recording?"

"I am," I said. "Just as a warning, this rental isn't high-end. I wouldn't count on the recording being crystal clear."

"You can *see* out of it, right?" Vann said. "It'll be fine. Record the handoff and then follow the recipient."

"I know my job," I reminded Vann. The asphalt of Chestnut Street gave way to cobblestones and I walked into the park where they kept the Liberty Bell, across the street from Independence Hall and the statue of George Washington. Both were awash with tourists and school groups being herded by exasperated adults. Occasional threeps dotted the area. I was not notably conspicuous in my rental threep.

"I see Ramsey," I said to Vann. She was hovering by the east side of the statue, looking at her phone and trying to act casual.

"Anyone coming up to her?"

"Not yet."

There was a tap on my shoulder. I turned and saw three tourists smiling at me. "Yes?" I said.

One of them held out her phone to me. "Would you photo?"

I looked at the tourists and took a guess at their country of origin. "Would you like me to take a photo of you, or did you want a photo of me?" I asked, and the translation came out in Spanish a fraction of a second later. I took the phone.

They were all very impressed with my fake

fluency. "A photo of the three of us, please, if you wouldn't mind. In front of the Independence Hall," the one who handed me the phone said, in Spanish.

"Sure," I said. "Let's go ahead and cross the street for a better shot."

"What the hell are you doing," Vann said. Her audio channel was still open to me.

"Blending in, if that's all right with you," I said, internally.

"You're an idiot."

"I've positioned myself for a better view of the exchange, actually." I motioned the three tourists to stand in front of the Washington statue, and held up the phone and took several shots with Ramsey also in the frame. The tourists smiled and waved and were oblivious to everything but getting their picture taken, as tourists often are. They thanked me and took their phone back and positioned themselves on the west side of the statue and then took selfies with their phones at arm's length, because of course they did, why wouldn't they.

I looked up from them just in time to see a man in a hoodie walk up to Ramsey. He was also carrying a plastic Wawa bag. He held it up to her, swapped out his bag for hers, smiled, and then walked away without a word.

"Got it on video and following," I said internally to Vann. I took a step to follow the man with the bag and almost missed the threep who walked up to Ramsey, pulled a handgun out of its own bag, and shot her directly in the head and then in the chest.

Ramsey went down. The tourists at the statue and everyone else started screaming and running. The threep collapsed, inert, gun still in its hand. Whoever had been using it had exited it and left it behind. It was a very expensive act.

"What just happened?" Vann asked. I assumed she was looking out of the lobby and seeing people scattering.

"Ramsey's shot," I said. "A threep."

"I'm coming. Go after the bag."

"Ramsey's —"

"Go after the bag, Chris!"

I could see the man, walking east on Chestnut, turning right on Independence as people ran past him. I also started running, toward him.

I turned the corner onto Independence and saw the man half a street down, looking back directly at me as he walked. He broke left across the street and started running. I chased after him.

The Sebring-Warner Pallas model is not fast by any stretch of the imagination. But one thing you get used to when you walk around in a threep is navigating through crowds and busy sidewalks, since non-Hadens will literally walk into threeps because they don't see them as quite human. It's not intentional. It's one of those unconscious biases that people don't even know they have.

Well, most of the time it's unintentional. Some people are just assholes.

The point is that I was not running faster than the man I was following. But I was gaining on him. Because I was doing a better job of threading through people as we ran.

The dude took a right on Locust, heading toward Washington Square, picking up speed because there were fewer people. As he did he shook the supplements out of the Wawa bag and then jammed his right hand into his hoodie pocket and pulled out a knife. He was going to tear open the bag and destroy the evidence. By this time his hoodie had fallen back from his head. His face was mostly away from me, but as he turned slightly I could see the earpiece lodged into his ear.

He leapt onto Sixth, avoided the traffic, and headed into Washington Square —

— and tripped over the curb, slamming

himself into the sidewalk pavement and sending the IV bag and the knife sprawling.

That's convenient, I thought, stepped onto Sixth to cross over and immobilize the dude before he could take off again, and then heard the revving of an engine a fraction of a second before a car intentionally and unapologetically ran into my threep, sprawling it in a southward direction on Sixth.

I picked my head up just in time to see the dude, bleeding, jam himself into the back seat of the car, IV bag in hand. I struggled to get my threep up off the asphalt and got up just in time to stare into the car, which revved up and hit me again. It dragged the threep under its carriage and cracked the head of the threep against the pavement so hard that I could hear the shattering of the head case a second before I lost connection entirely.

The rental threep was comprehensively trashed.

I ported myself back into my own threep in the valet parking of the Hotel Monaco, found my way out into the street, and ran toward Independence Hall, which by this time was crawling with park rangers and Philadelphia police. One of the latter went out of his way to intercept me. I flashed my ID onto my chest screen and got through, to find Vann standing over Ramsey's dead body. She saw me.

"Where's the bag?" she asked.

"Gone. With the guy who took it."

Vann nodded and then motioned to Ramsey. "This wasn't subtle at all. Murdering an FBI agent right out in the open."

"They don't want anything leading back to them." I pointed to the bag that Ramsey had traded for. "What's in there?"

"A fucking box of doughnuts," Vann said. "I don't think the exchange meant anything. I think the Wawa bags were just a way of identifying themselves to each other."

There was a commotion and three suits appeared. One of them was Lara Burgess, head of the Bureau's Philadelphia branch. The Philly FBI office was two blocks away. They could have run here, and it looked like they did. The suits flanking Burgess moved to tend to Ramsey. Burgess turned her attention to us.

"Agent Vann," Burgess said, "you have exactly ten seconds to tell me what the fuck is going on and why one of my agents is dead."

"Agent Ramsey is dead because she took a bribe to destroy evidence in my investigation, and the people who bribed her paid her off with a double tap, Director Burgess."

"Bullshit."

"Shane," Vann said.

"I have her confession recorded, Director Burgess," I said. "Just tell me where you want me to send it." Burgess looked at me, confused, and then I realized the last time she saw me I was in another threep entirely. She figured it out after a second and turned her attention back to Vann.

Who was ready for her. "So, Director Burgess, your agent went out of her way to fuck up an ongoing investigation, and we both know how you went out of your way just a couple of days ago to run interference for her against us."

Burgess stiffened up at that. "Watch yourself, Agent Vann."

"That's funny," Vann said. "Your agent interferes with our investigation for a bribe, your lab is sloppy enough to let her fuck up its evidence, and you tried to screw us to cover for your agent's fuckup, and you're telling me to watch myself. How about this, Burgess. I'm going to give you two choices here. The first is that from here on out, you give me and Shane everything we need to do our job, top priority, no bullshit, in which case we all make nice. The second choice is that you don't, in which case, fuck you, and I'm going to make it my mission to make sure at the end of all this, you release a statement about how you have left the Bureau to spend more time with your family. You can count on that. So tell me, Director Burgess, which of these you want. You have exactly ten seconds."

You wouldn't be able to tell it from my threep, but I was gawking at Vann in open admiration. It's one thing to bad cop an electrician or a medical assistant or even an FBI agent. But playing bad cop to an actual director of the Bureau took some chutzpah. And here Vann was doing it. Without blinking.

It was Burgess who blinked instead. "What do you need from me?"

"I need you to gather Alton Ortiz and Keshia Sanborn for me, right now, and deliver them to the Bureau. We need a room to talk to them in. I need your lab, the one that fucked up, to redeem itself and give us top priority for analysis." She pointed to the threep next to Ramsey. "I need everything on this thing and who was piloting it, and on the gun it used to kill Ramsey. I need a sandwich because I haven't had lunch yet."

"I can do all that," Burgess said.

"As in, now," Vann said.

"I understand you, Agent Vann."

Vann turned to me. "What do you want

368

for Christmas?" she said.

"I need to run a license plate and access to all the closed-circuit cameras in the area," I said. "I also need to get out an APB on three individuals."

"Who are they?" Burgess asked.

"I can give you their images soon. We'll need to run them through the database. I also need a monitor. You can put it in the room you set aside for us. And I, uh, need someone to go get the threep I left on Sixth."

Burgess looked at me. "Left?"

"It got hit. Twice." I pointed down Chestnut, toward the rental place. "And someone's going to need to go explain what happened to the threep."

"I assume you're going to try to put the cost of this threep onto our budget, Agent Shane?"

I looked at Vann, who shrugged. "No, Director Burgess. This one's on me."

"You don't seem to have very good luck with threeps, Shane."

"You wouldn't be the first to notice that, Director."

Burgess nodded. "I'll give you everything you've asked for, and put a priority on it all, Agent Vann, Agent Shane. But, Vann, a small request."

"What is it, Director Burgess?"

"Try not to be as much of an asshole today to everyone else as you've just been to me." She nodded at Ramsey's body. "Everyone in the office lost a colleague today. And whether or not she was indeed taking bribes, the fact of the matter is she was liked by everyone. If you run her down today, there's a very good chance someone will shoot you."

"Didn't your parents teach you to look both ways before you walk out into the street?" Vann asked. She was watching the video where I got hit by the car, and used the conference monitor's remote control to scrub the replay back and forth. She was enjoying the sudden jerk in perspective as my threep went flying.

"I don't think looking both ways will matter when a car is specifically aiming at you," I said.

"Maybe not," Vann allowed. Before she could continue, Keshia Sanborn and Alton Ortiz were escorted into the conference room by two agents. The agents sat them down and left, quickly.

Keshia Sanborn didn't waste time. "This is *outrageous,*" she said. "It would be bad enough for you to haul my client in here, but grabbing *me* —"

"Shut up," Vann said, and then turned to me. "Show them."

I popped a video up on the monitor in the conference room. It was of Ramsey handing over the IV bag, and then being shot in the head and chest. Ortiz winced at the image. Sanborn looked at it, uncomprehending.

"What is this?" she asked.

"This is a video of an FBI agent being shot to death after she handed off that second IV bag to someone who bribed her to get it," Vann said. "You know, Ms. Sanborn, the one that stood the best chance of clearing your client of the murder charge we're going to lay at his feet."

Sanborn opened her mouth to say something, then closed it quickly.

"Oh, look at that," Vann said. "It's always nice when a lawyer remembers they might need a lawyer themselves."

"What is going on?" Ortiz said, to me.

"As near as we can tell, your lawyer has been feeding information about your case to a third party," I said. "That third party has been consistently setting you up to be the fall guy for Duane Chapman's murder by tampering with, destroying, or hiding evidence." I scrubbed back in the video to the handoff. "Here, for example. That IV

371

bag is gone now. We don't know where it is."

"And if we hadn't lied to your lawyer about where we were going to be, we'd all be over at Chapman's town house now, looking for it in vain, because we wouldn't know it had been stolen," Vann said. "We wouldn't be able to find it, and that would make us angry and suspicious at you, Mr. Ortiz. And then you would be in a much worse position, and Ms. Sanborn here would be pushing that plea bargain on you again."

Ortiz turned to Sanborn. "Is any of this true?" he said to her.

"Alton, look," Sanborn began.

Ortiz put his hand up. "You should have said 'no,' " he said. "That's what you should have said right off. You are so *fucking* fired."

Vann tapped on the conference room glass to get the attention of the agents, and signaled for one of them to come back in. "Take her out but keep her around," she said, pointing to Sanborn. Sanborn left without uttering a word.

After Sanborn left I turned to Ortiz. "You're entitled to a lawyer," I said.

Ortiz laughed, bitterly. "Yeah, because that's been working out so well for me up to this point." He put his head in his hands and held it there for a couple of minutes. Then he dropped his hands, took a deep breath, and looked at the two of us. "Just ask me your questions."

"Why did you run from us earlier this week?" Vann asked.

"Because Duane's apartment burned down and I thought you guys knew about my cousin."

"You didn't ask your cousin to burn down the apartment," I said.

"No, but it burned down anyway. When I saw you, I panicked. I don't have any excuse."

"You knew Duane was having an affair with Kim Silva."

"Yes. We were friends. He told me right off."

"You were also having an affair with Marla Chapman."

"Yes."

"Why?" Vann asked.

Ortiz looked at her, confused. "What do you mean, why? Because I could, I guess. Because Duane was screwing someone else, and I wasn't having sex with anyone, and Marla wanted to and made the move on me, and I didn't think it mattered."

"Did you love Marla Chapman?" I asked.

"No. It wasn't about that. Marla was

angry and I was horny. I liked Marla. I think she liked me. But I think for her it was more about getting her own back."

"And you were okay with this," Vann said.

"Agent Vann, I'm not proud of the fact I was happy to be getting laid," Ortiz said. "But I was."

"So you didn't want Duane dead?" I asked.

"No, of course I didn't. And Marla never said she wanted him dead, either, if that's what you're going to ask next."

"So she didn't want him dead, but she did want him divorced," I said. "And you were happy to help with that."

"Agent Shane, I think I have it on pretty good authority that the marriage wasn't going to last," Ortiz said. "I didn't see the harm in helping the two of them get it over with. Like ripping off a Band-Aid."

"So you ask your cousin to help you on the same day Duane dies."

"I asked Pedro before then. The outage we planned just happened to be on the same day."

"It's a hell of a coincidence," Vann said.

Ortiz held his hands out, pleadingly. "I don't know what to tell you, Agent Vann."

"How did you get connected with Ms. Sanborn?" I asked.

"She got hold of me," Ortiz said. "Told me the league expressed concern about my situation and offered pro bono assistance. I don't have money for lawyers. I was happy to get someone for free."

"And what did you tell her?" Vann asked.

"What do you mean what did I tell her? I told her everything. I told her about Marla and me, I told her about Duane and Kim Silva, I told her about Duane sneaking Silva's supplements —"

"But you didn't tell her about the second bag," I said.

"It slipped my mind. I told her about the apartment, and everything in it. I even told them about the stupid cat."

"The cat?" I said.

"Yeah, a cat," Ortiz said. "Silva kept a cat in the apartment. Duane said Silva said she had a surprise for him and it involved the cat staying alive, so he better treat the cat nicely."

"What sort of surprise?"

"I don't know. I don't think Duane knew either. He knew there was a data vault on the cat's collar, so it was probably something on that, but he never asked what was on it."

"And *did* he treat the cat nicely?" Vann asked.

"Hell, I don't know. He must have, because Silva and he were still doing it. You don't screw around with someone who hates your pets. What happened to the cat, anyway?"

"It's dead," Vann said, glancing over to me.

"Someone killed the *cat*? Jesus Christ."

"Silva thinks Duane was in love with her," I said to Ortiz.

Ortiz shrugged. "Maybe?"

"Just maybe?"

"Duane liked her. And they had similar . . . I think *tastes* is the best way to put it. Duane was a little out there. Did you see the threeps he had at the apartment?" I nodded. "Duane used them all. He liked to switch things up. And that's something he couldn't really do with Marla."

"Because her plumbing was all permanently one gender," Vann said.

"Because Marla is very vanilla," Ortiz said. "She liked what she liked and only liked what she liked."

"And you were fine with that."

"I'm pretty uncomplicated myself. Duane was more complicated and Silva was happy to be complicated with him. Is that love? I don't think so. But Duane was good with it."

"Do you think Marla Chapman would

take a shot at Kim Silva?" I asked.

"Maybe? Marla was angry a lot. But she didn't have a gun in the house and I'm pretty sure she didn't know how to shoot. And she sure as hell wasn't suicidal. I can see her trying to go after Silva, sure. If not to kill her then to cause her pain. But not the way they said she did. And she wouldn't have killed herself afterward. Trust me on that one."

"And you covered all of this with Sanborn."

"We haven't talked much about Marla's death, but the rest of it, yeah," Ortiz said. "Why wouldn't I? She's my lawyer. Was my lawyer. I thought she was on my side." Ortiz fell silent and looked at the monitor, where Ramsey was handing off the Wawa bag to the man in the hoodie. "So you're saying this is my fault."

"What do you mean?" I asked.

Ortiz pointed at Ramsey. "I mean if I hadn't said anything about the second IV bag in front of Sanborn, this agent would still be alive. That's on me."

"Agent Ramsey made her own choices," Vann said.

"Okay, but one of her choices was to go get that bag. The bag I told you and my lawyer about."

"You were played, Mr. Ortiz," Vann said. "That's all. If you want to feel responsible for what happened because you were duped, that's on you. But maybe don't."

Ortiz nodded at this and then looked back and forth between the both of us. "So what now?"

"We're not going to hold you, if that's what you're asking," I said. "But I think you should stay in our custody for a couple of days."

"Because someone might try to kill me like they killed Duane and Marla."

"I think it would be good to err on the side of caution," I said.

"Hell yes it would," Ortiz said, and looked back at the monitor. "So this guy took the IV bag."

"Yes."

"So there's no evidence that I didn't kill Duane."

"We didn't need the bag to prove your innocence," Vann said. "We needed it to prove someone else's guilt."

"But you don't even have that." Ortiz pointed to the monitor. "He's got the bag. And you don't have him, right?"

"No, we don't," I said.

"So you have nothing."

I turned to Vann. "Can we show him?"

378

"I don't see why not," Vann said.

I reached over to Vann's satchel on the conference room table, opened it and took something from it, and placed it in front of Ortiz. It was an evidence bag with syringes in it.

"What is this?" he asked.

"Syringes full of the IV supplement mixture," I said. "Before the handoff we took some out of the bag. It's being processed now."

"Because we're not stupid, you see," Vann said.

CHAPTER TWENTY-ONE

"Let's run this down quickly," Burgess said to us, in the conference room. She pulled out a legal pad. "First, the supplement bag you provided contains the pharmaceutical compound that was trademarked under the name Attentex. The lab thanks you, incidentally, for telling them specifically what to look for. It made things go much more quickly."

"Delighted to help," Vann said.

Burgess looked up at this to judge Vann's level of sarcasm, but kept going. "Second, the Philadelphia ME also reran bloodwork to look for Attentex. She did not find it."

"Really," I said.

"She did not," Burgess said. "But she said she found compounds that are components of Attentex. Apparently it breaks down over time. She started talking about hydrogen bonds and I told her I didn't care, just to send the full report, which she's going to do

380

in the next few minutes. The short version is this is as close as you're going to get to that particular smoking gun."

"Good enough," I said. "What's next?"

Burgess flipped the page on her legal pad. "Your license plate was lifted off another car a few days ago, so that's mostly a dead end, except for the fact that a car with that license plate — a different car — was caught blowing through a toll on the Mass Pike last night. Brighton/Cambridge exit. No electronic payment setup so the plate was photographed to be charged."

"That would explain Marla Chapman showing up at Kim Silva's place," I said to Vann.

"Could be," Vann said.

"Now, the three men in the car," Burgess continued. "These are delightful people, incidentally. Agent Shane, the man you chased through town was Christian Erickson, your basic low-life scrub who has done a little bit of time for all sorts of minor things all around the Eastern Seaboard. We're working with the Philly police on this one. They have someone parked outside his last known residence."

"He's not going to show up there," Vann said.

"He's not a rocket scientist. He might.

Now. The driver of the vehicle is Terry Abbot. He did time a few years ago for assault and battery but has kept out of trouble since then. Well, until today, anyway. He was a livery driver for a long time but is recently employed privately as a driver by some company named Leavitt Shipping."

"Anything shady about Leavitt?" I asked.

"Not that we can find in the very little time you have given us to look," Burgess said. "It's a local company, been around since the 1930s, was acquired by some multinational about ten years ago."

"Which one?"

Burgess flipped to the next page of her legal pad. "Richu Enterprises? I don't know them."

"They're based out of Singapore," I said.

Burgess looked over at me. "And you have this information right at your fingertips how, Agent Shane?"

"It's been a long week."

"I don't doubt that. We also have Philly PD looking for Mr. Abbot. Your third man was a bit of a mystery to us since he had no criminal record to speak of, so he didn't turn up in our databases. But since you stood still long enough to get a nonfuzzy shot of him, Agent Shane —"

"There was a reason I stood in front of a

moving car," I said to Vann, who shrugged.

"— we went ahead and did an image search of him on the Internet. And through the magic of social media we have one Phillip Tucker, originally of Ipswich, England, whose online profiles have him as an executive assistant to a Martin Lau, who is —"

"Legal counsel for Richu," I said.

"I have him as counsel for Leavitt Shipping, but yes," Burgess said. "Neither Lau nor Tucker are citizens, so when they attempt to leave the country they will be invited to a chat by our colleagues at border control."

"They're already gone," Vann said.

"It's possible," Burgess agreed. "In which case they won't be coming back anytime soon." She set her legal pad down. "Now. What does all of this mean to you?"

"It means it's time for you to bring Ms. Sanborn in, Director Burgess."

"Vann, one of my agents died today. I need to know what's going on."

"Bring in Sanborn, Burgess," Vann said. "And then stay in the room."

Burgess stood up. "Fine. Just so you know, Sanborn got herself a lawyer."

"That's fine," Vann said. "We like lawyers."

■ ■ ■ ■

"Ms. Sanborn has nothing to say to you," Sanborn's lawyer, a particularly unctuous fellow named Dawson Curtis, said. He sat next to his client, who as promised was keeping her mouth shut. They were on one side of the conference room table. Vann and Burgess and I were on the other.

"I don't need her to talk," Vann said. "What I need her and you to do is listen. And look." Vann shoved the evidence bag of syringes at the two of them. "That's the evidence that shows that Ortiz didn't murder Chapman but that someone else did. We have it despite your client's attempt to make it disappear. We have warrants for her phones and computers and every single scrap of communication she's had for the last three years. Her former client Alton Ortiz is working with us and has told us everything he's disclosed to her."

"He's currently under federal protection very far away from here, incidentally," I said.

"Yes he most certainly is," Vann agreed. "Because of your client, a federal agent is dead and we have evidence linking her to the assault of another federal agent —"

I waved here.

"— not to mention an entire raft of other charges." Vann turned her attention to Sanborn. "You were in the room when we read out the charges to your former client. Most of those accrue to you now."

"Plus others," I volunteered.

"Oh so many others," Vann said. "So, no, Sanborn. I don't need you to talk. I don't need you to do anything. We already *have* you. And what we already have you for is enough to keep you locked up until you are roughly older than the fucking moon. I didn't bring you here to talk, Sanborn. I brought you here just so I could have the pleasure of telling you how much I'm looking forward to having you rot away the rest of your goddamned life." Vann pushed up from the table, and then looked down at Curtis. "I'm done with your client."

"Wait," Sanborn said.

"No," Vann said. "You're not *talking,* Sanborn."

"Wait," Sanborn said again. It was obvious she was about a minute away from tears.

Vann waited.

"Keshia," Curtis said. Sanborn held up her hand. Curtis sighed but kept quiet.

"You told Alton that you weren't interested in him," Sanborn said. "That you would trade for higher-ups."

"We do trade for higher-ups," Vann said. "But not after an FBI agent has been shot dead in front of Independence Hall, Sanborn." Vann pointed at Burgess. "Tell Director Burgess here that you deserve leniency after one of her people was assassinated after receiving information you provided. I want to see you actually do it."

Sanborn looked over at Burgess, who was a stone. "I didn't know that was the plan."

"Oh, for fuck's sake," Vann said. "Duane Chapman's dead. Marla Chapman's dead. Alex Kaufmann's dead. Kim Silva was shot through the gut. For Christ's sake, someone tried to murder Silva's *cat.*" Vann sat back down. "All of that happened *before* you made whatever call you made today. So don't you dare tell me that you thought Agent Ramsey's death wasn't part of the *plan.*"

Sanborn started crying for real.

We all watched her sob for a bit, and then Curtis cleared his throat. "Let's talk about what you want," he said.

Vann pointed to Sanborn. "This is doing me just *fine,* Mr. Curtis."

Curtis blinked at this, and then turned to me. "Agent Shane?"

"We want all of it," I said. "Everything."

"That covers a lot," Curtis said.

"Yes it does," I said. "Your client is going to sit here and tell every little bit of it to the agents here in the Philadelphia office. She's going to tell them knowing that they know she helped kill their colleague."

"And when she's done, what then?" Curtis asked.

I looked over to Burgess. "Your agent. Your call," I said.

Burgess stared at Sanborn like she was a bug, and did that for close to a full minute. "She gives us everything and everyone and we'll talk," she finally said. "But let me be very clear, Mr. Curtis, Ms. Sanborn. *Someone* is going to spend the rest of their life in prison for the death of Agent Ramsey. If your client doesn't want it to be her, then she damn well better convince me it should be someone else. Are we clear?"

Curtis nodded. "May I have the room for a few minutes?" he asked. "I need to confer with my client."

"It's nice to know I'm not the only person you've strong-armed today," Burgess said to Vann, outside the conference room.

Vann shrugged. "It's my gift," she said.

"Interesting way of putting it," Burgess said. She motioned with her head to Sanborn, who was still crying. "Do you want to lead the interrogation?"

Vann shook her head. "We have other people to deal with before they can all get their stories straight. I only have one question for her and then your people can do the rest."

Curtis looked up and motioned us into the room. "How do you want to do this?" he asked when we were back in.

"That's on the director," Vann said. "What I need to know is this: Who at the league did she give her information to?"

"No one at the league," Sanborn said.

"No one," Vann said, skeptically.

Sanborn shook her head.

"You need to explain this, quick."

"I have hundreds of thousands of dollars in school loans. I have credit card debt. My parents are on a fixed income and my brother and sister don't help them out. I'm junior counsel for the NAHL. They don't pay us all that much. I'm broke, all right? Last year I was approached with a deal. Share confidential details of NAHL business and legal issues when I was asked to, and they'd help."

"So they give you money."

Sanborn shook her head. "My mom called to tell me my father has started selling driftwood sculptures to a private buyer for a ridiculous amount. Dad uses half of that to

388

pay down my loans because parents can do that tax-free. Nothing comes to me directly, but I get the benefit of it anyway."

"Who is the buyer?" I asked.

"He doesn't know. It's through an art dealer." Sanborn gave a little laugh. "Dad has been doing driftwood sculptures as a hobby since I was a kid, and now magically there's a market. He calls himself the Grandma Moses of driftwood."

"Why you?" Vann asked.

"I work in Oliver Medina's office. I see or hear just about everything."

"But the league told you to represent Ortiz."

Sanborn shook her head. "I suggested it after I was told to. Medina thought it was a good idea. He's a proponent of pro bono work."

"Who told you?" Vann asked. "Who is your contact?"

"It's mostly through encrypted texts at this point. But the first time, I talked to a woman. She said she was representing another interested party. This was when we were in Washington, D.C. We were laying down the initial groundwork for putting a franchise into the city."

"You met her while you were doing league business?" I asked.

"No, at the hotel bar. She bought me a drink and I thought she was trying to pick me up." Another small laugh. "I mean, I guess she did."

I thought about it for a moment and flipped up a picture on the conference room monitor. "Is this her?" I asked.

Sanborn looked and her eyes got wide. "Yes," she said. "How did you know?"

Vann and Burgess turned to look at the image.

It was Lena Fowler.

CHAPTER TWENTY-TWO

"I hear you destroyed yet another threep," Tony said, as I connected to him. Vann and I were heading toward Lena Fowler's house as quickly as we possibly could, which in the early evening Washington, D.C., traffic was not nearly fast enough. Vann was driving. As she was driving my parents' car, I was nervous about it.

"How did you hear about that?" I asked.

"You have me working with your people here in the FBI office enough that I've had time to develop my own sources," Tony said. "So is it true?"

"I did not destroy another threep," I said. "A car did."

"You got hit by a car."

"Twice."

"So, once for the experience and twice to be sure?" Tony asked. "Hey, weren't you hit by a car when you were a kid?"

"It was a truck."

"Same concept. Three times is a fetish, Chris," Tony said. "Which is your business. But it gets pretty pricey. You might want to take up a less expensive hobby, like cocaine."

"I'll keep it in mind," I said. "I need something from you, Tony."

"Of course you do," he said. "It's one of the things I like best about you."

"So the IV bag had Attentex in it."

"Of course it did."

"But Attentex isn't effective without corresponding electrical stimulation."

"That's what Tayla told us."

"So what I need you to do now is to find how to provide that electrical stimulation."

"Aside from the obvious answer of, however it was that Neuracel did it, I assume."

"You are correct. And here's the extra challenge."

"I can't wait."

"Figure out how it could have been done in a way that would affect Duane Chapman and Clemente Salcido and Kim Silva."

"Is that all? I thought you were going to ask something hard."

"And if you can get the answer to me in the next hour or so that would be great."

"Ah, okay, there it is," Tony said. "You

know I'm charging you out the ass for this one."

"With the amount of work I give you I think I should get a volume discount," I said.

"Yeah, no. There's that old saying: Fast, cheap, and good, you get to pick two. The two you just picked are fast and good. Cheap has just left the building."

"Then make it worth my money, Tony."

"I always do," he said, and disconnected.

"Tony's on it," I said.

"I don't know why we don't just hire him at the Bureau," Vann said.

"I asked him about it once. He said he makes more as a consultant and besides he's already got the security clearance so he's got the only cool thing about the gig."

"It's not the only cool thing," Vann said. "You also get to shoot people."

"That's not actually all *that* cool, though, is it," I said. "Blood. Death. Paperwork."

Vann looked over to me. "I'm having a long day, Chris. Indulge me."

We turned onto Fowler's street and immediately saw a festival of flashing red and blue lights in front of her house.

"Well, fuck me," Vann said, and drove up to the barrier set up in the road.

A cop came up and started making rotating motions. "Turn it around," he said.

Vann grabbed her wallet and flipped out her badge. "Tell me where to park," she said.

The cop was not impressed. "I told you to turn it around."

"And I told you to tell me where to park," Vann said. "But if you want to get into a pissing match about it, Officer" — she read his badge — "Wheeler, I'm sure we can find a way to have you be a school safety officer for the rest of your natural life."

Wheeler looked at Vann, exasperated. "What are you, an asshole?"

"Yes," Vann said. "I am an asshole. Now tell me where to park."

Wheeler decided Vann wasn't worth his time and moved on to the next car he wanted to turn around. Vann decided that the car was already in its parking space and got out.

"If we get towed, you're paying for it," I said.

Vann waved me forward, to Fowler's house. Inside, Arlington police milled around, trying to look important but mostly gawking. There was a detective in charge of the scene. Vann ordered him out of the house.

Fowler was dead, to begin with. But she wasn't the only dead person in the house.

"Does he look familiar to you?" Vann pointed to a man slumped on the floor of the living room. Roughly half his face had been carved away by the knife Fowler had in her dead hand, but what remained was indeed familiar.

"Terry Abbot," I said. You don't quickly forget the person who ran you over twice.

"Uh-huh." Vann walked into the kitchen. "And here we have Phillip Tucker. Dead as a doornail."

"How?"

"More stabbing, it looks like. All those years at the Western Hemisphere Institute taught her some skill with a knife."

I looked at Fowler, who had had a bullet applied directly to her forehead. It appeared to have been provided to her by Abbot, who was still clutching a gun. Fowler had another bullet wound, this one to her side. I was supposing that one came first.

"I've found contestant number three," Vann said, from farther inside the house. I followed her back to a bathroom, where a third man lay propped up between the toilet and the tub, a trail of blood behind him leading back to the kitchen.

"Martin Lau," I said.

"Abbot and Tucker had to really be moving to get back here in time for this," Vann said. "Whatever *this* is."

I went back to Fowler and bent down and noticed something on her wrist. It was a number written in black Sharpie: 73495. I called Vann over and we looked at it together.

"What is that, a zip code?" Vann said.

I looked it up internally and it came up a blank. "No," I said, but Vann was already looking around the living room. Abruptly she walked away, toward the back of the house. I got up and followed.

Vann was in Fowler's bedroom, sliding open the closet door. "There it is," she said. She turned to me and pointed into the closet. "Enter the code," she said.

I walked over to the closet and looked. There was a fire safe in there, with a keypad. I entered "73495." The safe door beeped and unlocked.

Inside the safe was a handgun with ammunition and magazine separately stored, a passport and a birth certificate, another passport and another birth certificate with a different name from the first set, about $5,000 in U.S. currency and another thousand in euros and pounds, and a large folder with a Post-it note on it.

The Post-it note said: *Agents Vann and Shane, FBI.*

Inside the folder was a truly impressive amount of highly incriminating evidence.

"She knew we were coming," I said, quickly thumbing through the pages.

"She saw the body count rising," Vann replied. "She knew we'd get back to her."

"There's something underneath the folder," I said. I reached in and pulled out a computer tablet. The screen was blank. I clicked the power button once, gently, and the screen woke up, showing a fish-eye view of the kitchen and living room from above, the carnage gently curving away from the focal point above the kitchen table.

Vann stared at the tablet for a moment and then walked out of the room. A second later she appeared on the screen as she walked into the living room.

"It's live," I yelled. I looked more closely at the screen and saw the timer. "And it's recording."

Vann walked back into the bedroom. She nodded at the tablet. "Can you scrub back?"

I nodded and moved the time frame backward. There was a bustle of activity as Arlington police scurried backward through the scene, followed by long minutes of nothing but dead people. Then the dead people sprang back to life and after a few seconds of reverse murder, arranged themselves at

Fowler's kitchen table. We stopped and let the video play forward in real time, with no sound.

The four of them sat at Fowler's table, with Fowler and Lau clearly arguing. This went on for a while, and then Lau said something to Abbot, sitting across from Fowler. Abbot wrenched out his gun and shot at Fowler, who moved to the side, reached under the table, and produced the knife. The knife slashed left, slicing Lau in the neck. He staggered and fell off his chair, clutching at his wound and struggling back away from Fowler.

Abbot fired again at least twice, missing both times. Fowler switched knife hands and slashed up at Abbot, slicing off a fair amount of his face and then slashing him a second time in the neck. Tucker by this time was up and trying to move frantically away from Fowler, who grabbed him and expertly nicked at least three of his major arteries. This kept her preoccupied enough that she didn't see the fallen Abbot raise his gun, and, when she turned to face him, shoot her in the forehead.

Fowler went down, still holding her knife. Abbot lowered his weapon and didn't move anymore.

"That was unpleasant," I said.

"Do you have that?" Vann asked me.

"Already transferred the recording."

Vann nodded and left the bedroom again. I set down the tablet, picked up the heavy file folder, and followed her into the kitchen. She reached the table and looked under it. Then she motioned for me to do the same.

There was a snub-nosed revolver taped to the underside of the table, and dangling tape from where the knife used to be.

"Why did she pick the knife?" I asked Vann.

"Pretty sure she just reached under and that's what she came up with."

"If she had gotten the gun, she might still be alive."

"If she was alive, I don't think she would have told us about the files. She'd still have wiggle room to come out on top." Vann pointed to the code on Fowler's dead wrist. "This is meant to be an 'if I'm going to hell, I'm taking you with me' gesture."

"Nice she thought of us when she did that."

"Well, then let's give her an honor guard," Vann said.

A man showed up in the doorway, flanked on either side by uniformed policemen, and stared down Vann. "Who the fuck are you to tell my people to vacate a crime scene?" he said.

"I think that's the Arlington chief of police," I said to Vann, helpfully. She looked at me witheringly.

"I asked you a question," the chief of police said.

"I'm the FBI," Vann told him. "And your people can have it back now. We got everything we came for."

"How are you holding up?" I asked Vann. "It's been a long day."

"I could use a smoke," Vann said, looking at me significantly.

"Parents' car," I said, as the car turned onto Kalorama Road.

"Your parents probably have a dozen cars," Vann said. "They wouldn't even know."

"Tell you what," I said, as the car parked itself at the curb across from the Tudor-style house we were about to visit. "You try that line of reasoning on my mother. If you can get her to go along with it, you can smoke in this car all you like. But you have to try it out on her."

"Pass," Vann said.

"She's very fond of you, you know."

"Not fond enough, apparently." Vann got

out of the car. We walked up the steps to the front door nestled in a pretty turret.

"We're here to see Amelie Parker," I said, to the woman who answered the door.

"It's nearly eleven at night," the woman said.

"Yes it is," Vann said. "Amelie Parker, please."

"She's indisposed right now. You can't come in."

"We insist," Vann said, and presented the woman with our warrant. The woman stared at it blankly for a moment.

"Who are you?" I asked the woman.

"Winifred Glover," she said. "Ms. Parker's nighttime caretaker."

"Ms. Glover, you have to let us into the house," I said. "We have a warrant for Ms. Parker's arrest."

Glover stared at us blankly again. "How . . . how are you going to arrest her?" she finally said. "She's a Haden."

"A transport is coming behind us," I said. "In the meantime, Ms. Glover, show us to her, please."

Glover looked genuinely miserable and confused. Vann, who was already going through nicotine withdrawal, was starting to look impatient. I held up a hand to keep her from snapping Glover's head off. "What is it?" I asked Glover.

"She's not here," Glover said, in an explosive rush. "Her body, I mean. It's gone. Her travel creche is gone. I came to the house for my shift and she wasn't here. I don't know where she is."

"Where is she usually?" I asked. Glover pointed to a large ground-floor room facing toward the back of the house. Vann went off toward it. I turned my attention back to Glover. "Did you ask the daytime caretaker where she went?"

"Carol wasn't here when I got here," she said. "No one was. I let myself in with my code and the house was empty."

"When was that?"

"Six tonight."

Vann walked back into the room. "Everything's unplugged," she said. "I'm checking the rest of the house." She headed off again.

"Does Ms. Parker usually go off unannounced?" I asked Glover.

"No," she said. "She only leaves the house — physically, I mean — once or twice a year. She will do it if her family are having the holidays somewhere remote enough that she might have trouble connecting through a threep. She did last year when the family had Christmas in Patagonia."

"And when she does that, how does she

usually travel?"

"She has a car come pick her up, of course," Glover said. "And then her family's company sends a jet for her. It has one with support for a Haden's creche."

"Which airport?"

"When I went with her we always went out of National."

"Vann!" I yelled.

"Oh, look, it's you again," Tony said, as he connected with me. "I just sent you what you asked me for earlier."

"Thank you," I said. "It was very helpful."

"If you got it, what are you getting touch with me now for? It's almost midnight."

"I have a hypothetical for you."

"Oh, this should be good."

"Let's say you or I am on a private jet out of National, heading toward Sarajevo."

"A little esoteric for a destination, but all right."

"If we wanted to connect with our private space, would we be able to?"

"This is a high-end private jet?"

"About as high-end as they come, yes."

"And hypothetically where is this plane right now?"

"Somewhere between Newfoundland and the southern tip of Ireland."

403

"Okay. Then, yeah, probably. Depending on where the plane is, the signal is either going to go through a floating wireless relay to the undersea cables, or is going to bounce off a satellite. If it's the former the lag is going to be pretty minimal. If it's the latter you've got like a three- to four-hundred-millisecond delay, because the speed of light is a thing that happens."

"Okay. Next hypothetical."

"Oh boy."

"Let's say there was a Haden fugitive from justice flying to a country without an extradition treaty with the United States."

"Sure. Like, possibly, Bosnia-Herzegovina."

"Yes."

"Theoretically."

"Correct. Now, let's say you have a warrant to access their private space, which is on a U.S. server, which you also have a warrant for."

"Belt and suspenders, got it."

"But the private space is encrypted."

"How encrypted?"

"Massively."

"And what kind of server is this? Shared server? Maintained by a third party who has access?"

"Private server, personal space designed

by others but personally maintained. No one in or out without the owner's key."

"Then your warrant's not very useful. You can take the server offline, if you want, and lock your theoretical fugitive out of their personal space. But if it's state-of-the-art encryption, you're not getting into it anytime soon. When did you want to be into it?"

"Hypothetically, before the plane lands."

"So, no. Not going to happen."

"Not at all."

"If you can find someone who worked on the space who left a back door into the place, maybe. Or if there's something so egregiously wonky with the code that it exploitably breaks the world. Or if our theoretical fugitive left an open-ended invite to a friend or family member. Then possibly."

"Let's go back one."

"Wonky code."

"Yes. How easy is that to exploit?"

Tony sighed, which is an affectation in a Haden but is effective nevertheless. "Chris, for God's sake, just tell me what server it is and what I'm looking for and how much time I have."

"So you're saying you can do it."

"I said no such thing. I'll try it. We'll see if it works. Send the relevant details over and

I'll get on it."

"You're the best, Tony."

"Yes I am. Just remember you said that when you get my invoice."

I disconnected and turned to Vann. We were both still in Parker's house. Glover, not knowing what else to do, had served Vann tea.

"Tony's on it," I said. "Ready for your part?"

Vann nodded and then turned. "Ms. Glover," she said.

Glover appeared from the kitchen. "Yes, Miss Vann."

Vann visibly winced at being called "miss." I decided not to say anything about it.

"Amelie's father is the CEO of Labram, is he not?"

"CEO, yes. Her grandfather is chairman."

"Do you know how to reach either?"

"I have contact numbers for both and for Amelie's mother and sister, in case of emergency."

"Let's start with the father," Vann said.

"It's very late for a phone call, Miss Vann."

"I know. He's going to want to take my call."

CHAPTER TWENTY-THREE

I rose up through the water of the lake and took stock of my surroundings. The jetty with the sailboat was roughly a hundred meters away. A healthy swim, virtual or real. I set myself into a lazy backstroke and slowly made my way to shore. I emerged out of the water with clothes sopping wet. They dried unrealistically quickly. By the time I made my way to the house, they and I were entirely dry.

None of the simulated house servants bothered me as I wandered through the house. Either they didn't register me at all or their programming dictated that since I was neither announced nor invited, I didn't need to be dealt with. I stepped in front of one servant to see what he would do and was amused by the quick emotionless spin he made to avoid me. I wasn't invisible, then. Merely unimportant.

The sound of music came from the second

floor of the mansion. I followed it up the stairs and found it emanating from a large, stately library room. Amelie Parker was in the room as well, on a chaise longue, reading a book. I peered at the spine. It was *The Great Gatsby,* which I thought was a little on the nose.

"How's the book?" I asked.

Parker startled and dropped the book. She stared at me as if I were a magically appearing ghost, which was fair, all things considered. "How?" she started, then stopped.

"I got in through your lake," I said. "The one you never had the coding finished for. It's actually more complicated than just that, of course. But basically that's how I did it."

Parker stared at me hard for a moment, silently, and then was confused again.

"You can't boot me out," I told her. "I glitched in, so your space isn't registering my invitation. As far as your server knows, I'm supposed to be here. Also, technically speaking, I have a warrant to be here as well. Your server is in U.S. territory."

"*Why* are you here?" Parker said.

"I wanted to tell you what I know," I said. "And then I wanted to give you a chance to turn yourself in voluntarily."

"Turn myself in," Amelie said, and smiled.

"For what?"

I walked into the room and admired the books on the shelves. They were all bound in leather and the simulated smell of the library was intoxicating. "This is a really beautiful room, Amelie," I said.

"Thank you."

"You killed Duane Chapman," I said. "Not intentionally, I know. He wasn't your target. Kim Silva was. But you didn't know Silva and Chapman were lovers. You didn't know she let him sample her Labram supplements."

"I don't know what you're talking about," Parker said.

I reached up and took a book down from the shelf, a classic children's book from Catherynne Valente. I held it up to Parker. "I love this book."

"I do too," she said, confused.

I set the book on the table near me and continued. "A few years ago your start-up company bought the intellectual property of a company called Neuracel, including a compound called Attentex," I said. "It wasn't useful as an additive in your supplements, because it caused seizures and other side effects. But you figured out another use for it. If you had enough information on individual Hilketa athletes, you could tailor their supplements so that the Attentex you put into it would subtly hamper their performance. It's pharmaceutically inert unless there's an electrical charge applied to the person taking it in, so you could pick and choose when and where to use it. It breaks down quickly in the bloodstream and doesn't show up in drug tests because no one's looking for positives on Attentex or its components."

"I don't remember this compound you're talking about," Parker said.

"Yes you do," I said. "Specifically, a year ago you did a test drive of Attentex on Clemente Salcido. He was coming on board to endorse Labram supplements, and the company had all the information they needed to create a supplement mix tailored specifically for him. You took that information, ran a few simulations to see how much Attentex you'd need to degrade his performance, and put it into his mix. But you miscalculated and he had seizures on the field. He was out of the league after that."

"Chris —"

"Why are you flying to Sarajevo?" I asked.

"I have investors there," Parker said, fazed by the sudden twist of questioning.

"For MobilOn."

"Yes, of course."

"You've been having difficulty finding investors in the U.S.?"

"I wouldn't say that," Parker said.

"Actually you are, compared to the funding you were getting with your previous start-up, the one you sold back to Labram for substantially more than it was worth," I said. "A lot of the companies you partnered with on that seem reluctant to go in with you on MobilOn. Your potential investors are skeptical that you will be able to keep it going long enough for it to be bought back by Labram for a premium. Too many better-funded and -connected companies jumping into the threep-sharing market. So you had to offer something extra to entice them."

"This is nuts."

"And what you offered them was the ability to affect Hilketa play," I continued. "Not in the North American league, where you don't have reach and the market is mature anyway. But in the upcoming European and Asian leagues. Labram has signed a deal to be the default supplier of supplements and performance creches in those leagues. It's already creating the limited liability corporations to fund the new franchises. Your family company already did all the hard work setting up the right set of circumstances. All you have to do is exploit them."

411

Parker didn't have anything to say to this.

"After Salcido, you did more tweaking of your Attentex formula and you were finally convinced you have something you could show your investors. So you told them that on the final pre-season game of the year, Kim Silva would have the worst game of her career — always just a fraction of a second too slow, always a step behind. Nothing so obvious that it would seem like she had been drugged. Just a step down from a franchise player to a journeyman. From a Kim Silva to a Duane Chapman, you could say. You told them they could bet on it. And some of them did.

"But you didn't know the box of supplements Labram sent dated to be used last Sunday — the box you doctored — was given to Chapman by Silva. She used the remainder of her previous week's box of supplements. There are always more sent than the Hilketa athletes use. And the precise mix you used for Silva — designed for her body and for her metabolism and her own brain — sent Chapman's brain into overdrive. It killed him while Silva was having one of the best games of her career."

"Your story doesn't make sense," Parker said. "If this supplement mix was meant for Silva, it wouldn't have affected Chapman at all. You said yourself it has to have another component to work."

"An electrical component," I agreed. "And this confused me at first. So I asked my friend Tony to help me with it, to find the one thing Silva and Chapman and Salcido had in common. And the answer was, they all used Labram creches for their bodies during play. The creche monitors every system in the player's body. And a year ago, right before the Salcido incident, every Labram creche had its operating system updated to offer mild intermittent electrical stimulation. The update notes say it helped to offer more accurate information for the data feeds the league sells to fans. And it did, enough so that the other creche manufacturers updated their operating systems with similar stimulation. But that's not why you did it."

"So I'm tweaking a player's creche during games now, is what I'm hearing. That still wouldn't explain Chapman."

"Well, see, that confused me, too," I said. "Because any creche that acted substantially differently from all the rest would stand out. But Tony reminded me that only the players with Attentex in their supplements would be affected. The same electrical stimulation could be sent to every creche. If all the

413

creches are operating the same way, it masks the problem. It's pretty ingenious, as long as you're not stupid or greedy about it. Target one or two players on a team for any game, make them play below their general level — or make sure they don't break out in any one game — and you change the game. You can dictate winners and losers. Or keep the same winners and losers and just mess with the spread."

I walked over and sat down in the chair across from Parker. "It's a great idea, except of course it's unethical and illegal and you entirely screwed it up and killed a player by accident. Now you need to smooth things over with your potential MobilOn investors, the ones you promised that you could fix Hilketa games for in return for their investment."

"These would be the same investors who are also investing in the foreign Hilketa leagues with Labram, right?" Parker said. "And they're going to bet on their own games. Because *that* won't be blindingly obvious."

"Not all of your investors are investing in the foreign leagues," I said. "Even if they have a history of working with Labram. And those that are, well. If they're smart enough to know how to launder money through your family's company, they're smart enough to place their bets without getting caught. The problem isn't *who* is betting, Amelie. The problem is that what you promised them became a mess, and every time you tried to fix the problem, it got worse. Chapman died. Kaufmann died.

"You learned through Keshia Sanborn that Kim Silva had information implicating Labram in money laundering, which would bring more eyes on what you were doing. So you leaked Silva and Chapman's affair to the *Hilketa News* and called in a favor from Martin Lau to make it look like Marla Chapman tried to kill Silva and then killed herself. You paid to have Rachel Ramsey contaminate the IV sample and when another bag showed up out of the blue you bribed Ramsey to get it and then killed her. You killed her, Amelie. The threep that was used to kill her and the tank that came through my window were both made at Van Diemen. When the Baltimore FBI showed up with warrants, they rolled right over. You were piloting both of these threeps.

"And when you finally realized you were in too deep and it was time to get the hell out of Dodge, you pointed Lau and his flunkies at Lena Fowler, your Integrator. You used to think her history made her silent and reliable, but she also knew more of your secrets than you preferred she knew. Lau would keep silent because his company had business with Labram, but Fowler was a loose end. And that catches us up to right now, and you on a plane to a country that doesn't have extradition."

Parker looked up at me for a moment, eyes full of confusion.

And then, finally, she couldn't keep a straight face any longer.

"It's a nice story, Chris," she said. "It's too bad you can't prove it."

"What do you mean?"

"We both know what that means. You talk a good game but it's speculation. You don't have proof of anything substantial."

"You mean because the cat is dead, and so is Fowler and anyone else who could give you up."

"I don't know anything about any of that," Parker said. "What I do know is if you had anything, you'd have arrested me by now. And as it stands, the point is moot. I'll be in Sarajevo in less than two hours. And I think I'll stay for a while in the country. It's beautiful there."

"It is," I said. "I've been."

"You can come visit," Parker said, and smiled. "I'll still need a celebrity spokesperson for MobilOn."

"So," I said. "You won't be turning yourself in voluntarily."

"No I won't. There's no reason for me to be doing that."

"Here's the problem," I said. "One, the cat's not dead." Parker's smile dropped. "In fact, he's by all indications quite popular with the FBI's forensics accountants, who are combing through Labram's finances quite thoroughly, including its purchase of your previous company. Once they're done running through that information, Donut the cat will be reunited with Kim Silva. Isn't that nice? But it means you wrecked our house for nothing. Our insurance will pay to fix the damage to the house and our threeps, and is putting my roommates up in a hotel for now, but I assume they'll come after you for it later. Be ready for that lawsuit."

Parker didn't say anything to that, so I continued.

"Two, before Fowler died — and before she killed Martin Lau, which I'm sure Richu Enterprises will be quite upset about — she left a very large pile of documents addressed to me and Agent Vann. A whole lot of it is about you, Amelie. She saw you flailing about and realized how much at risk she was from you. She wanted to return the favor."

"I don't believe you," Parker said. "And it wouldn't matter now even if I did."

"I knew you wouldn't believe me, so I've saved this part," I said. "While I was busy coming to visit you, my partner was having a chat with your father, catching him up on everything you've been up to. It turns out you weren't forthcoming with him about what you were offering as an extra entice-ment to invest in MobilOn. In fact, it doesn't seem like you clued him or any other family members in to what you were doing. And as a result, you've exposed Labram to intense government scrutiny and damaged the company's reputation with its investors, and with the North American Hilketa League, who it values as a key strategic partner. Your father isn't happy, Amelie. And it turns out, you're on his plane."

Parker blinked at this. "What does that mean?"

"It means you're not going to Sarajevo. In about thirty minutes, in fact, you'll be on the ground outside of Venice. There you'll be greeted by some nice Americans who will arrest you and, once your plane is fueled and your flight crew rested, take you back to Washington, D.C. Your dad's cutting you loose."

"He can't do that," Parker said.

"He *is* doing it," I said. "He's also putting Labram's money-laundering schemes — the really outrageous ones — on your plate. Along with the funding for those anti-Haden protesters that show up at every Hilketa game. Apparently Labram was funding them through some dummy public interest groups. Trying to push Hadens out of the game to open the non-Haden market faster is not a good look. And now that's on you, too."

Parker gaped. "That's all complete bullshit!"

"I don't disagree," I said. "But I'm not the one who has to deal with it." I stood up and looked around. "This is a beautiful room, Amelie. And a beautiful house. And if I were you I would spend the next several hours enjoying it as much as I possibly could."

"Thanks for the advice," she said, coldly.

"You're welcome," I said. I walked to the doorway to the library. When I got there, I turned. "Oh, and, Amelie?"

"What?"

"Thank you for the job offer. I must decline."

EPILOGUE

The image of Duane Chapman went up on the giant scoreboard and the fans of the Boston Bays, present for the Friday night season opener, let out a cheer. And from the field Kim Silva, present but on the injured list, waved to the fans. The cheers became even louder, both because Silva was the Bays' star player and because by now every Hilketa fan on the planet knew she and Chapman had been star-crossed lovers.

Vann and I watched all of this from the owner's skybox, guests by way of the Bays thanking us for solving the murders of Duane and Marla Chapman.

"It's a nice tribute," I said, gesturing to the field.

"It's all right," Vann said.

I glanced over to her. "Don't get too excited," I said.

She nodded her head toward the field. "This isn't why I'm here."

The door to the skybox opened and Bob Kreisberg walked in with Oliver Medina. Kreisberg spied me and Vann and steamed right over, extending a hand to both of us in turn and thanking us for our efforts. At one point he became weepy talking about Duane Chapman. We listened politely and offered our condolences. After a few more minutes of thanks and a gentle refusal of season tickets, Kreisberg bade us farewell and wandered over to say hello to my parents.

"What just *happened,*" Vann said to me, under her breath.

"It's fine," I said. "You're fine. You've made an old man very happy."

"Remind me not to do *that* again," Vann said, and then Oliver Medina came up to the two of us.

"Agent Vann," he said, nodding to her, and then to me. "Agent Shane." Medina stopped and cocked his head at me. "I was sorry to hear your father decided not to invest in our Washington franchise," he said.

"I think he had questions about the long-term stability of the league," I said.

"He's wrong about that, but right now I can't say I don't understand his position," said Medina. "In any event, thank you for everything you've done for the league. Both

421

of you. It's been a hell of a week around here."

"It certainly has," I agreed.

"It's not over yet," Vann said.

"Oh?" Medina looked at Vann with interest.

"We still have a death outstanding," Vann said. "Alex Kaufmann."

Medina pursed his lips. "Well, I thought he was collaborating with Amelie Parker," he said. "She was working to fix the games and he was facilitating the Labram deal for supplements and creches that would have let her do it. A deal we've canceled now."

"Yes, that would have looked bad for everyone," Vann said.

"As I understand it Parker had her Integrator kill Kaufmann and then make it look like he'd been hanged," Medina said. "You said she was in his room before he died. She was trained by the army. And Parker needed him out of the way."

"All true," Vann said. "Except the first part."

"Lena Fowler wasn't in Kaufmann's hotel room to kill him," I said. "She was his lover. They met when she was integrating for Parker but then they started a relationship on the side. He got her the room next to his for the Washington game. And she didn't kill him. Kaufmann hung himself and she found him a few minutes later."

"And you know this how?" Medina asked.

Vann nodded to me. I handed Medina a piece of paper I was carrying. "This is a copy," I said. "Obviously."

Medina frowned and glanced at the page.

"It's a suicide note, addressed to Fowler," Vann said. "The sentence I want to bring to your attention is the first one. 'Medina says all of this will fall on me.'"

Medina frowned. "You think this implicates me in what Alex and Amelie were doing?"

"I think when Kaufmann saw Chapman drop dead he knew exactly what was happening," Vann said. "The drug that was supposed to slow Silva down killed someone else instead. I think he panicked and pulled the data feed. Then when he figured out he just made things worse, he put in a call to you."

"So you knew," I said. "Either you knew what was going on with Parker and Kaufmann beforehand because you were involved, or you learned about it then."

"Either way, you did nothing while other people died. Including an FBI agent," Vann said.

"And if you knew what Parker and Kaufmann were up to, then you probably knew that Keshia Sanborn was feeding Parker the whole time, too. And that she was setting up Alton Ortiz to take a deal to take the heat off her."

"And the league," Vann said.

Medina took this all in and handed the suicide note back to me. "Why do you think Fowler took the note out of the room?" he asked me.

"She took the note because it was hers," I said. "It was addressed *to* her. It was *for* her."

Medina gave a small shrug. "If she had left it, or just not come into the room at all, she would have saved you a considerable amount of trouble trying to piece together Alex's death. Why do you think she chose not to stay in the room? Or to call the police?"

"I don't know," I said.

"And now we'll never know, because both of them are dead."

"You should tell us what the two of you talked about before he hung himself," Vann said to Medina.

"Of course I won't," he said. "A deputy commissioner of the league was talking to the league's general counsel about a league matter. A matter which I note is not yet

424

entirely resolved. Aside from the obvious issue of attorney-client privilege, it would be irresponsible for me to discuss an ongoing concern."

"Kaufmann said you said all of this would fall on him."

" 'All of this' is a very inexact term, Agent Vann."

"You could narrow it down for us."

"I believe I've already explained the concept of attorney-client privilege," Medina said, and smiled. "Agent Vann, Agent Shane, this will sound odd, but I appreciate your antagonism right now. It means that you want to do right by Alex. I think he'd appreciate that. He'd also tell you to stop wasting your time concocting conspiracy theories. But mostly he'd thank you."

"If we find out you had any involvement with what Parker was up to, your attorney-client privilege goes out the window," Vann said.

"Then I better hope you don't find anything," Medina said, genially. "And if you do, I better hope you can't make it stick." He nodded at the both of us. "Agents," he said, and headed to join Kreisberg.

"Well, he's a smug bastard," Vann said to me.

"Do you buy what he says?" I asked.

"That he didn't know?"

"He didn't say he didn't know. He just said he wouldn't tell."

"So you think he did know."

"If he didn't, then he's bad at his job," Vann said. "I don't think he's bad at his job."

I looked down at the field, where the first half of play had begun. "Dad says the league's finances are about to implode," I said. "That the foreign teams are the league's plan to stay alive long enough to get non-Hadens into the sport, and the league into financial stability. The league had to know Labram's foreign team companies were money-laundering shells."

"Yes," Vann said. "They knew."

"If they knew that, then how much further a step is it to what Parker was planning? To fixing games for profit?" I asked. "If they knew they could get away with it and no one would care, do you really think they wouldn't?"

On the field, one of the Boston Bays wrenched the head off an opponent.

The crowd roared.

"I think I need a cigarette," Vann said.

ACKNOWLEDGMENTS

First and as always I want to give attention and appreciation to everyone else involved in the production of this book. At Tor, this means of course my editor, Patrick Nielsen Hayden, assisted by Anita Okoye; Irene Gallo and Peter Lutjen, who have once again created a simply wonderful cover; Sona Vogel, who had to catch my errors and inconsistencies, of which there are unfortunately many; Heather Saunders for the feel of the book on the page; Alexa Saarela and Patty Garcia, who let people know my books exist in the world. And Tom Doherty, as ever.

Thank you also to Bella Pagan and her team at Tor UK, and to Steve Feldberg and everyone at Audible.

Many, many thanks to "Team Scalzi" — Ethan Ellenberg, Bibi Lewis, Joel Gotler, and Matt Sugarman. Agents and lawyers are wonderful.

427

This novel took me rather longer than usual to write, for a number of reasons but one big one being simply that 2017 was a raging trash fire of a year, filled with horrible people trying to do horrible things and often succeeding. It's harder to bear down creatively when the world is burning.

Head On is important to me, not only because I like the world and love the characters who are in it, but also because, simply, it's here and done. Every novel I try to do something new with my writing — push a boundary of some form or another to keep growing as a writer and a creative person. This time around, it turns out the "new thing" is writing a novel when an entire planet is trying to pull focus. I think this is going to be a good skill to have, because I doubt 2018 will be any better on this score. I'd really, really like to be wrong! I guess we'll see.

With that said, friends and family helped me get through the year with sanity intact. There are too many of you to list in the acknowledgments, but if you consider yourself a friend of mine, know your friendship was appreciated in this year more than ever. I'd like to particularly thank Mary Robinette Kowal, however, who gave me encouragement on this book at precisely the right moment.

Finally and inevitably, thanks to my wife, Kristine. The process of writing books is opaque to most people; you can't tell from a book cover whether the book took six weeks, six months, or six years to write, or what the state of mind of the author was while it's being written. I suspect that will be the same with this novel. The only reason you'll know it took me longer than usual to write is that I'm telling you now.

But Krissy knows just how long each novel takes because she has to live with me while I'm writing them, and she sees pretty much every stage of the process. For this one, the process was — how to put it — *more process-y* than it's been with others. She encouraged me, supported me, and loved me through it. She is the best of people, and every day I am reminded how stupendously, genuinely lucky I am that I get to be with her. I hope each of you in your life has someone like her in it.

— John Scalzi
12/20/17

ABOUT THE AUTHOR

John Scalzi is one of the most popular and acclaimed science fiction authors to emerge in the last decade. His massively successful debut *Old Man's War* won him science fiction's John W. Campbell Award for Best New Writer. His *New York Times* bestsellers include *The Last Colony, Fuzzy Nation,* and *Redshirts,* the latter winning the 2013 Hugo Award for Best Novel. Material from his widely read blog, Whatever (whatever.scalzi .com), has also earned him two other Hugo Awards. Scalzi also serves as critic-at-large for the *Los Angeles Times.* He lives in Ohio with his wife and daughter.

The employees of Thorndike Press hope you have enjoyed this Large Print book. All our Thorndike, Wheeler, and Kennebec Large Print titles are designed for easy reading, and all our books are made to last. Other Thorndike Press Large Print books are available at your library, through selected bookstores, or directly from us.

For information about titles, please call:
(800) 223-1244

or visit our website at:
gale.com/thorndike

To share your comments, please write:

Publisher
Thorndike Press
10 Water St., Suite 310
Waterville, ME 04901